Bookshop
by the Sea

ALSO BY DENISE HUNTER

Bookshop
by the Sea

DENISE
HUNTER

THOMAS NELSON
Since 1798

Published in Nashville, Tennessee, by Thomas Nelson. Thomas Nelson is a registered trademark of HarperCollins Christian Publishing, Inc.

Interior design by Emily Ghattas

Thomas Nelson titles may be purchased in bulk for educational, business, fundraising, or sales promotional use. For information, please email SpecialMarkets@ThomasNelson.com.

Scripture quotations are taken from the King James Version. Public domain. And from the Holy Bible, New International Version®, NIV®. Copyright © 1973, 1978, 1984, 2011 by Biblica, Inc.® Used by permission of Zondervan. All rights reserved worldwide. www.zondervan.com. The "NIV" and "New International Version" are trademarks registered in the United States Patent and Trademark Office by Biblica, Inc.®

Publisher's Note: This novel is a work of fiction. Names, characters, places, and incidents are either products of the author's imagination or used fictitiously. All characters are fictional, and any similarity to people living or dead is purely coincidental.

Library of Congress Cataloging-in-Publication Data

Names: Hunter, Denise, 1968- author.
Title: Bookshop by the sea / Denise Hunter.
Description: Nashville, Tennessee : Thomas Nelson, [2021] | Summary: "From the bestselling author of The Convenient Groom (now a beloved Hallmark Original movie) comes a sweet and sizzling story of second chances and unexpected happy endings"-- Provided by publisher.
Identifiers: LCCN 2020045153 (print) | LCCN 2020045154 (ebook) | ISBN 9780785240471 (paperback) | ISBN 9780785240488 (epub) | ISBN 9780785240495
Subjects: GSAFD: Love stories. | Christian fiction.
Classification: LCC PS3608.U5925 B78 2021 (print) | LCC PS3608.U5925 (ebook) | DDC 813/.6--dc23
LC record available at https://lccn.loc.gov/2020045153
LC ebook record available at https://lccn.loc.gov/2020045154

Printed in the United States of America
HB 04.24.2023

chapter

one

Eleven months had not been long enough to prepare Sophie Lawson for the sight of him. Presently, Aiden Maddox sauntered into the Dock House like he owned the place, the din in the restaurant rising at his arrival. One at a time the groomsmen grasped his hand and pulled him in for a shoulder bump.

Seven minutes late.

Aiden swept Sophie's sister into a hug, giving her a peck on the cheek. His masculine frame dwarfed Jenna's slight build. The bride-to-be accepted his affection with apparent warmth that tweaked a thread of betrayal in Sophie's frayed heart.

Since she hadn't seen him in seven years—and since he was otherwise occupied—she allowed herself a quick assessment. He'd dressed up a pair of jeans with a blue sports coat that she knew, even from across the room, matched his eyes perfectly. At the moment he was talking to Grant, his best friend and Jenna's fiancé, smiling that same crooked smile that used to set her pulse thrumming. Aiden tossed his head back, laughing with abandon.

He looked much the same, just a little less boy and a little more man. His shoulders were broader, and he sported a five o'clock shadow. He still had those sensual lips, the top one curving like a heart, dipping low in the middle. But she didn't have to stalk him on social media to know what he looked like now when they knew so many of the same—

His eyes locked on hers.

Sophie's fingers tightened on the chair she stood behind. Her quick peek had turned into a prolonged stare.

She jerked her gaze away, pushed in the chair, and sought escape. Open French doors led onto the deck where the party would soon dine. The May breeze skittered over her skin as she slipped outside. Twilight's rosy hue lit the landscape, the marina with all its boats, and the shimmering harbor. Water rippled against the pilings, and somewhere nearby hardware pinged on a sailboat mast.

Sophie straightened the name cards she'd placed earlier on the long rectangular table. She had put herself to the right of the bride, Grant to the left, and Aiden just beyond him, a safe three chairs from her own. Her father would be on Sophie's other side, but that couldn't be helped. She had to keep him away from her twin brother, Seth, and their maternal grandmother.

Sophie glanced at her watch. Their dad was now ten minutes late. She sent him a text. It was her job to run interference tonight, which included overseeing her dad's movements and keeping Grant's grandfather from the booze.

She ignored the erratic thumping of her heart—which had little to do with her assignments—and instead focused on positive things. The flickering votives, the white twinkle lights, the jazz music flowing through the speakers, and the savory scents of grilled steak and fresh garlic.

In the eleven months they'd been engaged, Jenna and Grant had gone back and forth a dozen times on the menu, requiring Sophie to call the restaurant as many times. But all that was behind them now. The stage was perfectly set for a beautiful rehearsal dinner.

As she reached for a votive, the hair on her arms lifted. The oxygen was suddenly too thick to breathe. She didn't have to turn around—Aiden had followed her outside.

"Hello, Sophie." The sound of her name on his lips made something twist hard and tight inside. Anger, that's what it was.

She stared into eyes that gazed at her with fondness. *Fondness.* As though he had any right to look at her that way. At least he wasn't presuming to hug her as he had the others. Surely he knew she wouldn't welcome an embrace.

"Aiden." She crossed her arms. "I see you made it."

"Were you counting down the minutes?"

"Somebody has to keep things on schedule. Your seat is there, beside Grant. Dinner will be served soon." She turned to go.

"Wait, Sophie. I haven't had a chance to tell you . . . I'm sorry about your mom. She was a wonderful lady. Closest thing I ever had to a mother."

His words triggered that soft spot she'd always had for the motherless boy.

Do not feel sorry for him.

"Thank you."

"You were good to her. And she was so proud of you."

"Yes, well . . ." Sophie shuffled her feet. Toyed with the skirt of her sundress.

"Your dad must be devastated."

She blinked at him. Her dad was the last person who had a right to be devastated. Hadn't Aiden heard? Why had Grant never mentioned it?

Aiden looked back into the restaurant. "Hard to believe little Jenna's getting married. Seems like yesterday she was begging us to drive her to the movies to meet some boy."

"Well, she's twenty-two now, and she's found her perfect match. Grant will take good care of her." If Aiden noticed the bite behind her words he ignored it.

"They're good together." Aiden shoved his hands into his pockets. "And Seth graduated from Appalachian State, I hear."

"With his masters. He just got hired on as project manager at a consulting firm." She glanced around for an escape, but the entire bridal party was still inside.

"And you, Sophie? What are you up to?"

She really didn't want to talk to him about her dreams but decided to offer the bare minimum for civility's sake. "I'm moving to Piper's Cove. Going to open a bookshop."

The corner of his mouth ticked up. "Wow, that's great. A bookshop, huh?"

She just smiled in response. Politeness dictated that she ask about his life, his business. But she couldn't bring herself to do it. "I should go in and—"

"You look wonderful, by the way." His gaze grew intense. "You always have, but I think you're even more beautiful now."

She steeled herself against his charm. It didn't mean anything. Words were easy. And who did he think he was, coming here, saying things like that to her?

Think of Jenna. Keep it cordial.

"You look well too," she squeezed out.

His eyes twinkled in that familiar way, those silver flecks dancing. "Did that hurt much?"

"Only a little."

He chuckled.

She checked her watch. They couldn't wait any longer for their dad. "I should go and round everyone up. We're running late."

"I thought this was the Fosters' shindig—parents of the groom and all."

Grant's parents had paid for the meal—for the entire wedding actually, since the Lawsons' bank account was in poor shape. But the details had been left to Sophie, and in the wake of her mother's death, she'd been happy for other things to focus on.

"I'm just helping out."

Granny May appeared at their side, her small frame erect behind a walker adorned with an old-fashioned bicycle horn. Tonight her thinning white hair was coiffed within an inch of its life, and her kelly-green blouse set off her peachy skin tone.

"Hello, Granny." Sophie stooped down to hug her maternal grandmother, a bouquet of Cinnabar assaulting her nostrils. "You look beautiful tonight."

"I look like an old, shriveled-up prune—what can you expect at seventy-six? But you look lovely, dear."

Granny turned a scowl on Aiden. "I see you found the back door quick enough."

Aiden blinked. "Um, good to see you, Granny May."

"That's Mrs. Alexander to you."

Sophie cleared her throat and addressed her grandmother. "Have you had a chance to meet Edward Drury yet—Grant's grandfather?"

"Is he the one at the bar, taking down the whiskey shots?"

Sophie winced. Not already. "I should introduce the two of you later. He's really nice, and Grant thinks the two of you might hit it off."

"His cornbread's not baked in the middle if he thinks I need a man in my life at this point." She found Aiden over the rim of her glasses. "Don't you have a plane to jump out of or something?"

"Granny . . ." Sophie took the woman's elbow. "Why don't you help me round everyone up? We're running behind schedule."

As Sophie strolled back inside the restaurant, she felt Aiden's eyes on her back. Her face flushed with heat. Her legs felt like wobbly stilts. She thought she'd been prepared for this.

She would survive this weekend. She just had to get through dinner and the rehearsal tonight, then the wedding and reception tomorrow. Two days. Then she could count on him to leave—because leaving was what Aiden Maddox did best.

6

❧

Aiden watched Sophie's retreat, his gaze lingering on her tall, slender form. She still had that regal look about her—square shoulders, elegant ballerina neck, grace in motion. Her sleek and shiny brown hair wasn't waist-length anymore, though it flowed well past her shoulders. It would no doubt still feel soft as butter if he ran his fingers through it. Not that she'd give him the chance.

He looked away. Okay, so he was still attracted to her. Not a surprise, really. But he hadn't expected her to be standoffish. Not that he thought they'd be best of friends or anything, but he expected to have congenial, perhaps even wistful, conversations. He sure hadn't realized her hard feelings had survived all these years.

Not that he didn't have some remorse about leaving—he couldn't regret a business that had become so successful. But he had grieved the loss of their relationship.

Within moments of Sophie's departure, the party began trickling outside. A celebratory vibe stirred in the air as they took their seats. Sophie was too far away for conversation. He couldn't even see her from here—but that had probably been the plan.

Once everyone was seated Mr. Foster welcomed them, then offered a poignant blessing. Afterward they tucked into their salads while Aiden made conversation with the bridesmaid and groomsman seated across from him. All the while thoughts of Sophie lingered in the back of his mind.

Soon the waitstaff swooped away empty salad plates,

replacing them with entrées. He barely noticed the savory smell of his steak as Sophie's laughter carried to his ears. He'd always loved her laugh, unrestrained and melodic. Infectious. He looked her way, wondering what had provoked it, but Grant still blocked his view.

Aiden stabbed a piece of steak. What had gotten into him tonight? Ever since his eyes fastened on hers across the restaurant, an ache clawed in his chest. He'd thought about her a lot over the years, of course. She was his first love. He sometimes missed the quiet conversations on her porch swing, missed her generous heart and dedication to whatever she set her mind to. And he missed teasing her about all of it. He'd never known anyone so darn dependable, much less a teenager. But then, she'd had to be those things.

As if on cue her dad stepped out onto the deck. Although Craig Lawson's impeccable suit and neatly combed auburn hair indicated he cared about his daughter's big event, his late arrival suggested otherwise.

"Daddy, you're here." Beaming, Jenna stood and embraced her father.

Beside Aiden, Seth stiffened, scowling at his dad before taking a drink. What was this? Had there been a fallout between father and son?

Sophie gave her dad a hug and invited him to take a seat beside her. But her posture was stiff, her smile tight. Had something happened in the aftermath of Rose's death? Sometimes great loss brought a family closer together, and other times it tore them apart.

Grant must know what had gone awry with the Lawsons. But when he'd started dating Jenna a year and a half ago, Aiden had given him strict orders to keep all news of Sophie and her family to himself. He'd loved her so much. He didn't want to keep looking back and missing her. Best to just keep moving forward—or so he told himself.

"It seems like the weather's supposed to hold out through tomorrow," one of the groomsmen said.

Aiden was glad for the distraction. "They're calling for sunny skies on your big day, Grant."

"It's not supposed to start raining until Sunday."

"That'll give everyone plenty of time to get back home," Seth said.

A tropical storm was headed this way. It had caused some stress over the past week as they watched it develop in the Caribbean waters and swing northward.

Except for Aiden and one of Grant's college buddies, everyone had driven from Raleigh and would return after the reception Saturday night. Aiden had a late flight back to Charleston.

Empty plates were removed one at a time as conversation carried on at the table. The sun sank quietly in the sky, the twinkle lights glimmering off the harbor.

Mr. Foster rose, holding his glass aloft. "I'd like to toast my son and his soon-to-be wife." He went on to say kind things about the happy couple, throwing in a couple jokes along the way. Then with watery eyes he wound things down. "Grant, I know you'll treat your bride with all the love and kindness she deserves. Jenna . . . Welcome to the family, sweetheart."

"Hear, hear!"

As the group quieted once again, Jenna's dad stood and cleared his throat. "I don't know if I can even talk after that."

The group chuckled, but Seth stiffened beside him again. Aiden didn't think he was imagining the mounting tension in the room.

"Hard to believe my baby girl's about to tie the knot." Craig turned to address the bride-to-be. "Jenna, you bring joy to everyone who knows you. And it seems you've found a young man who makes you happy. I wish you many years of joy together."

"Hear, hear!"

Amidst the din Seth raised his glass. "To dear old Dad . . . May these two lovebirds end up a lot better off than—"

Sophie shot to her feet. "To Jenna and Grant . . . the happy couple we're celebrating tonight. Um, I know the words of King Solomon sum up the way my sister feels. 'I found him whom my soul loveth.' I'm so happy for you both. To a long and happy union."

There was another round of clinking glasses as servers set out slices of cheesecake, and the group went back to their respective conversations.

Aiden cast a glance down the table. How many crises would Sophie end up averting before this weekend was over?

chapter

two

Might as well get this over with.

Sophie kissed Pippa's furry brown head and set her down in the master bedroom of the Fosters' beach cottage. While the rescue Yorkie was nothing but a sweetheart for Sophie, she was distrustful of strangers, something Sophie assumed was left over from her early days. Jenna had begged for the dog for her eighteenth birthday, but the responsibilities of dog ownership had soon fallen upon Sophie. Jenna hadn't seemed to mind when Pippa chose Sophie as her master.

She glanced around the room, making sure there was nothing for Pippa to get into. Thanks to the Fosters' generosity, the beach house would be Sophie's home for three weeks while she spruced up the building that would house Bookshop by the Sea. Then she'd move into the space above the shop.

Her belongings were already unpacked and put away. Well,

what she had with her. Most of her things were in storage. She was glad to be in Piper's Cove, after arranging all the pieces from Raleigh, making multiple trips back and forth. Finally, she was ready to pursue her dream.

But she couldn't think about that right now. First, the rehearsal. The mental checklist for the next two days was long and emotionally exhausting, and she found herself eager to tick all the boxes.

Pippa stared at her with sad brown eyes, her fluffy black tail drooping. Sophie tossed the dog her favorite squeaky toy. "I know, honey, but it'll only be for a little while. Be a good girl. Play with Bunny."

Sophie closed the door behind her and made her way through the crowded living room, following a path that took her around the armchair where Aiden was chatting with Dana, one of the bridesmaids. Sophie slipped through the sliding glass door. Time to get this show on the road.

A warm, salty breeze drifted over the deserted beach. Tomorrow white chairs would be aligned in tidy rows, and a gazebo, draped with chiffon and dripping with wisteria, would stand center stage near the shoreline.

She had so many memories in this beach town, most of them good, before her mom fell ill and her dad bailed. They came here every summer, staying in rental homes. She and her siblings played at the shoreline all afternoon, turning browner by the day, while their parents watched from the beach under the shade of an umbrella. Evenings were for riding bikes along the boardwalk. Each night Sophie dropped into her bed with a book, sun-tired and happy. That Jenna had decided to have her wedding here attested to the fond memories attached to this place.

Sophie joined Jenna at the deck railing, placing an arm around her sister's shoulder. "Everything all right, sweetie?"

Jenna turned to her, eyes shimmering with tears. "I can't believe I'm getting married tomorrow. Grant's everything I dreamed of, Soph."

Sophie's shoulders released the tension the tears had automatically induced. "I'm so happy for you. He's a good man."

"He really is." Jenna dabbed at her eyes. "And I'm already ruining my makeup."

Sophie produced a tissue. "You look beautiful. Grant's a lucky man, too, you know."

"Thanks. Is Dad keeping away from Seth?"

"Don't you worry about that. I'll handle any problems that arise, but I'm sure they'll both be on their best behavior." Though Seth's impromptu toast gave her cause to question that statement.

She squeezed Jenna's shoulders, noting the fading light. "We should get going before we lose daylight."

They quickly went over the order of ceremony.

"So after the parents are seated," Jenna said, "the harpist will strike up 'A Thousand Years,' and Dana and Erik will walk down the aisle, followed by—"

"Wait. I—I thought you wanted the groomsmen waiting up front with Grant and Pastor Dave. The bridesmaids were going to walk down the aisle alone."

"No, I told you, didn't I? We changed it a couple weeks ago.

Dana and Sarah were worried about walking alone on the sand. They want strong arms to hang on to."

Sophie imagined her arm curled around Aiden's, tucked close into his side. *Deep breaths.* "Oh. Sure. Of course. Whatever you want, honey." They talked through the remaining order, working out minor details.

"Okay," Jenna said finally. "I think we're all set."

"I'll go get the others."

Fifteen minutes later Pastor Dave and Grant stood near the shoreline as twilight encroached. The wedding party gathered on the deck, watching the ushers pretend to seat the Fosters.

Sophie felt a twin twinge and searched the group for her brother. Sure enough, across the deck her dad had cornered Seth. Jaw knotted, her brother stared toward the water.

Daggonit, Dad. Now is not the time.

Sophie made her way over and touched her father's arm. "Dad, we'll need you over here with Jenna. It'll be your turn soon."

Seth gave her a grateful look as she led their dad to the steps where Jenna waited. Seth had been vocal about his disapproval of Dad's participation in the ceremony, but this was Jenna's day. He'd promised to behave, but if their dad kept trying to engage him, things could go sideways in a hurry.

Things could not go sideways.

"All right," Sophie called over the chatter. "Here we go. Everyone get in order of the procession."

Everyone shifted, moving into place. Sophie kicked off her

sandals. For the wedding they'd wear little wisps of decorative lace, extending from their second toes to their ankles, but tonight they were barefooting it.

Aiden appeared at her side, offering his arm and a crooked smile. "I see you're still taking care of everyone."

Sophie bristled, remembering that last argument seven years ago. He'd been too immature to understand her family obligations.

"Well, I am the maid of honor after all."

"I didn't mean anything by—"

"Here we go, everyone." Sophie tapped the button on her phone, and the beginning strains of "A Thousand Years" flowed from the speaker.

The couples strolled down the aisle two by two. And then it was Sophie and Aiden's turn.

She reluctantly took his arm, trying to imagine that her right side was numb and that she didn't feel the warmth of his body or smell his subtle piney scent.

Aiden kept his gaze forward. "What I said before—I didn't mean it as an insult."

She kept a smile on her face. "Sounded like one."

"Listen . . . Maybe we should start over."

"Like before you arrived or before you left?" What was wrong with her? She was supposed to be smoothing things over. Keeping the peace. He just raised her hackles. Their strife seemed discordant with the harmonic music and festive atmosphere.

He sighed. "Okay, maybe I should start with an apology then."

"That's not necessary. Let's just get through this, Aiden."

It had been her motto for the last seven years. Through Aiden's abrupt departure, her father's abandonment, and her mother's long illness and death eight months ago.

But now her mom was gone, Seth was self-sustaining, and her sister was getting married. Sophie was finally, *finally*, on the verge of having her own life. Nothing was going to ruin it. Certainly not Aiden Maddox.

"All I meant was that you took care of your family when they needed you. You should be proud of that."

"I don't need your approval."

He gave a wry chuckle. "What *do* you need from me, Sophie?"

"I don't need anything from you." This was taking forever. She glanced behind her, making sure Jenna and their dad were ready. "Can we speed this up a little?"

"Eager to be rid of me?"

She held her tongue. She'd been dreading this little reunion ever since Grant slid that engagement ring on Jenna's finger. Even though Aiden moved to Charleston shortly after he graduated, he remained close to Grant.

But not to his girlfriend. No, he just dumped her like yesterday's garbage.

Sophie shook the thought. For all of their forward progress it seemed they were on a treadmill. Her arm was far from numb. Rather, the springy hairs of his forearm tickled the soft flesh of her wrist. She curled her fingers into fists to avoid touching him unnecessarily. And his familiar smell was about to drive her crazy. It took her right back to high school prom, talks on her porch, making out in his Chevy truck.

"Look, Sophie . . ." His smoky voice made gooseflesh rise on her arms. "I'm really sorry about how I left. You didn't deserve that, but I did try to call that once—"

"Now is not the time, Aiden."

Yes, there'd been *one* phone call three months after he'd left. One voice mail, begging her to return his call. He hadn't said it outright, but she'd gotten the feeling maybe he felt like he'd made a mistake. But Sophie had her hands full with caring for her family. And she wasn't eager to pursue a long-distance relationship with someone who'd left her behind so easily.

He glanced her way. "I wasn't ready for the kind of—"

"Not now."

"—relationship we had. I was eighteen, and I had things I wanted to do. I didn't know who I was, and I was too young to—"

"*Aiden.* Can we talk about this later?"

"When?"

"I don't know." The guys were going out after the rehearsal, and the girls were holing up at the beach house. "After the reception tomorrow night."

"I have to leave early, my flight."

"During the reception then, but not until after the toast." Her maid-of-honor duties would keep her busy until then.

"All right. Save me a dance. We'll talk then."

They'd finally reached the front. "Fine."

Sophie gladly let go of Aiden's arm and took her spot just to the left of center. Only when she realized she'd committed to dancing with the man who'd broken her heart did her practiced smile slip.

chapter

three

Sophie blinked back a tear as she watched Jenna and Grant sway under thousands of white twinkle lights. The band had set up on the upper deck, the strains of "All of Me" drifting on the evening air.

Jenna's mermaid gown shimmered, the cut of the dress making the most of her petite figure. Their mother's diamond pendant glittered above her V-shaped neckline. Though the necklace had been given to Sophie, Jenna had begged to wear it as her "something old" and promised to take good care of it. Someday, Sophie wanted to wear the heirloom at her own wedding—but that day felt eons away.

Grant placed a kiss on his bride's forehead. Sophie couldn't believe her baby sister was married. Jenna had skated through her teenage dating years, breaking hearts along the way, but had never fallen head over heels.

Then in college Grant had come along, and it had been love at first sight. Jenna, having never suffered a broken heart, was a firm believer in fairy tales. It worried Sophie a little, her expectations. But Grant really was one of the good ones—his taste in best friends aside—and Sophie believed he'd treat Jenna right.

Sophie was tempted to sink into a chair, but she was afraid she wouldn't be able to get back up. Having gotten little sleep last night, she was running on adrenaline. She'd made it through that long—thankfully silent—walk down the aisle with Aiden. Held back tears through the emotional ceremony. Smiled her way through the pictures, many of them putting her in close contact with Aiden. Chatted her way through the dinner and gotten through her toast—the ending of which she'd had to rewrite since she borrowed it last night.

She'd almost made it.

Sophie swept her gaze around the room, locating her dad near the railing with Sheila, his date. He was entitled to bring someone, but she wished he hadn't. The presence of the thirty-something brunette had done nothing to soothe Seth's bitterness.

Sophie spotted Grant's grandfather on the beach with other relatives. He swayed slightly as he sipped from a flask. Sophie sighed. Later she would ask him to dance and swipe the thing from him if she had to wrestle him to the ground. She couldn't allow him to ruin Jenna's day.

Granny May was seated on one of the benches, watching the bride and groom dance, a soft smile making her seem years younger.

Sophie caught sight of Aiden on the other side of the deck.

Dana's hand rested lightly on his bicep as he seemingly hung on to every word.

For the first time today Sophie allowed her gaze to linger on him. He looked like sin in that black tux. His hands were tucked in his pants pockets, the jacket lapels flaring apart to reveal the crisp white shirt and broad chest beneath it. The physicality of his job had kept him in excellent shape.

His dark-brown curls were artfully tousled tonight, fluttering in the breeze. In the shadows his deep-set eyes remained a mystery. His face was shaved smooth, highlighting his cheekbones and exposing the sharp cut of his jawline. There was a ticklish spot right under that jaw. She used to—

His gaze locked on to hers.

She couldn't look away. They'd always been connected this way. If he was nearby she knew exactly where he was. There'd been times she'd thought of him and somehow knew he was thinking of her right then too. It was the same feeling she had with Seth—the twin thing.

But Aiden wasn't her twin. Aiden wasn't her anything.

The crowd broke out in applause. The music had ended. She jerked her gaze from Aiden as the band started a popular line-dance tune. Time for the wedding party to earn its keep.

Erik appeared at her side, extending his hand and a charming grin. "Wanna dance?"

"Sure." Sophie took his hand and joined the growing throng on the makeshift dance floor. They did the energetic moves, side by side, exchanging laughter when he goofed up a move or hammed it up.

Minutes later the band segued into another crowd-pleaser, and the dancing continued. From the middle of the pack Sophie kept an eye out for trouble. Seth was dancing beside one of the bridesmaids, seemingly having a good time. Their dad was at a table with Sheila, watching the fun from the sidelines. During the fourth song she lost sight of Grant's grandfather.

The song ended and the band struck up a slow tune.

Erik held out his hands. "Dance with me?"

She'd done her dancing duty, and she really should find Mr. Drury. But one glance at Erik's puppy dog eyes and she acquiesced.

Erik's hands settled at her waist as the bluesy ballad wove around them. Others had also coupled up, leaving the dance floor full.

"It was a nice wedding, wasn't it?" Erik said. "Grant seems really happy."

"He and Jenna are a good match. You were there when it happened, weren't you? When they met?"

"I was." Erik laughed, his eyes crinkling at the corners. "Just like that, he was gone. He didn't get her number that night either, and he moped around until he finally found her on Facebook."

Sophie had heard the story before. She watched the newly-weds swaying under the lights, gazing at each other as if there were no one else around. "Jenna was the same. She called me the next day and told me she'd met the man she was going to marry. And here I thought she was being fanciful."

His eyes twinkled down at her. "Have you ever fallen for someone like that? Love at first sight or whatever?"

"Not—not that suddenly."

"Me neither."

But she was remembering the way Aiden had appeared out of nowhere her junior year of high school. She'd been trying to get a pack of jelly beans from the school vending machine, but it was stuck. He strode right up to her in that black leather jacket, tipped the machine, and freed her snack. Once he retrieved the package, he held it out, his eyes pinning her with a smoldering look she felt to the tips of her toes. Even then there was a connection. He flirted with her for weeks before he finally asked her out.

Across the deck Aiden and Dana turned in a slow circle. The woman was pressed against his chest, her head resting on his shoulder.

Sophie's heart squeezed. He was only dancing with Dana out of obligation. Word was, he was dating someone back home. With Sophie's sister dating—and now married to—Aiden's best friend, she sometimes got wind of information she hadn't asked for and didn't want. Apparently Aiden was quite the heartbreaker these days.

Dana looked up at Aiden, saying something, and he smiled down at her.

Erik shifted them around, causing Sophie to lose sight of Aiden and Dana. "You can't seem to stop staring at your ex."

"What? No, I'm not—I'm keeping my eyes on everyone. Grandpa Edward and my dad and Seth . . . I'm making sure nothing gets out of hand."

His eyes twinkled. "If you say so. You are a very diligent

sister. Grant told me how you took care of your mom when she was ill. That's admirable."

"It was a labor of love. My mom was an amazing woman."

"I'm sure she was. I'm sorry for your loss."

"Thank you, Erik."

"Jenna said you got into Duke?"

Turning down that scholarship had been one of the most difficult things she'd ever done. She lifted her shoulder. "I don't need a college degree to get where I want to go."

"Ah, that's right. The bookshop. How'd that come about?"

"I've always been an avid reader, and I worked at a library in Raleigh. I love how books can transport you to another place. You get caught up in the characters' lives, and they become your friends. I guess I want to share my love of reading with others."

When she'd been caring for her mom, reading had been a necessary part of her mental health—and a pastime she shared with her mother. She spent many afternoons those last months reading all their favorites aloud to her mom. They spent hours planning out every detail of her bookshop all the way up until Mom's last days. But Sophie didn't want to think about that today, not on Jenna's happy day.

"I thought bookstores weren't doing too good these days, what with e-books and everything."

"Independent stores are actually experiencing growth right now. And there's not a bookshop around for fifty miles, so I'll have no competition."

The song ended, but the band moved into another slow ballad.

"What about you? Jenna said you have one more year of school. Business administration?"

"Business management. I plan to take over my dad's restaurant when I graduate. The degree was his requirement."

"Sounds reasonable."

Aiden appeared at their side. "May I cut in?"

Before she could put him off, Erik stepped away. He hiked an amused brow at her. "To be continued."

Aiden slid smoothly into Erik's place, but that was the only thing that was the same about this dance. She was suddenly conscious of the warmth of his hands at her waist, of the taut stretch of muscles beneath her palms. Of the graze of his lips at her temple.

⁂

Ever since he'd spotted Sophie in Erik's arms, Aiden had been counting the seconds before he could ditch Dana and take the man's place. Aiden drew Sophie close until his arms stretched around her.

And yes, he was making a point of dancing closer to her than Erik had. It filled some primal need he couldn't quite figure out. He couldn't seem to help himself. That she didn't resist his efforts made him a little heady.

He wanted to ask if she was interested in Erik, but he didn't want to waste precious time talking about some other guy. Aiden needed to make things right with Sophie, if he could. That had been his solitary goal since last night when he'd realized she still held him in contempt.

"You've been avoiding me," he said softly into her ear.

"I've been attending to my duties."

It was more than that, and he couldn't blame her. "I really am sorry for how I left. You deserved better."

He waited for her response while their feet shuffled, while their thighs brushed. He grazed his palms across the low arch of her back, still remembering the curves he'd mapped out years ago.

"Forget it," she said finally. "Water under the bridge."

"I didn't mean to hurt you, Sophie."

She stiffened.

He leaned back until their eyes met.

"I counted on you, Aiden. That was a big deal for me."

Guilt pricked him hard. Sophie'd had precious few people in her life she could lean on. She'd spilled all her secrets to him, and he'd thanked her by running off.

"I called you after I left."

"I remember."

"You never called me back. But even so I picked up my phone so many times, wanting to tell you things, wanting to know how your day was going."

"Why didn't you?"

He gazed into her solemn brown eyes, wanting to give her an answer that would somehow heal the wound. It was a question he'd asked himself a million times. But he never arrived at a reasonable explanation.

"I don't know," he said finally. It was the most honest answer he could give her.

But not the one she'd been hoping for apparently. Her lips pursed as she broke eye contact to stare over his shoulder.

"That's God's honest truth, Sophie. I loved you. And I left you. Both of those things are true."

At the hurt and confusion in her eyes, he wished he could call back the words. He didn't want to cause her more pain. "Maybe I'm just not cut out for all that stuff." She'd been the first girl he'd broken up with, but heaven knew she hadn't been the last.

As far as healthy relationships went, he hadn't had much of an example. His mom left when he was so young he barely remembered her. And after the divorce his dad seemed to have no interest in finding another wife. Aiden wasn't even sure he believed in happily ever after. At least, not for himself.

"Or maybe you just took the easy way out," Sophie said.

Only leaving her hadn't been easy at all. "I was young and stupid. What can I say?"

Probably not that, because his reply made Sophie bristle.

Ross Givens had offered him part ownership in Extreme Adventures in exchange for sweat equity. And for a guy with little money to his name and no college opportunity, it seemed like a dream come true.

It paid off too. Aiden was now doing quite well financially. *But you lost Sophie*, his stubborn heart reminded him.

The song was winding down too quickly, the strains of the outro playing. *Dig deep, Maddox. And fast.* "I really am sorry I hurt you, Sophie."

She gave him a placid smile and a small nod that did nothing to alleviate his guilt.

The last note of the song played out, and a faster rhythm rose to take its place. Sophie drew back, her hands sliding away. "I should go check on some things."

"Wait, we're not finished."

"I think we are." She turned to go.

He caught her hand gently. "Come on. I have to leave soon, and I don't want to go with things unsettled between us."

"Things have been unsettled for years, and it hasn't seemed to bother you until now. But fine. If you need to hear you're forgiven . . . you're forgiven. It was a long time ago, and we were *both* young and stupid. Let's leave it at that. I hope you have a safe trip home."

He winced. He knew he'd been stupid, but hearing that Sophie considered herself the same for falling for him was a punch to the gut.

By the time he thought of something to say, it was too late. Sophie was making a beeline across the deck toward Mr. Drury. She coaxed him onto the dance floor.

At least it wasn't Erik. But that knowledge was small comfort in light of the obvious resentment Sophie still harbored against him.

chapter

four

The rest of the evening seemed to pass in fast-forward.
Sophie danced with Mr. Drury, effectively confiscating his flask.
But he was already wasted, and later he bumped into one of the
bridesmaids, knocking her to the sand. Sophie smoothed things
over and ushered Mr. Drury back to the dance floor before he
could cause any more trouble.

From there she spotted her dad and Seth in a heated dis-
cussion down on the beach. She handed Mr. Drury over to his
daughter, Grant's mother, and went to head off the conflict.

Her dad was as desperate for Seth's forgiveness as Seth was
to avoid him, and Craig didn't know when to quit. Sophie coaxed
Seth back to the party while Sheila distracted their dad.

In the middle of it all she received a scolding from Granny
May. "Why in heaven's name were you dancing with that
horrible boy?"

"It was just a dance, Granny."

"What you need is a nice young man—and it so happens my friend Dora has an eligible grandson who—"

"No thank you." She gave Granny's arm a gentle squeeze, then excused herself.

She had no delusions that that was the end of it, however.

All through the evening she'd been aware of Aiden's presence, on the dance floor, mingling with the groomsmen, chatting with the newlyweds. She was having a drink with Erik when she caught Aiden's eye across the deck. He lifted a hand as he descended the deck stairs, giving her a sad little smile.

Sophie waved good-bye and went back to her conversation, refusing to dwell on the fact that Aiden was leaving and she might never see him again. It was for the best. When Erik asked for her number, she gladly gave it to him. He was nice and fun and easy to talk to, and apparently she needed a distraction.

The party wound down over the next hour, and finally it was time to see the newlyweds off. They were traveling to the Bahamas, which had narrowly escaped damage from the storm now heading their way.

Family and close friends gathered at the limo to see the lovebirds off. As Grant held the door, Sophie gave Jenna a long hug.

"I love you, honey." The words didn't do justice to all the emotions bubbling inside. "Have the most wonderful time."

"Are you sure you don't want help with the cleanup? Sheila and Granny May offered to stay."

Sophie was too tired to deal with her father and Sheila or

Granny's aggressive matchmaking. "I've got all the time in the world."

"If you're sure. Thank you for all you've done. You're the best sister a girl could ask for."

Sophie drew back and palmed Jenna's cheek. "Be happy."

"I'll make sure of it," Grant said.

Sophie gave him a final hug, and as they slid into the car she called, "Let me know when you get there."

The crowd cheered as the couple drove away, and Sophie blinked back happy tears as the taillights disappeared down Bayside Drive. Her baby sister was officially married.

More good-byes were said, and finally the last of the guests left. Sophie went back into the quiet house and released an anxious Pippa from the bedroom. The terrier bounced around, trembling with happiness to see her mama again.

"That wasn't so bad, was it?"

Pippa whined pitifully and Sophie chuckled. "Well, it's over now anyway."

After changing into yoga pants and a T-shirt she took Pippa outside, lingering awhile since the poor darling had been cooped up.

Once she had Pippa settled inside again, Sophie began to set the place to rights, starting with the deck. A drizzle began as she was picking up the last of the trash. She'd take down the twinkle lights in the morning. According to the forecast it would rain for a while before the actual storm hit, so she'd have time to safeguard the house as well.

She thought of the big dead oak tree outside her bookshop

and prayed it withstood the gale-force winds approaching. She couldn't afford—and didn't have time for—a damaged roof right now.

The caterers had cleared away the food and dishes, so there was only random trash in the house to deal with. When she was finished picking up, she carefully slid the furniture back into place.

It was almost midnight by the time Sophie fell into bed with a copy of *She Means Business*, trying to dredge up the excitement that had been building for months. Excitement about her new life and her new shop.

But the gloomy cloud that had been hanging over her the past few hours refused to budge. She tried to blame it on some kind of empty nest syndrome. Her family was gone and she was officially alone. But if she was honest, the sense of loss had begun before the crowd's departure, before her sister's departure even. It began the second Aiden Maddox raised his hand in good-bye.

Nonsense. He'd been out of her life for seven years now. They didn't even live in the same state.

And yet . . .

Sophie gave her head a shake as she pulled Pippa close, snuggling her baby. "Well, sweet girl. I guess it's just you and me now."

⁂

Aiden needed something to distract him from thoughts of Sophie. From the memory of her guarded eyes and evasive manner. At least she'd returned his wave when he left instead of pretending she didn't see him.

He settled into the seat at the airport gate and pulled out his earbuds. He had only himself to blame. He'd lived with his decision to leave her, but somehow coming face-to-face with the pain he'd caused her made it all fresh again. He'd spent the drive to the airport pondering why he ever left her.

Yes, the opportunity at Extreme Adventures had been an excellent one, and nobody loved the thrill of an adrenaline rush as much as he. But he loved Sophie and knew she couldn't go to Charleston with him. He not only hurt her, he hurt himself. Even as busy as they were, getting the business off the ground, he was neck deep in heartache for months.

He was opening his favorite music app when a text came in from the airline. His stomach dropped as his eyes caught on the word *canceled*.

No.

He looked at the gate screen and saw the same word repeated there. A commotion began around him as fellow travelers realized their plans had been upended.

A line was already forming at the desk near the jet bridge. Aiden hopped on his phone and checked the radar. He knew he'd been cutting it close. But the storm was slow moving, hanging over Georgia for two days. Now it appeared to be moving faster, however.

Further investigation showed the Charleston airport had closed. He'd have to book another flight, no earlier than tomorrow—and that was if he was lucky. The timing would be tricky because once the Charleston airport was open, it would be only a matter of hours before the storm would close this airport.

Driving home was a last resort. Even without the storm, it was a five-hour drive. And with all the inlets and rivers, he could almost count on flooding. No, it would be better to take his chances with the airlines.

Tomorrow was Sunday; his business was closed anyway. The ESTA ceremony wasn't until Tuesday, and since he was up for the award, he had to be there. But he should be fine. He waited in line at the desk and tried to be patient while other travelers rearranged their plans.

When it was finally his turn he rebooked for the next evening. The storm would be out of Charleston and not yet here, in full force at least. Maybe it would even dissipate, as often happened as they moved north.

New schedule in hand, he hitched his backpack onto his shoulder and turned his thoughts to accommodations. With the approaching storm and canceled flights, hotels would be booked. The Fosters' beach house wasn't far away. Everyone would be long gone by now.

He'd have to get another rental car, but that wasn't a big deal. He checked his watch. Too late to bother the Fosters with a call, but they wouldn't mind his bunking there for the night. And he knew just where they kept the spare key.

chapter

five

Sophie had no idea how long she'd been trying to fall asleep, but it had been a while. She turned over in bed, nudging Pippa aside with her knee. The dog didn't even stir.

It had been an exciting, emotional day, so it would make sense if she were lying here reminiscing about how beautiful Jenna looked as she walked down the aisle or about the sweet expression that fell over Grant's face as he watched his bride approach.

It would even make sense if she were anticipating the opening of her bookshop—her dreams finally coming to fruition at the ripe, old age of twenty-five. Or excited about being on her own for the first time ever. She had so much to look forward to.

But none of those things were stealing her thoughts tonight. It was the memory of Aiden's hands at the small of her back. The soft scrape of his voice in her ear. The plaintive look in his soulful eyes as he'd apologized.

That's right. He apologized. I've forgiven him. The end.

Sophie shifted again, trying to find a comfortable spot on the pillow, which hadn't given her a moment's trouble the past two nights.

Rain pattered on the roof, falling steadily now. She was thankful the weather wouldn't prevent her from starting on her shop tomorrow. She already had five gallons of Coastal Blue waiting in her store, along with primer, rollers, brushes, tape, tarps, and a six-foot ladder.

An image of Aiden's face flashed in her mind. The way he'd stared at her when they were dancing, all his usual bluff and bluster nowhere to be seen. His eyes had gone soft, full of concern. Regret etched clearly on the planes of his face.

Where was all that regret when he'd left her, plate full and already overwhelmed by her responsibilities? Where was he when she was up nights with her mom, helping Seth through calculus, and dealing with Jenna and her lack of regard for her curfew?

A soft thump sounded over the patter of rain. Sophie opened her eyes to the darkness, listening. Probably just normal house sounds. The past two nights there had been four other girls bumping around, so Sophie wasn't necessarily familiar with the house's creaks and clanks.

Something thumped and Sophie bolted upright. Her heart knocked against her ribs, heavy and fast. It sounded as if it had come from the entryway. Maybe it was just the wind, knocking tree branches against the house. Maybe it hadn't been as loud as she'd imagined—Pippa still slept undisturbed after all.

But those assurances did nothing to settle her pulse or slow the speed of her thoughts. Especially since no trees stood near the house. Besides, Pippa had once slept through a blaring fire truck siren when her neighbor had a middle-of-the-night emergency.

Another thump had Sophie snatching her phone off the nightstand, her feet sliding to the floor. That one had definitely come from the entry. She stood, clutching her phone to her chest. Should she call 911? She'd peek out her bedroom door first to see if anything was amiss. She dialed the first two numbers before making her way across the cool wood floor.

The air-conditioning kicked on, the sudden sound making her jump. Maybe that's all the noises had been—the machinations of the cooling unit. As she inched her way to the door, she was grateful that the humming covered the sounds of her movement. But it would also hide the sounds of a potential intruder.

She eased open the door and winced as the hinges creaked. Back on the bed, Pippa remained a still shadow, huddled near the head of the bed.

Sophie peeked out the doorway and into the short hallway. Her eyes had adjusted to the darkness, but a little light snuck in from the windows in the living room. She'd have to go farther.

She padded down the hallway, along the right-hand wall, her breaths coming in quiet little pants now. When she reached the living room threshold, Sophie swept her gaze over the darkened space. No moving shadows that she could see.

A noise sounded to her right. The front door. The knob clicked.

She lurched for a weapon on the entry table. Her hands

closed around something. She raised it over her head, wishing she'd taken time to dial that final "1."

Too late now. A hulking shadow came through the doorway.

She brought the object down hard. It shattered on contact as a scream tore from her throat.

"What the—?"

In a blink she was knocked back against the foyer wall. Weight pressing. Arm at her throat.

She grabbed at it, pulling, but her efforts were ineffectual. He was big and strong, towering over her. A thousand pounds of pressure. Her legs trapped.

She couldn't scream. Couldn't breathe.

Shuffling sounds. Then a light, bright and glaring.

Her wide eyes fixed on a male face. A familiar face.

"Aiden?" she tried to say, but nothing came out.

He blinked down at her, the hardened mask slipping away. He dropped his arms and backed away. "Sophie. What are you doing here?"

Air. She dragged in a breath. Intense relief slumped her shoulders. Thank God it was only Aiden. For a minute she'd thought she was a goner. Her lungs expanded again and again, trying to keep pace with her rattled heart.

"What are you doing here?" Irritation rose over the feeling of relief. "You're supposed to be on your way home."

"My flight got canceled. I thought I'd bunk here."

"Ever heard of a hotel?"

"I didn't think the Fosters would mind. Why are you still here?"

"The Fosters gave me permission to stay while I renovate my shop," she said in a tone that conveyed *she* had the owners' consent.

His hand touched his temple, his finger coming away with blood.

The delicate glass hadn't been substantial enough to do much harm, but it had left a nice cut. However, the fright he'd given her assuaged any feelings of guilt.

His jaw knotted. "What were you doing, taking on an intruder with some flimsy knickknack? You could've been killed."

She bristled. "You can't sneak into an occupied house and lecture me on safety measures."

"I wasn't sneaking, and I didn't know it was occupied."

"Well, maybe you could've knocked—or at least called! How'd you even get in?"

"They keep a key under the flowerpot."

That would've been nice to know. "Well, you can put it right back and head to the nearest hotel. I hear the Sunny Daze is very nice."

"All the hotels are going to be full, Sophie. There's a storm on the way, remember?"

The storm. He was right. She could almost feel the walls closing in on her. She didn't want to be trapped in this house with Aiden. This was supposed to be *her* time. *Her* empty nest. Even though, okay, it wasn't exactly her nest.

But she could hardly send him out to sleep on the beach in the rain. She gritted her teeth. "How long?"

"I've already rebooked my flight. I'll be out of your hair by noon tomorrow. You won't even know I'm here."

Ha. She'd know where he was every single second.

They stood glaring at each other, neither willing to give an inch.

She couldn't believe him, barging in here in the middle of the night and scaring her half to death. Practically choking her. She rubbed her throat, aware that beneath the surface, some foolish part of her was glad he hadn't left after all.

And that only made her grind her teeth.

As did the way his eyes softened as they drifted to her throat. "Did I hurt you?"

"I'm fine. You can take one of the rooms upstairs. And be sure to wash your own bedding before you leave." She turned to go.

"Wait." He grabbed her arm. "Don't move."

She followed his gaze to the glass fragments on the foyer floor.

"Be right back." He passed her, the shards crunching under his shoes as he headed toward the kitchen.

Sophie pressed her palm to her chest, taking a minute to breathe. This couldn't be happening. She was really sound asleep, and this was only a nightmare. But the sounds of him bumping around the kitchen were all too real, as was the adrenaline still coursing through her veins.

Aiden returned to the foyer, broom and dustpan in hand. Blood dripped from the cut at his temple as he swept up the shards. He retrieved her phone, which she must've dropped.

When he finished he set aside the tools. "We can vacuum in the morning."

Sophie stiffened as he lifted her off her feet. "What are you—?"

He carried her to the area rug and set her down.

The contact was over before she knew it, but it left her even more shaken than before.

He grabbed a backpack she hadn't noticed and slung it over his shoulder. "I'll head upstairs. Good night."

"Good night." Sophie hurried back to her room and closed the door behind her. With shaking hands she plugged in her phone, settled in the bed beside her sleeping dog, and stared up at the darkened ceiling.

And she thought she'd had trouble sleeping before.

chapter

six

Aiden's eyes popped open to gray light filtering through the drapes. A quick scan of the room reminded him where he was. Who he was with.

He touched his temple. Last night's run-in had actually happened. Sophie really had attempted to assault him with some figurine. He really had shoved her against the wall with brute force. He winced at the memory. He'd probably left bruises. He knew for a fact he'd scared her half to death.

Way to go, Maddox. Give her one more reason to hate you.

Yes, her presence at the house had been a surprise. But it hadn't been a bad one. He had unfinished business with Sophie Lawson. Maybe God was giving him another chance to make peace with her. Real peace.

He checked his phone and it was only seven. He sent a text to Tiffany, letting her know his trip had been delayed. He'd met

41

the woman when she'd been hired by the private airstrip they used for tandem jumps. He and Tiffany hit it off right away and had been talking for about three months. It was getting to be time to make their relationship exclusive, but Aiden hadn't yet pulled the trigger.

He wasn't sure why. She was adventurous and fun and easy to talk to. With her thick blonde hair and slim athletic build, she wasn't exactly hard on the eyes either. Why wasn't he more eager to take things to the next level? He shook away the question. He had enough worries at the moment.

Aiden listened for sounds downstairs. Nothing but silence. That wasn't unexpected, given the hour and the time they'd gone to bed.

He checked the website for the Charleston airport. Still closed but expected to open "soon." Then he checked his weather app, hoping for more good news—but what he saw there weighted his chest like a lead brick.

❧

At the sound of a whine and the feel Pippa's tongue licking her cheek, Sophie opened her eyes.

"What?" Sophie croaked. "It's too early."

The faint light coming through the curtain's slit promised it was still early, but a quick check of her phone refuted the notion. After eleven? She hadn't slept this late in years. Everything from the night before came rushing back. The scare, Aiden's appearance. He was *here*.

She fell back against her pillows, her nose detecting familiar and tempting aromas: coffee and bacon. Someone had been up awhile—and apparently helped himself to her groceries.

Like it or not, she would have to face him once again. But he'd be gone in less than an hour. And it would take her half that time to shower and get dressed.

She took a moment to check her texts. Jenna and Grant had arrived safely in the Bahamas. She sent a quick response and moved toward the shower, her muscles aching from last night's short but brutal battle.

Stupid Aiden.

She helped Pippa onto the floor. Usually she let out the dog first thing, but Pippa had had a potty break late last night. And Sophie wasn't facing Aiden without clean hair and a bare minimum of makeup.

"Give me a minute to shower, and we'll go outside."

Pippa cocked her head, eyes twinkling and tail wagging at her favorite word.

"Who's a good girl? Huh? My little Pippa is, yes she is."

The Yorkie followed her into the bathroom and occupied herself by sniffing every nook and cranny while Sophie showered. After toweling off and dressing in shorts and a T-shirt, she dried her hair straight and applied foundation and mascara. By the time she finished it was eleven thirty.

She looked down at Pippa. "See, that didn't take long. And now we only have thirty minutes with our unwelcome guest. Isn't that right?"

At the sounds coming from the kitchen her pulse found a

new gear. She paused before opening the door, steeling herself against Aiden's innate appeal. "Let's get this over with."

Pippa squeezed through the door before Sophie had it fully opened. The dog lifted her nose, and her ears twitched toward the sounds coming from the kitchen.

Sophie crossed the threshold of the living room as Pippa reached the kitchen. Aiden stood at the stove, wearing well-fitting jeans and a black T-shirt that showed off an impressive pair of biceps.

"Good morning." A smile formed as his gaze fell to Pippa. "Who's this little guy?"

"Careful," Sophie said as he squatted down. "She doesn't really like—"

Pippa sniffed his hand, then gave it a lick. Two licks, three. The dog gave a little yap—her playful yap—and stood there, tail wagging, looking up at Aiden with wide, adoring eyes.

Sophie scowled at the little traitor.

Aiden laughed at the dog and ruffled her head. "Wanna play, girl? You wanna play?"

"Come on, Pippa. Let's go outside."

Hearing her favorite word again, Pippa trotted over to Sophie, who leashed the dog. Once outside, Sophie noticed the strands of lights had been taken down. The patio furniture had also been removed. The dog did her business in record time, which Sophie was grateful for since it was still raining.

When she returned inside, Pippa gave a quick shake on the rug and ran to her dog dishes beside the pantry. Aiden had apparently filled them with fresh water and kibble.

"She's cute." He turned back to the stove and flipped an egg. "How long have you had her?"

"Four years."

The granite island had been set for two. A platter of bacon sat in the center beside a tall stack of pancakes. A bowl of fresh fruit rounded out the meal. He'd been at this awhile.

She felt a prick of guilt for wanting to rush him out the door. "Thank you for making breakfast. You didn't have to."

"The fridge was well stocked—hopefully you didn't have other plans for the food."

"Other than eating it, no."

He scooped up the eggs and settled them on the plates at the island while Sophie filled their glasses with orange juice. It appeared she'd have to make it through one last meal with her ex-boyfriend. She checked the oven clock. One quick meal.

They settled at the bar stools, and Aiden offered up a prayer. Sophie didn't hear a word. She was too consumed by her awareness of him, inches away. She focused on the quiet sounds of Pippa munching on her kibble.

When he finished the prayer, Sophie dug in, suddenly ravenous. She'd been too busy socializing during the reception to eat much. The bacon was lightly crispy, just the way she liked it. And he seemed to have remembered the way she drank her coffee, a little sugar and plenty of cream.

So he had a good memory. That didn't mean anything.

"You okay? Did I hurt you last night?"

"I'm fine." She had a couple bruises, and it hurt a little to swallow, but she kept that to herself. She glanced at the fresh scab on his temple and resisted the urge to ask how his head was doing.

"Thanks for clearing off the patio," she said instead, wanting to keep the conversation neutral. "I was going to do that this morning."

"I felt bad leaving the party early."

"Understandable."

"So, you're going to be opening your bookshop soon . . . Will you be renting an apartment in town?"

"My shop's on the boardwalk, and it has a small apartment upstairs. It needs a little work, but I hope to have it livable soon after my grand opening."

"So . . . you're staying here in the cottage until then?"

Something in his expression made dread spring to life in her chest. "Yes. Why? Is that a problem?"

"Of course not." He stirred an egg around on his plate. "Have you checked the weather lately?"

"Not this morning. Why?" She reached for her phone. "What's going on?"

"The, ah, tropical storm was upgraded to a Category 1 hurricane."

"Okay. Well, that's not too bad." She'd need to make storm preparations, but she planned on that anyway. She'd still have the afternoon and evening to start painting her shop.

"It's also picked up speed." The intensity in his eyes conveyed something more than his words. "It'll be barreling down on us in a few hours."

"So, what's the big—?" Her stomach bottomed out as realization hit. "Your flight."

He held her gaze for a full five seconds. "It's already canceled."

Sophie dropped her fork, and it clanked against her plate. That dread worked its way through her blood like poison. "And I suppose you'll be wanting to stay here tonight."

He tilted his head, giving her a helpless look. "I really don't have another option, Soph."

"Have you even checked the hotels?"

"Come on, you know they're full up."

"An Airbnb, then, or a—"

"In the middle of a hurricane? Everyone's boarding up—which is what we should be doing here soon."

Sophie sat back in her chair, her appetite gone regardless of the food still left on her plate. He was right, but that only irritated her more. She didn't know why his presence bothered her so much. What they'd had together was long gone. She'd moved on and he was with someone else now.

She was a different person than she'd been then. More mature, more resilient, and yes, maybe a little more jaded, as Jenna had said. Although Sophie preferred to call it realistic. Having a few walls to guard herself was perfectly acceptable as long as there was an operable doorway.

But if she looked more closely at the situation, she could see Aiden was a threat to her mental well-being. She was afraid she'd open that door and wind up with more sorrow and regret. Maybe he wasn't the same person either. But he still exuded a certain charm she found irresistible. And he definitely had a way of trampling hearts—she'd learned that the hard way.

On the other hand, how much damage could the man do in twenty-four hours? She was afraid she knew the answer to that one.

She closed her eyes. *What are You trying to do to me, God?*

"Sophie?"

She opened her eyes and fell right into those twin pools of blue.

"It's just one night. I'm sure the airport will open in the morning, and I'll get out of your hair."

He made it sound so easy. "Fine, Aiden. It looks as though we don't really have a choice. And it's a big house."

"Meaning . . . I should stay out of your way?"

"Don't you think that's best? How's your girlfriend going to feel about you being cooped up here with your ex?"

"She's not my—" He sighed, looking away. "Listen, maybe this will be a good time to find some closure. I don't feel like things are really settled between us."

"As far as I'm concerned things are as settled as they're ever going to be."

He gave her a long, soulful look, the same one that had always made her want to palm his scruffy cheek and whisper soothing words. But why should she comfort him? *She* was the one who needed comfort at the moment.

She got up from the bar stool and took her plate to the sink. "We should get the windows covered before the storm moves in."

chapter

seven

The rain was coming down harder. Sophie was soaked to the skin by the time she finished securing the colonial storm shutters. Since Aiden was so fond of heights, she let him handle the upstairs windows. He was still on a ladder, closing the last shutter. The process had taken longer than she'd anticipated, and the storm would soon be bearing down on the cove.

She dashed through the open doorway and stood dripping on the rug while she shrugged from her raincoat.

Pippa looked up at her with questioning eyes, head cocked, ears perked. "It's gonna be okay, sweetie. Just a little storm." Sophie swept the trembling dog into her arms. "Let's go find Mama a dry set of clothes."

She took her time in the bedroom, especially once she heard Aiden come back inside. She soon heard him moving around overhead. They could just keep to their own spaces. There was no reason they had to hunker down together.

In the bathroom she picked up her blow-dryer and looked at Pippa staring at the ceiling. "We don't like him, you know. He's the enemy."

Pippa gave a playful yap.

"Yeah, yeah, he's got his charms, but trust me on this. He'll only break your heart."

Her phone buzzed. Sophie set down her hair dryer, grateful for the distraction—a text from Seth.

Everything okay? I felt a twin twinge and checked the weather.
The storm was upgraded to a Cat 1.

Sophie replied. We're all boarded up, and the patio furniture is secure. I'll wait it out until it blows over.

She was eager to get started on her shop. She'd waited so long for this, but she'd have to be patient. She could use her time wisely—finish her business book or scour *Publishers Weekly* for upcoming releases the local readers and tourists might like.

She set down her phone and tugged a comb through her damp strands. If she were here alone she'd let it air dry. But it tended to dry frizzy, and for some ridiculous reason she didn't want Aiden seeing her at her worst. *He should know what he's missing*, she thought, though the excuse rang hollow.

Another text came in. Wait. We?

She skimmed her previous text. She had said "we," hadn't she? Now she either had to lie or tell her brother that Aiden was here.

Aiden's flight got canceled, so he came back here.

His reply boomeranged back. You've got to be kidding me.

Three little dots told her he wasn't finished, so she waited. Might as well let him get it all out of his system.

What right does he have, imposing on you after what he did?
You should kick his butt to the curb.

Chill. He didn't even know I was here. It was a surprise to both of us. She skipped the part where he'd nearly strangled her. And the hotels are full up because of the storm.

A cascade of texts followed.

You don't have to let him stay there, Sophie.
You don't owe him anything.
He dumped you out of nowhere.
At the worst possible time.

Seth must've run out of steam because there was a long pause before his next message.

He's going to suck you right back in.

He was only stating Sophie's deepest fear. And he hadn't said anything she hadn't already thought herself. But it was nice to know Seth was looking out for her, trying to protect her.

I know you're only concerned, but give me some credit. I've
learned a few things since then. I'll be fine. We'll keep to our
own spaces, and he'll be out of my hair tomorrow.

I don't like it.

For what it's worth, I don't either. It was time to end the
conversation. I hope you have a nice day. I'll check in with you
tomorrow.

Wait. I hate to bother you with this right now, but I have a
document I wrote for work. Nobody edits like you . . . I want to
make a good impression.

Sophie paused, a feeling of reservation sweeping over her.
Seth wasn't a kid anymore. He wasn't even in college. He was a
grown man with a grown-up job. And Sophie should probably
start letting him fend for himself.

On the other hand she liked helping out. And she didn't
have anything better to do.

No problem. Send it over.

I need it by tomorrow. ☹

Naturally. She sighed. While she preferred to plan ahead, her
twin brother liked to fly by the seat of his pants. It often ended
up putting her in panic mode.

I'll be waiting out a storm, so I won't have anything better
to do.

Maybe having something productive to work on would keep
her from falling into Aiden's arms again. Remembering how safe
she'd once felt in his embrace, she shivered.

She texted Seth. Oh, so you're actually doing me a favor?

Ha-ha. It's a matter of perspective.

She sent the eye roll emoji.

Seriously, thanks, Sis! I owe you one.

You owe me about a thousand. But you're welcome. Talk soon.

Sophie pocketed her phone and blow-dried her hair. When
she was finished she still heard Aiden moving overhead, so she
made her way to the living room where her laptop waited. If anyone should be confined to his room, it should be him.

With the storm shutters closed the living area was unnat-
urally dark. It was odd not being able to see outside, especially
when she could hear the rain pummeling the roof and the wind
whistling through the eaves.

She sat down with her laptop. Her brother's document had
arrived, but Sophie checked the weather first. Sure enough, the
radar showed the eye of the storm making landfall near Myrtle
Beach as the outer edges of the hurricane swept over Piper's Cove.

Still a Category 1, which could produce winds up to ninety-five miles per hour.

She lifted Pippa onto the couch, and the dog set her head on the crook of Sophie's elbow, trembling. Sophie stroked her little head. "It's okay, girl. It's just a little storm. We're safe in here."

The dog peered at her with such trust, Sophie's heart squeezed tight. For such a little thing, she brought Sophie so much joy and comfort. Pippa's soft fur had caught many of her tears, especially after her mom passed.

"What would I do without you, girl? Huh?"

After one final stroke she opened her brother's file and gave it a quick scan. He'd failed to mention the document was eighteen pages long.

Sophie sighed. So much for scouring *Publishers Weekly*.

Something smacked the side of the house, making Sophie jump. Pippa burrowed into her side, and Sophie slid an arm around her. "You're okay, sweetie. It can't hurt you."

Sophie had made it through twelve pages of her brother's document, fixing punctuation and clarifying points here and there. He was a decent writer, but just like with his college essays, he tended to write the first draft and leave the rest to her.

A sound from the stairs drew her attention. Aiden descended, dressed in a fresh pair of jeans and a white T-shirt, his dark hair still slightly damp. He'd always filled out his clothes quite nicely, and that ability had only improved since he'd been gone.

She dropped her gaze to the laptop's screen.

"It's breezing up out there," he said.

"Storm's over us now. Hopefully it won't get any worse."

When he stopped at the bottom of the steps, Pippa hopped from the couch and trotted over, tail swishing.

"Hey, pretty girl." He ruffled the dog's fur, taking a minute to mock fight. The dog ate up his attention, hunching down and yapping playfully.

"I don't know about you," Aiden said a moment later, "but I'm getting hungry. Fortunately you stocked up on groceries. Why don't I fix us some grilled cheese sandwiches?"

She closed the laptop. "I can do it."

"No need. Let me. I'm running out of things to do."

Had he texted his girlfriend about the delay? Did he tell her where he was and who he was with? Was she upset he was hunkering down for a storm with his ex-girlfriend?

Whatever transpired between the couple was none of her business.

"Sure," Sophie said. "Sounds good."

She frowned as Pippa followed him into the kitchen, right on his heels. One would think the dog would sense the friction between them and take her mama's side.

Sophie went back to editing the document, only vaguely aware of a pan clanking, the sucking sound of the refrigerator opening, and Aiden's voice crooning to Pippa.

Soon a quiet sizzle sounded, and she drew in the scent of the butter browning in the skillet. Her stomach gave a hard growl. Breakfast had been hours ago, and she hadn't eaten much.

She got a few pages edited before Aiden called her into the

kitchen. He'd brought out the fruit left over from breakfast and added a bag of SunChips to the island.

"Bon appétit," he said after offering a quick prayer.

His easy prayers made her think his spiritual walk had progressed in the last seven years. While he'd attended church with his dad, he'd never taken spiritual things very seriously.

"Do you attend church in Charleston?" she asked.

"Yeah, I do. Why do you ask?"

"Just wondering."

"It's a large church that one of my customers invited me to. They have a lot of programs, very mission minded."

"That's great."

"I guess you'll have to find someplace to attend now that you're moving here."

"That won't be hard. The options are pretty limited. The town mayor invited me to hers, and I've visited a couple times. I think I'll probably make it my new church home."

She'd been hit or miss while caring for her mother. And even afterward. Come to think of it, her prayer life hadn't been anything to write home about lately either. Maybe once her shop was up and running, it would be time to get back to some good habits.

"It's nice to have a church family when your real family lives far away. You already know the mayor?"

"She came by the store the day I took possession of it." She and Alanda had hit it off right away. Besides being the mayor, she owned several buildings on the boardwalk.

Sophie bit into the sandwich, noting the crispy crust and

rich, buttery flavor. She remembered Aiden's pathetic attempts in the kitchen when they'd been dating.

"Your cooking skills have improved." She instantly regretted the reference to the past.

"It was either learn to cook or starve to death. My specialty is steak on the grill, but that's not really an option at the moment."

He probably cooked for his girlfriends. According to Grant there'd been a revolving carousel of women. Aiden probably added a baked potato to the menu, set a nice table with flowers, and treated them to that crooked grin of his from across the table.

She didn't even want to think about what might happen afterward. Though he and Sophie had played with fire for months, they'd never gone all the way. But she still remembered those bold, confident kisses, his steady fingers plowing through her hair, his weight pressed against her.

Enough of that, Sophie.

When they finished the meal Sophie stood. "I'll do the dishes."

"Thanks." He brought his plate to the sink and paused. "Want me to dry?"

She could feel his warmth at her back. "That's okay. I've got it."

"Okay. Well . . . I have some phone calls to make."

She deflated at the quiet sound of his retreating footsteps. She wasn't disappointed he'd fled to his room. She'd practically told him it was what she expected after all.

But as she settled back on the sofa with her laptop, she couldn't help feeling a little lonely, even with Pippa curled up in the crook of her knees.

What was wrong with her? It had been years since she'd had the luxury of spare time and privacy. She was just feeling claustrophobic with the windows all boarded up.

She went back to Seth's document, making corrections. Once she finished she'd curl up with the new Kristin Hannah novel she'd snagged from her inventory.

She hadn't gotten far on the document when a text came in from Jenna. She'd sent pictures of two strappy dresses, asking which one she should wear to tonight's beach party. Sophie chose the red one and also offered her opinion on shoes, then returned to the document.

A while later her dad texted her for intel on Seth. She suggested that Dad should give her brother space but had a feeling he'd ignore her advice. Lately his patience had worn thin—he was tired of waiting for Seth to forgive him—and he too often put Sophie in the middle.

She was finally finishing up the document when Granny May called.

"What in the world are you doing?" Granny said by way of greeting.

Sophie sighed. The family grapevine was alive and well. "I see you've been talking to Seth."

"How could you let that man stay there, Sophia Rose? Is he there right now? Put him on the phone."

"He's upstairs and I'm not putting him on the phone."

"You should throw him out in the storm, is what you should do."

"Whatever happened to 'forgive, and you will be forgiven'?"

Her grandma sputtered. "Well, a serpent changes his skin, not his fangs."

"Granny, he's not a serpent. He was an eighteen-year-old boy who made a decision to leave."

"He made a selfish decision that broke your tender little heart."

Sophie couldn't argue with that. And she couldn't fault her grandmother for feeling resentful. She'd been the one who picked up the pieces as Sophie mourned him.

"Just remember. He may look like an angel, but he's got the devil's own charm. Don't you fall for it this time around."

Sophie rolled her eyes. "The storm will pass and he'll be gone tomorrow. Until then we'll keep to our corners. All right? You don't have to worry about me. I'm a big girl."

"I can't help it. You've had way too much put on you, and I blame myself."

"It's not your fault Mama was sick, Granny, and you did everything you could to help. You were wonderful emotional support." Granny's health had kept her from being her daughter's primary caregiver, and she was forever apologizing for it. "I don't know how I can thank you for always being there for me."

"Hmmm. Funny you should mention that . . ."

Sophie sighed. "Why do I feel like I've been set up?"

"'Set up' is exactly the right way to put it. I told my friend to give her grandson your phone number and—"

"Granny—"

"—he should be calling soon. He's a resident here at Dr. Wald's office, and he graduated at the top of his class from Stanford."

"You shouldn't have done that."

"He's a *pediatrician*, sweetheart."

"I'm sure he's lovely, but I want to focus on getting my bookshop off the ground right now, Granny."

"Nonsense, you've always been a good multitasker. He's a man of faith, and he's quite the looker too. I stalked him on Facebook. You should do the same. Look him up. It'll give you something else to focus on while that snake tries to slither his way back into your heart."

"He's not—" Sophie rubbed her eyes. Her grandma was a force, and sometimes it was easier to give in than fight. "All right. Fine. I'll look him up."

"That's my girl. His name is Joshua Stevens, with a *v*. Sophie Stevens, doesn't that have a nice ring to it?"

"Granny, you are getting way ahead of—"

"I have to go. Just keep your phone on. You don't want to miss his call. And I'll be checking in on you too."

"Oh, jeez—maybe he could start with a text or something."

Nothing but silence was on the other end.

"Granny?"

Great. Her grandmother had already hung up.

Sophie set down her phone, emotionally wrung out from the conversation. She gave her head a shake, then went back to her laptop, waking up the screen. Just as she opened an email to her brother, the lights flickered off.

chapter

eight

A beep sounded from somewhere in the house, and the bedroom went dark. Aiden stilled, waiting for the light to flicker back on. But thirty seconds later he gave up. Using his phone's flashlight he left the room and headed downstairs. "Sophie?"

"Right here." Her voice came from the sofa, where the glow of her phone screen lit her face.

Pippa whined, no doubt sensing the tension.

"Looks like we've lost electricity," she said.

"Probably a line down somewhere."

"Maybe it'll come back on."

He couldn't miss the hopeful tone in her voice. "They won't be able to work on it until the storm passes. I'll text the Fosters and see if they have a generator." Wouldn't that be nice? Otherwise they were looking at twenty-four hours together in a candlelit home with no distractions.

"Good idea."

Aiden sent the text and didn't have to wait but a minute for the reply. His stomach filled with lead. "They don't have one. I'll hunt down the flashlights and candles."

She frowned down at her laptop. "I don't suppose you happen to have a hot spot on your phone?"

"No, why?"

"I was working on something for Seth, and he needs it back by tomorrow morning. I'm finished but I have no way of sending it now."

As far as he could see that was the least of his worries. His flight had been canceled, and if he didn't get one by Tuesday morning he'd miss the ESTA ceremony—and what could turn out to be the biggest moment of his career.

They had no electricity, little water, and the storm was just getting underway. And his phone battery was already half gone. Of course, he could use his car charger, but it was parked outside. And as much as he liked a good adrenaline rush, running through a hurricane was definitely ill advised.

As if on cue a loud *thwack* sounded against the side of the house. He headed to the utility room, and while he rummaged through a drawer he heard Sophie on the phone with her brother. Her soothing tone indicated Seth was upset.

Back when he and Sophie had dated, her mother had become too ill to parent properly. Since her dad worked long hours, Sophie stepped up to the plate. She grew up fast, trying to keep her family together.

Aiden had admired her sacrificial spirit more than he could say. But her siblings took advantage of her selflessness and sense of duty. He hoped they'd grown out of that, but it looked like they hadn't—at least not from where Aiden was sitting.

"I don't know if that's safe," Sophie said on the phone. "Anyway, there's nothing open. The document you sent really isn't that rough. If you went through it one more time you'd probably be able to—"

Aiden opened an overhead cabinet. Ah, there they were. Three flashlights, a collection of candles, and a lighter. Perfect. He grabbed everything and carried it to the kitchen island.

"Maybe you could get an extension," Sophie said. "I'm sure the electricity won't be—I know you're just starting your job but—"

Aiden checked the flashlights. Only one of them worked, but he knew where the extra batteries were. He located them and replaced the dead ones.

"I'm not going to start over. I'd have to make all those changes on my phone, and it would take all night."

Aiden wanted to snatch the phone away and tell Seth to solve his own problems and let his sister move on with her life. Instead Aiden flipped the switch on a flashlight. Its beam flooded across the kitchen.

Sophie gave a hard sigh. "Okay, Seth. Fine. I'll check around and see if I can figure something out."

Aiden looked her way as she said a hasty good-bye and began tapping something into her phone. She wasn't seriously considering going outside.

She must've sensed his appraisal because she looked up at him, her face aglow in the light of the screen. "What?"

He couldn't miss the defensive tone in her voice. "You can't go out there in this, Sophie."

"I'm going to see if Alanda—the mayor—still has power. She doesn't live far from here."

He scowled at her. "In case you haven't noticed a hurricane is on our doorstep."

"You risk your life on a daily basis, and you're worried about me going out in a storm?"

"I don't—" He palmed the back of his neck, refusing to defend his job or mention all the safety precautions he took.

"It's only a Category 1, and I'll be safe inside my SUV."

"And if a power line comes down? Or some projectile pierces the windshield? What will you do then?"

"That's highly unlikely." Sophie stared at her phone and seemed to sink in on herself. "Her power's out too. And I don't have anyone else's number."

The amount of relief he felt was disturbing. But why shouldn't he care about Sophie's well-being? Of course he didn't want her hurt or injured. He wasn't a monster.

She was tapping away at her phone again.

"What are you doing now?"

"Maybe the shops are closed, but the hotels are definitely open, and they'll have generators."

"I'm not sure Wi-Fi will be their number-one priority."

"That's what I'm checking on."

Shaking his head, he went upstairs to fill the bathtub with water. When he was finished Sophie was still on the phone, so he went to the master bath and filled the tub in there too. He tried not to notice the flowery scent of her shampoo hanging in the air or the delicates draped over the towel bar.

Afterward he made his way back to the living room. "The tubs are filled, and we have plenty of candles and flashlights. You should probably unplug your—What are you doing?" A rhetorical question since he could plainly see she was slipping into her raincoat.

"The Marriott still has power and Wi-Fi, and they agreed to let me use it."

"The Marriott is at least fifteen miles away."

"Great. I can charge my phone as I drive." Caught in the beam of his flashlight, she snatched up her purse and laptop.

He imagined all manner of trouble that could happen during the thirty-minute drive. If she got stuck he'd have to go after her. And God help her if anything terrible happened—the emergency crews no doubt had their hands full.

"Stay here, Pippa." Using her phone to light her path, Sophie whizzed past him on her way to the garage. "Be back soon."

"I'm going with you."

She stopped so suddenly he nearly plowed into her.

"I don't need a babysitter, Aiden. I can take care of myself."

"I'm going with you," he repeated in a no-nonsense tone.

They stared each other down, neither giving an inch for a good thirty seconds. Maybe he couldn't stop anything bad from happening, but he was trained in emergency medical response. That had to count for something.

"Fine," she finally said. "Suit yourself."

chapter

nine

The pummeling rain was so loud Sophie couldn't even hear the Tahoe's engine. She backed out and started down Bayside Drive. Her wipers were on full blast, but it was still hard to see the road. And even though it was only four o'clock in the afternoon, it seemed much later.

Leaves and small branches flew past. A piece of cardboard fluttered by on a gust of wind.

"You realize this is crazy, right?" Aiden called over the noise.

"Nobody said you had to come."

"Just drive slowly. And watch for downed lines."

"I don't remember you being such a control freak."

"I don't remember you being such a daredevil."

Sophie pressed her lips together. He was one to talk. The man jumped out of planes, hang glided, paraglided, and bungee jumped off bridges. In high school he'd never passed up a dare. Driving through a storm should be a walk in the park for him.

66

"Seth really needs this document." She wished she didn't feel the need to defend herself. "He's just starting this job and wants to make a good impression."

When Aiden remained quiet Sophie glanced his way. Face set, he stared out the windshield.

"What?" she asked.

"Nothing."

"It's his first grown-up job. It's a big deal."

"I didn't say anything."

"You didn't have to." Sophie loosened her grip on the steering wheel. She wasn't normally this prickly, but apparently Aiden brought out the worst in her these days. Besides, he couldn't possibly understand her devotion. He didn't even have siblings, much less a twin.

"Watch out." Aiden pointed out some flooding on the side of the road, and Sophie steered around it.

At this pace the fifteen-minute drive was going to take at least double that, and driving in the storm was making her tense.

She searched for neutral ground to fill the silence. "How's your dad doing these days? I haven't seen him in forever."

"He's doing well. Still climbing around roofs for a living."

Dan Maddox was a roofer, an independent contractor. He was also a gem of a guy who'd always been good to Sophie. He had all of Aiden's good looks and charm, but unlike his son he was a homebody. Aiden must've gotten his adventurous spirit from his mother.

"He must miss you." Aiden was his only child, and as far as she knew, he rarely went home.

"We stay in touch. He's become a good friend—someone to kick ideas around with. And believe it or not, he's pretty good on the advice front."

"I can see that."

"He comes to visit a couple times a year for a week or two. We put him to work at the office, and he loves it."

The office. Sophie couldn't seem to stop the little twinge of jealousy. He'd chosen that business over her. Still, maybe it was time to put it in the past.

"How is the business going?"

"Really well. It's grown steadily every year, and last year profits were up 11 percent over the year before."

Business ownership was now something they had in common. And knowing the challenges of a new start-up, she couldn't help but be a little proud of him. "That's impressive. You still enjoy it?" Sophie drove around another large puddle. They hadn't passed a single car.

"I do. And I think you'll enjoy running your own business."

"Hope so. What's your role in the business, exactly?"

"I used to do a little of everything. But we've acquired more help recently, and each team member is more specialized now. I mostly do tandem skydiving. And the last couple years I've been working on some safety innovations off the clock."

"Sounds interesting." Aiden hadn't done particularly well in school. She knew he sometimes felt stupid as he struggled through some of his classes, but he was anything but. Aiden was an out-of-the-box thinker. It didn't surprise her that he was tinkering with gizmos and gadgets.

68

Something hit the side of the car. She hoped this hadn't been a terrible mistake. They were far enough into the drive that it made no sense to turn back now.

"Have you heard from Jenna and Grant?" he asked after a tense moment passed.

"They arrived safely and are attending a beach party tonight." She frowned at the inclement weather. "Must be nice, huh?"

"In a couple days you'll never know there was a storm but for the cleanup. The two of you still seem close."

"She's my baby sister."

He went quiet as Sophie navigated something in the road, which turned out to be part of a beach umbrella.

"So a bookshop . . . Tell me how that came about. I remember you being something of a bookworm back in the day."

"Reading's always been my favorite pastime. I can't imagine anything better than talking about books all day long."

She didn't mention the months she and her mom had spent planning the shop she'd one day own. Too personal. Opening this shop felt like a sacred assignment. One she had to get right. And this storm wasn't helping matters.

"You made such good grades. I always thought you'd go to college. You dreamed about getting into Duke."

"How do you know I didn't go to college?"

He was quiet so long, she glanced over.

He cleared his throat. "I looked you up once on Facebook."

Her heart squeezed uncomfortably. "You did, huh?"

"Moment of weakness. I thought for sure you'd get in to Duke."

"I did."

She thought she'd said it too quietly to be heard, but his head whipped around. "You got in? And you didn't go?"

"Someone had to stay home and care for my mom." Duke had been close enough she could've come home weekends. But with her dad gone, she needed to be a full-time caregiver.

"Oh, Sophie." His tone was weighted with compassion.

Her eyes stung with tears at the unexpected empathy, and she was glad it was almost dark outside. "It all worked out. I'm doing exactly what I want to be doing. Four years of college would've been a waste for me."

Silence hung in the air for a long moment.

"Well," he said finally, "you've always put your whole heart into everything you do. I have no doubt you'll run the best bookshop around."

His words warmed a place deep inside. Reminded her how much he'd always believed in her. "Thanks."

They went quiet as the wind picked up. It buffeted the car, and Sophie had to fight to stay on the road. She'd be glad when this drive was over and they were safe at home again.

Or would she? Then there would be hours of quiet—and darkness. How would they occupy themselves until the storm passed? She didn't even want to think about that right now. One thing at a time.

The storm only seemed to worsen as she drove. She took two detours due to flooding. She ran over something she hadn't seen in the road, something big and solid. The loud *thump* made her grimace. How had she missed that? She slowed down.

Surprisingly, Aiden said nothing.

Several minutes later she turned into a full Marriott parking lot. "Finally."

"Pull up under the shelter. While you run in I'll check under the car for damage."

Sophie grabbed her laptop, dashed inside, and found the woman she'd spoken with on the phone. They chatted a few minutes. The lobby was packed, people milling about, probably stir-crazy as they waited out the storm.

There were no open seats so once she was in possession of the password she found an unoccupied part of the counter, opened an email, and attached the document. Seconds later it *whooshed* into cyberspace, and Sophie released a sigh. All of that for thirty seconds of Wi-Fi. She texted her brother, letting him know the document was in his in-box.

"You be careful out there now," the woman at the front desk called when Sophie thanked her again.

"Will do."

Now she just had to brave the storm for another thirty minutes. In anticipation of the long drive, she stretched her neck and rotated her tense shoulders. A headache brewed at the base of her skull.

Aiden waited for her just inside the front doors.

"All done." As her gaze locked on his, her smile slipped. "What is it?"

"We have an oil leak."

She winced. She'd known that thump hadn't sounded good. The last thing she needed was an expensive car repair. "Is it bad?"

He lifted a shoulder. "It's hard to see exactly where the oil's coming from or how much is leaking."

"But we'll be okay to drive back home, won't we?"

"Probably . . . Best-case scenario it's a slow leak, and you can have it looked at later."

"And worst-case scenario?"

"You don't want to know." He looked at the front desk. "Maybe we should check their availability, just in case."

"The lady at the desk already told me they're full. Anyway, I can't leave Pippa home alone. She'd be frantic. We have to go back—we really don't have much choice."

He gave her a long look, then nodded. "All right. Want me to drive?"

She handed over the keys. "Be my guest."

❦

Aiden hunched over the steering wheel, straining to see the road through wipers that swished frantically back and forth. The storm had worsened. Trees bowed deeply and random objects flittered and flew under formidable gusts of wind. Sophie remained quiet, seeming to recognize his need for focus.

They'd been on the road for twelve minutes when the oil light blinked on. Aiden's stomach dropped at the orange glow. The Tahoe must be losing oil fast for the light to have come on so quickly. He didn't like the looks of this.

Sophie just had to bail out her brother. Aiden stuffed back his irritation—and the I-told-you-so that begged for release.

He made an effort to temper his tone. "The oil light just came on."

"Oh no." Sophie peered over at the dashboard. "What do you think we should do? We can still make it home, can't we?"

"Maybe. We're about halfway there. But one thing I know for sure—we don't want to run out of oil."

She paused for a beat. "Is that the worst-case scenario you were talking about?"

"The engine could seize up, and you'll be looking at a lot of money. On the other hand, if we pull over now we might be stuck waiting for help for hours."

Her gaze burned into the side of his head. "Let's keep going then."

And they did. But six minutes later a deafening clunking sound tore through the vehicle.

chapter

ten

"What is that?" The repetitive clunking sounds were even louder than the storm.

Tension seemed to roll off Aiden in waves as the vehicle rolled to a stop. He put it in Park and shut off the ignition. The SUV shuddered in the wind and, with the wipers no longer moving, the windshield quickly became a deluge of water.

"I don't know, but it doesn't sound good. Hopefully we caught it in time." Aiden released his seat belt.

"Caught what in time?"

"The engine."

She frowned at him. "The engine might be ruined?"

"Worst-case scenario." His brows drew together. "If you ask me, you should charge your brother for the repairs."

She rolled her eyes. "Well, I didn't ask you, and this isn't his fault."

"Really?"

If anything it was Sophie's fault. She was the one who'd insisted on making the trip. But she wasn't keen on pointing that out.

"I'm calling 911." She dialed the digits and reported the trouble, using her phone to figure out their exact location. A few minutes later the operator told her she'd send help.

Sophie tapped the button to disconnect. *Sit tight*, the operator had said. Sophie was trapped in a car with the man who'd broken her heart, and he blamed her for this. She checked her watch—almost five o'clock.

"Did they say how long they'd be?" Aiden asked.

"She warned me it might be a while."

Aiden sank back in his seat, heaving a sigh. "Great."

ॐ

Aiden's phone went dead. Playing *Alto's Adventure* for two hours had been a waste of battery, but he knew he'd go crazy without something to do. Shortly after Sophie had gotten off the phone, she'd begun making some kind of list on her laptop.

Aiden texted his dad to tell him he was still in Piper's Cove. He was excited about getting the roofing contract for an apartment complex, and they texted back and forth for a while.

Then he checked in with Ross via text, updating him on his situation and assuring him he'd be back in time for the ESTA ceremony. Surely the airport would open in time. He thought about texting Tiffany to kill time, but that felt weird with Sophie only inches away. Anyway, what if Tiffany called instead of answering his text? Awkward. He hadn't exactly told her he was riding out the storm with his ex-girlfriend.

He hadn't exactly told Tiffany about Sophie at all. He hadn't known the woman that long, and he wasn't in the habit of opening up to someone he was only casually dating. He didn't want to think about Tiffany right now.

Bright lights shone through the rivulets of water running down the windshield. It appeared help might be arriving. He could only hope.

"Finally." Sophie echoed his thoughts as she closed her laptop and gathered her things.

The lights got brighter and closer. Aiden lowered the window enough to make eye contact with a fiftyish policeman with a military haircut. Deep frown lines creased the man's face, indicating a perpetual scowl.

"Well, what are you waiting for?" He peered around Aiden to Sophie. "She can ride up front."

"Yes, sir." Aiden raised the window and handed Sophie the keys.

They exited the SUV and dashed to the other vehicle. By the time Aiden got inside he was soaking wet. He hadn't brought a raincoat to Piper's Cove, as he'd expected to be home before the storm hit.

He buckled up and dried his face with the damp tail of his T-shirt.

"Address?" The officer's gravelly voice indicated the consumption of many packs of cigarettes.

Sophie rattled off the address.

The officer scowled at Aiden in the rearview mirror. "This is a bad night to be out. You might exercise some common sense next time we have a hurricane moving through the area."

Aiden frowned at the back of Sophie's head. "We appreciate the ride."

"There are people out there with real emergencies, you know. Woman had a chair come through a window and knock her out cold. Fire started inside a garage, and a little boy is on his way to the ER. And that's to say nothing of the everyday emergencies like heart attacks and strokes." He mumbled something, but Aiden only caught the words *stupidity* and *common sense*.

Sophie was apparently too busy on her phone to respond.

"Sounds like you've had a rough night," Aiden said.

"You don't know the half of it." The officer kept up a running monologue, and he had nothing positive to say.

Of all the cops in Piper's Cove, they'd had to get this one. Feeling tenser by the moment, he tuned out the man. What a long afternoon. Aiden tried to feel sorry for Sophie, who was in for some expensive car repairs. But she'd been the one who'd insisted on this ill-conceived adventure.

As soon as they pulled into the drive, Aiden unbuckled his belt, as relieved to escape the officer as he was to be back at the house.

"Do everyone a favor and stay put till the storm's over," the officer growled.

"Yes, sir." He ground out a thank-you, then he dashed through the rain, following Sophie up the porch steps and into the house.

꧁꧂

Sophie dried the last plate and set it in the cabinet. The kitchen was now sparkling clean—at least she thought it was. Hard to tell when she was working by candlelight. She dried her hands on the towel. She'd officially run out of ways to occupy herself.

Aiden was in the living room, working a crossword puzzle by candlelight. He'd been silent since that officer had dropped them off.

What in the world were they going to do for the rest of the night?

Unable to stall any longer, she returned to the living room and sat across from him on the sofa's end. She lifted Pippa onto the couch, and the dog curled up at her side, propping her head on Sophie's leg.

Sophie petted Pippa's trembling body. The little darling was traumatized from having been left home alone. She could relate to the dog's anxiety. Sophie had never been claustrophobic, but with the windows boarded, the temperature rising, and darkness pressing in, she was feeling a little cramped now. And okay, Aiden's presence wasn't helping either.

"Run out of ways to avoid me?"

Aiden was studying her, the golden candlelight flickering on his face, an enigmatic look in his eyes. He was a gorgeous man, she couldn't deny that.

And she didn't see any point in denying his accusation. "You seemed upset with me. I thought it best if we went to our own corners for a while."

He set aside the crossword puzzle, his shoulders sinking in a sigh. "I'm not upset with you. Well, okay, I *was* upset, but I'm over it. I'm not going to be like Officer Cranky Pants about all this, and honestly there's so much underlying stuff between us—" He gave her a pained look. "I'd really just like to get it settled once and for all, Sophie."

Oh, that. She'd been hoping he'd let it go. She didn't want to relive what had happened between them. Didn't want to feel the pain of betrayal and heartache. That wound had scabbed over, and she didn't want to tear it away for fear it might conceal a festering infection.

"I'm not ready to talk about it, Aiden."

"It's been seven years. When do you think you'll be ready?"

A valid question.

As if reading her mind, Pippa stood up on the couch and whined, giving Sophie that look she knew so well.

"She has to go out. I should've thought about that. I can't take her out there in this."

Aiden pushed to his feet. "I set up something in the garage earlier. I'll take her."

Sophie wasn't sure when Aiden had had time for that, but she was grateful. She set Pippa on the floor. "Thanks."

"Come on, girl. Let's go potty."

The dog followed Aiden to the garage door.

Sophie sank into the sofa cushions, grateful for the reprieve, no matter how short. But when he returned she would have to relive the worst day of her life—whether she wanted to or not.

chapter
eleven

Raleigh, North Carolina
Seven years ago

Sophie stared at the acceptance letter from Duke University. The euphoria she'd experienced upon retrieving it from the mailbox only hours before had been stomped out by the discovery she'd made upon entering her house.

She tucked the letter in her nightstand drawer, her little secret. Going to Duke, returning home on weekends, was no longer an option. She'd have to be here every day.

Things had been depressing around the house since her mom's doctor told them she'd soon be permanently bedridden. Multiple sclerosis, especially the type her mom had, was a scary illness. Rose Lawson had no chance of improvement, only a certainty that things would get progressively worse.

Sophie checked her watch. She was supposed to meet Aiden at his house when he got off work in fifteen minutes. He had some kind of big news. And boy, did she have news of her own. But she didn't want to leave Mama alone.

She sent Aiden a text asking him to come here instead.

He responded quickly. I guess we can talk on the porch.

She frowned at the message, her stomach tightening at the way he'd phrased it. Their relationship had been a little strained since their argument last week when she canceled yet another date to take care of her mother. Sometimes he didn't understand the weight of her responsibilities. He'd blown the situation all out of proportion.

A knock sounded on her bedroom door, and Sophie blinked back tears before she opened it. Jenna looked paler than usual, her blue eyes watery and bloodshot. Tears streaked her carefully applied makeup.

Upon sight of her sister's distress, Sophie wanted to burst into tears herself. But she had to be strong for her sister. She could fall apart later, in Aiden's arms.

She ushered Jenna into the room and closed the door behind her. She didn't want their mother to overhear. She was napping on the couch and had enough stress of her own right now.

"How could he do this to us?" Jenna whispered.

Sophie led her to the bed, where they sat down. Their dad had been gone when they'd gotten home from school, and he'd taken all his belongings with him. Even now Sophie could hardly comprehend the magnitude of his betrayal. "I don't know. I mean, he's been a little distant lately but—"

"And short-tempered with Mama."

"Still . . . I never dreamed he'd abandon her like this."

"Abandon *all* of us." Jenna looked up at Sophie, eyes awash in fresh tears. "It really hurts that he'd do that to us. Just leave us like he doesn't love us. Like we don't need him anymore!"

Sophie had a fist-size ache in her chest. She wished Seth were here to participate in this conversation, but he'd reacted to the news with anger. Just taken off in his old Mustang, and they hadn't heard from him since. Maybe he'd burn off his anger. Mom didn't need that right now.

"What are we going to do?" Jenna whispered. "She's going to be bedridden soon, and we're still in school. Who's going to take care of her? We can't afford home care. Especially not now."

"It's going to be fine, honey. Mrs. Collins will watch her during the day." Their neighbor had been a godsend. "And I'll quit my job at the library and take care of her the rest of the day."

"But you and Seth are leaving for college in the fall!" Jenna's eyes were wide with panic. "How am I going to manage all by myself?"

"Don't worry about that. I can go to school here." The thought of that acceptance letter made her stomach twist. "I didn't really want to leave Mama anyway, and now I have double reason to stay. You and Seth—your lives will go on as they always have, I promise."

"Oh, Sophie." Jenna's eyes locked on hers. "You'd do that for us?"

She put her arm around Jenna. "Of course I would. You're my baby sister. But we have to be strong for Mama right now. This is hard enough on her without having to bear our sadness too. She must feel so betrayed."

"I'll be strong for her." Jenna dabbed at her tears. "Do you think Daddy might come back? Maybe he was overwhelmed by her prognosis."

Sophie wished that were true. But as good a provider as their dad had always been, he was also selfish. In retrospect, she could see the red flags. The way he'd progressively left her mother's care to others. How distant he'd become with them. The only time he stayed with their mom was on Sunday mornings, and Sophie suspected that was more about skipping church than it was about caring for his wife.

"He's not going far—he'll be just across town, and I'm sure he'll want us to visit." Although Sophie didn't even want to see his face at this point.

She gave Jenna one last hug. "I'm going to check on Mama, then Aiden's coming over. We'll be out on the porch talking. Are you going to be okay?"

Jenna dried her tears with her sleeves, sniffling. "I think I'll work on my history paper. It'll give me something else to focus on. Have you heard from Seth?"

"No, but I'll try him again." Sophie tapped out a text asking if he was okay. He sent one back immediately.

I'll be fine. Don't worry about me. I'm at Spencer's house.

She showed the text to Jenna. "See, he's fine. He'll talk things out with Spencer."

Jenna returned to her room, and Sophie checked the mirror before heading to the living room. Her mother lay on the sofa, curled on her side. She looked so peaceful in sleep, but she had puffy bags under her eyes from crying.

Sophie pulled an afghan from the back of the couch and draped it over her mom's sleeping form. *It's okay, Mama. I'm going to take care of you.*

The sound of Aiden's truck filtered through the walls. Sophie would recognize that rumble anywhere. She slipped on a sweater and slid out the door, eager to be with him after this rotten day.

As he jumped from his truck, peace rolled over her. She loved his manly swagger and the crooked smile he gave her. When he joined her on the porch she pressed into his solid chest. What would she do without him? Even when her whole world was spinning out of control, he was here to make sense of it all.

He wrapped his arms around her, chuckling. "Well, that's a nice greeting."

"What a day. You have no idea how glad I am to see you."

He squeezed her before letting go. "Tell me about it."

He looked so happy, and she didn't want to ruin his good mood just yet. "You first. What's this opportunity you're bursting to tell me about? I could use some good news."

"Let's sit down." He led her to the swing. The familiar glide and squeak of the chains had a calming effect on her. They'd spent hours out here talking and snuggling and making out. It was their special spot.

He clasped her hand and rested it on his thigh. "You

remember that big house Dad and I roofed last fall? The one in Windemere?"

"The one with all the gables?"

"Right. I think I told you the owner, Ross Givens, and I struck up a conversation and realized we had common ground. He used to own an outfitters business in Colorado, and he was getting ready to open an extreme sporting business in Charleston."

"Yeah." Sophie nodded, a feeling of dread worming its way into her heart. "I remember."

"Well, Ross called me last week and made me an offer. I almost told you about it then, but I wanted to think on it first. Sophie . . ." His gaze sharpened on hers. "He wants me as a partner in that business. He wants me to move to Charleston and handle the adventure side of it. At first we'd just offer kite surfing, wakeboarding, parasailing, and stuff. Eventually he wants to offer tandem jumping—he has a buddy who runs an airfield nearby."

Something cold swept through Sophie, numbing her from the inside out. She couldn't seem to unfreeze her tongue from the roof of her mouth.

"I told Ross today . . . I'm going to do it. I'm taking him up on his offer. I get to be his partner in this, Sophie. I don't have to invest money or anything—my part's all sweat equity because I'm bringing a lot of experience to the business. We're signing papers later today. It's going to happen fast because he wants to be up and running by spring break."

"You're leaving?"

Aiden blinked at her, some of the joy slipping from his face.

"Hey, Jelly Bean . . . Don't be sad. I know Charleston's a bit of a drive—"

"Four hours!"

"—but this is a great opportunity. How can I pass it up? This is a chance to be a business owner, and it won't cost me a dime."

"I—I thought you were going to take over your dad's company someday." He'd mentioned it a time or two. They'd settle here and raise a family. A band tightened around her throat.

"Aw, you know that's not really my thing. I mean, I can roof as well as the next guy, but the thought of doing it for the rest of my life? It doesn't exactly ring any bells, you know? And we barely get by on the profits. I want more than that for my life."

Sophie gave her head a shake. She couldn't believe this was happening. Or that he was so excited to be—to be *leaving* her. She'd thought they were spending the rest of their lives together. They hadn't talked about it in great detail, but the subject had come up a time or two.

"I thought we were—" She swallowed hard and forced the words out. "I thought you loved me."

He squeezed her hand. "Ah, honey, I do love you. Come on, Soph, be happy for me. It's only a few hours' drive. You can visit me all the time. Maybe even move down there after graduation. There are some good schools there."

She jerked her hand from his. There was so much wrong with what he'd said she hardly knew where to start. "I can't move there, Aiden."

Especially not now. She opened her mouth to tell him all about her dad's desertion. About how she had to stay in Raleigh now and be her mother's primary caregiver, possibly for years. *Hopefully* for years.

But the look on his face told her that wouldn't matter. Nothing she said would change his mind about leaving. And she wasn't going to beg him—or guilt him—into staying. She had her pride.

"Try to understand," he said. "This is a once-in-a-lifetime opportunity. Hitching my future to Ross's wagon is smart. He's successful in everything he does—he's a freaking millionaire. And he wants *me.*"

So do I, she thought weakly. But that didn't seem to matter to him. He had stars in his eyes, and they were blinding him to everything else, including her.

"I can't believe you made this decision without even talking to me."

"I know I should've said something earlier, but I didn't want to muddy the waters. Come on, Soph. This doesn't have to be the end or anything. We can keep in touch and see what happens."

She flinched. *See what happens?* Those words, more than anything else he'd said, showed she'd perceived their relationship much differently than he had—regardless of his heat-of-the-moment proclamations.

She left the swing, crossing her arms against the sudden chill in the air. She was shaking, trembling from the inside out. "I think you should go now, Aiden."

He rose, giving her that puppy dog look. "Come on, Sophie . . ."

"I mean it, Aiden." Her voice somehow sounded like steel

even though she was melting inside. "If you want to go, then go. But don't think I'm going to follow you or hang around here waiting on you."

He searched her face somberly, his eyes drooping sadly at the corners, his smile long gone.

Sophie didn't wait to see what he'd say or do next. She had her own life, her own problems to deal with, and he was leaving her here to do it. Without another word she turned away from him, opened the door, and slipped inside.

chapter

twelve

Piper's Cove
Present Day

The potty run was taking longer than Aiden anticipated.
Pippa didn't seem to know what to do on the newspapers he'd
spread across the floor. She must've never been paper-trained.

He guided her back to the papers. "Go potty, girl," he said
for the tenth time.

The dog peered up at him mournfully, eyes glowing in the
beam of light, tail drooping.

"It's okay. Go ahead and potty."

He left her there and wandered around the perimeter of the
garage, surveying the tools organized on the Peg-Board. Mr.
Foster was a tidy man. The walls were bright white, and the
concrete floor was clean enough to eat off of.

If Aiden was honest, he didn't mind that Pippa was taking

her own sweet time. Part of him dreaded the upcoming conversation with Sophie even though it was necessary. He was afraid he wouldn't have answers for her questions about what he'd done.

What if, when they walked away from each other this time, they were no closer to a resolution? What if Sophie still hated him? What if leaving her still felt like the biggest mistake of his life?

The jingle of Pippa's dog tags pulled him from his thoughts. The dog had done her business on the newspaper. She stared up at him, pride shining in her eyes.

"Good girl, Pippa. Just needed a little privacy, huh? Let's go see Mama."

Pippa darted to the door, tail wagging.

Aiden wished he felt as optimistic as the dog. He closed the garage door behind him and returned to the living room.

Sophie lifted Pippa onto the sofa. "All better now, sweetie?"

"She wasn't too crazy about the newspaper, but she finally went."

Sophie looked at him across the candlelit room. "Thank you."

A long beat of silence hung between them, punctuated by the pounding of rain and the rattling of shutters. He sensed her reluctance to return to the topic at hand. She probably wouldn't bring it up again if he didn't.

"There's something I never told you," she blurted.

His gaze fastened on hers. This was going to happen then. "All right . . ."

Sophie stroked Pippa as if she needed to occupy her hands with some meaningless task. "The night you came over to tell me you were leaving . . . It was the same day my dad left us."

Aiden reared back. "Left you?"

"When I got home from school that day, my mom was a wreck. All my dad's stuff was gone. He left us—and he never came back."

Aiden felt all the breath leave his body. "Oh, Sophie. I didn't know."

How had no one told him this? Well, it wasn't as if he'd ever spoken to Sophie again. And once Grant had started dating Jenna, Aiden had shut him down whenever he brought up Sophie or her family. It was somehow easier if Aiden knew nothing about her life.

"He divorced your mom? When she was all but bedridden?" Craig Lawson had left his family to fend for itself at the worst possible time. Heat flushed through Aiden's body.

"In record time."

Aiden wished he could take back the condolences he'd offered the man last night. He thought it odd that Craig had moved on so quickly after Rose's death, but that sometimes happened after a spouse's long illness. Aiden wanted to throat punch the guy now. No wonder there'd been so much tension between Craig and Seth during the wedding festivities. It was a wonder Jenna had even wanted her father to walk her down the aisle.

"But if he left," Aiden said, "who took care of your—?"

The sudden realization made his stomach harden. Reliable Sophie. Dependable Sophie. Always ready to help those she loved.

"You did." Another realization struck. "That's why you turned down Duke."

She looked down at Pippa. "I don't regret a single moment I spent with Mama. She was a great woman and a wonderful mother. I would've taken care of her the rest of her life if I'd had the opportunity."

Her words barely registered because something else hit him. "Wait. Your dad left the same day we talked on the porch? The same day I told you I was leaving?"

She gave him a wry grin. "I seem to recall mentioning I'd had a bad day."

A bad— He closed his eyes in a long blink. "Sophie, why didn't you tell me? Why didn't you stop me, why didn't you—?"

"What for, Aiden?" She lifted a shoulder, looking hopeless in the golden glow of the candlelight. "You were leaving. Nothing was going to stop you, least of all me."

He opened his mouth to say it wasn't true. But then he recalled his mindset that day. The euphoria. The way Ross's offer had made him feel wanted and needed.

And despite the ache of disappointment that welled up at his own selfishness, she was right. It gutted him now to think of Sophie sitting on that porch swing, hearing him tell her he was leaving right after her father had deserted them. "I am so sorry. I feel like a total jerk."

"You didn't know."

A heavy weight settled inside him at what he'd done to someone he'd supposedly loved.

He scrubbed a hand over his face, a humorless laugh escaping. "No wonder you hate me so much."

And here he'd thought a sincere apology would fix everything. But Aiden knew what it felt like to be abandoned. He barely even remembered his mom, but her departure had left scars that ran so deep they were untouchable.

"I don't hate you." He barely heard her words over the storm. "You obviously didn't feel the same way about me that I felt about you. I guess you couldn't help that."

He leaned forward, elbows on knees. "But I did, Sophie. I loved you like crazy. What we had was special."

"It's okay, Aiden. You don't have to spare my feelings."

"It's the truth. After I left I thought about you every day. I missed you. And while, yes, the business eventually became a success and I loved what I was doing . . . a part of me felt empty without you." Still did. But she wouldn't believe him even if he told her—and he probably shouldn't, as he was sort of dating someone else.

"You were my person, Soph. The one I went to when things were falling apart or when they were going great, and I needed someone to be happy for me. You were my biggest cheerleader. Remember when I got a C in algebra, and my dad was disappointed even though I'd done my best? You gave me a hug and said you were proud of me. You told me I was smart. Nobody had ever told me that before." Even now, the memory of that moment made his throat thicken.

"You are smart," she said softly.

The corner of his lip turned up. "See what I mean? You always saw the best in me."

And then he'd dumped her for a job opportunity. His smile fell as he rose from his chair, suddenly needing to be beside her.

Sophie tensed as the cushion beside her sank under Aiden's weight. She withdrew her hand from Pippa and set it in her lap.

He seemed regretful, and part of her was glad for that. But his contrition also made her more vulnerable. She'd always been so vulnerable to him.

He set his hand on hers, his gaze piercing hers. He could make her feel so many things with just a touch—and she was feeling them all right now. Remembering how in love with him she'd been. How hurt she was when he left. How long it had taken to get over him.

She had gotten over him, hadn't she? It was hard to tell when he was looking at her like this.

"I was such an idiot," he said. "I went over to your house high on myself because somebody believed in me. And I hurt the person who'd always believed in me the most. I don't know what I was thinking."

"You were thinking I'd give up all my dreams to follow you."

A frown creased his brow. "I don't think I ever believed that. I knew how much Duke meant to you. And I knew you wouldn't move so far away from your mom."

Sophie pulled her hand from his and lifted Pippa onto her lap. She needed comfort—and a buffer.

Neither of them spoke for a moment. Rain battered the roof. The shutters clattered. Somewhere in the distance a siren sounded.

"I did love you, Sophie. I hope you believe that."

Just not enough. She tried for a smile. "It's okay, Aiden."

"I didn't deserve you, you know. I didn't deserve a girl who'd given up all her dreams to take care of her siblings and her dying mother. I was far too selfish to ever do that."

Sophie remembered all the times she'd felt used up. The times she'd been resentful, like when Seth left for college and when Jenna went out on weekend nights with her friends. All of Sophie's friends had gone off to college and gradually drifted away. "Don't give me too much credit. I'm plenty selfish."

"That's not the way I see you. And I doubt that's the way anyone else sees you either. But, Sophie . . ." he said gently, eyes softening on her. "You should've told me about your dad leaving that day. I might not have done anything differently, but you didn't even give me the option of changing my mind."

He was right. Not telling him had been her choice. Maybe he wouldn't have done anything differently, but she hadn't given him the chance to find out.

"You're right. I'm sorry."

He nodded, but she could tell he still had a cloud hanging over him. He hadn't forgiven himself for leaving without a backward glance. Sophie wanted to give him the release he longed for, but she was also afraid to remove that last barrier. It was the only thing keeping her safe from him.

That and the girlfriend. And the fact that he'd be leaving as soon as the last raindrop fell.

Also problematic: She wasn't angry with him anymore. He'd been so young, and even if he didn't realize it, the depth of his feelings had probably scared him. She knew what abandonment did to a person. There was a reason she hadn't fallen for anyone else after him. People left. No one knew that better than her.

"I really am sorry, Sophie."

She gave him a smile that wasn't all that hard to dredge up. "Don't worry, Aiden. I forgive you."

His features went soft in the candlelight. But a moment later he lifted an impish brow. "Thought you already forgave me."

Remembering the dismissive words she'd thrown at him during their dance, she smiled. "Yeah, well, this time I mean it."

His eyes swept over her face. He nudged her shoulder. "Thank you."

She nudged his back. "You're welcome."

A long, quiet moment passed between them.

Then his lips turned up in that cocky half smile she used to love. "Do you think the Fosters still keep that cabinet full of old-school games?"

"I happen to know for a fact that they do."

chapter

thirteen

Aiden pouted. *"The popper's broken."*

Sophie rolled her eyes at his antics. He'd always been a sore loser. "It is not. The dice jumped, and you're going home. Sorry."

"You're not sorry." He eyed Sophie as she moved his red piece back home. "You're enjoying this."

"Well, you killed me at Yahtzee so, yes, a little bit."

He hit the pop-die but didn't get the number he needed, so he deferred to her.

Sophie got a "two" and moved her last remaining blue piece. The rain still pattered on the roof overhead. Over the past couple hours the house had grown warm and stifling.

"So, have you stayed here a lot with Grant and his family?" Sophie asked.

"Couple times. It's a nice getaway, and they don't use it much during the week."

"Beautiful place. It was nice of them to let me stay while I get my shop up and running. I sure hope I get it open in time."

"There's some kind of deadline?"

"Have you heard of Nathaniel Quinn, the author?"

"He's had a couple books adapted into movies, hasn't he?"

"Yes. Well, his upcoming novel is set here in Piper's Cove, and I'm hosting his book release party a week from Tuesday. It's going to be huge. I have flyers up all over the region and a web-page devoted to the event. I sent out press releases, and the local media will be there, not to mention all his fans."

"Wow, how'd you score that gig?"

"Rosewood Press contacted the mayor, asking who could host it. I initially wasn't planning to open the shop until mid-June, but I couldn't pass up the opportunity for so much expo-sure. By the time the party's over, every reader in a hundred-mile radius will know about Bookshop by the Sea."

"Talk about an influx of capital."

She needed it too. The cost of a website designer and renova-tion materials had drained her savings. Not to mention the fees associated with registering her business and getting her permits.

"So you see why I have to open on time. I had the renovation scheduled out to the day, and because of the storm I'm already behind."

"You should be able to start tomorrow afternoon, though. The storm's supposed to let up in the late morning."

"I'll be fine as long as I don't encounter unexpected problems. The shelves have to go in over the weekend, so the walls and floors need to be finished by then."

"Is your apartment ready for occupancy?" He pushed the popper, then scowled when he had to pass his turn again.

"Not quite but that'll have to wait until next week." She stroked Pippa's back. "We'll be quite cozy up there, won't we, girl? And we'll have our pick of books to curl up with at night."

"You always did have your nose in a book." His tone held a hint of affection.

"What about you? I always thought maybe you'd be a reader when you got older—spy novels or true crime, maybe?"

He arched a brow. "Sorry to disappoint."

"Not at all? Not even when you're super bored or stuck at the doctor's office?"

"Do magazines and newspapers count?" Aiden's phone buzzed with an incoming text. He checked the phone, then set it down without responding.

Sophie moved her piece. "Is that your girlfriend?"

His eyes met hers across the coffee table, then darted away. "Yeah."

"You can answer if you want to."

"It's nothing that can't wait."

Sophie was curious about the woman. What did she look like? What did she do for a living? Did Aiden tremble when he touched her the way he had when he'd touched Sophie?

She shook the thought away. "How'd the two of you meet?"

He took a sip of his iced tea, then took another turn, finally getting the right number. "She's a pilot at the airstrip we use for jumps."

"A pilot." Looked as if Aiden had paired up with a fellow

adrenaline junkie. She flew the plane and he jumped out of it. There must be camaraderie in that. "So you work together."

"Sometimes. There are several pilots. Tiffany also handles paperwork in the office, so she doesn't fly as much as some of the others."

Tiffany. "That's nice."

"What about you? Boyfriend?"

She shot him a wry grin. "When would I have had time for that?"

"I guess you've put your life on hold to some degree. But surely you've dated."

"Very little." She could count them on two fingers, actually, but she wasn't owning up to that. "And with no one who interested me."

She felt his perusal and wondered what he was thinking. Heat bloomed in her cheeks as she stroked Pippa's head.

"You deserve someone special, Sophie. Maybe now that you have a new beginning you'll find him."

His blue eyes were mere shadows in the flickering candlelight. "Maybe I will." Their gazes held for a long, poignant moment. Years ago she'd thought he was her special someone. She would've staked her life on it. Her heart felt as if it might pound right out of her chest.

He still affected her like no other man. When he'd arrived at the house she only wanted to avoid him. But now, only one day later, she dreaded his leaving. What in the world? If she wasn't careful she'd lose her heart before the storm even passed. Maybe she'd lost a bit of it already.

She jerked her eyes back to the game board and rolled the dice, getting the number she needed to send her final piece home.

She glanced triumphantly at Aiden as she took care of business with a flair. "I'm so sorry. I'm afraid you've lost."

"You're not one bit sorry. Best two out of three."

She glanced at her watch. It wasn't that late, but this—the darkness, the candlelight, the conversation—was too intimate. Too dangerous.

"It's getting late." She swigged the last of her drink and rose to her feet. "I think I'll turn in while we're even."

After she helped him put away the games, he knelt down and gave Pippa some love. When he straightened, his expression was an enigma in the flickering shadows.

"Here, take a flashlight. Good night, Sophie. Sleep well."

"Night, Aiden." She scooped up Pippa and headed to her room, feeling his eyes on her until she closed the door.

She leaned against it, setting a kiss on Pippa's head. "Don't get too attached, sweetie," she whispered. "He'll be leaving soon."

chapter

fourteen

Sophie awakened to darkness. She'd slept like a rock but had no notion what time it was. Pippa didn't stir as she stretched toward the flashlight on her nightstand and flipped it on. It was after nine o'clock in the morning.

She searched for her dog in the jumbled bedding. "Pippa?" Not finding her, Sophie shone the light around the room. The door was cracked open.

Rain pattered on the roof, and the wind howled as she slipped from bed and out the door. "Pippa?"

"She's in here." In the living room Aiden was seated in the armchair, the screen of his phone lighting his face.

Pippa jumped from his lap and skittered over to greet her.

"She was whining earlier so I took her to the garage to do her business. She's getting to be an old pro."

"Thank you." Sophie smoothed her hair, which probably looked like a skein of yarn. "I can't believe I slept this late."

"You must've needed it. And it's so dark it's impossible to know the time." He handed her the phone. "I charged it in my car all night. You've got a few messages."

"Thanks." Her notifications showed an unknown caller, a text from Seth, two from Jenna, and one from Erik. She and the groomsman had texted back and forth a bit, but hours went by between her texts and his responses. It was a little annoying.

"I scheduled a flight for tonight," he said.

Her stomach plummeted. "That's great."

"The storm will be over early this afternoon, and we can get the house back in order before I go."

"Thank you. I appreciate the help. Hope there's not much damage."

"Doubt it. The house has been through much worse. I helped myself to a protein bar earlier. There's plenty left."

"I'd kill for coffee."

"Too bad there's no fireplace—I could heat some water."

"How long do you think the electricity will be out?"

"Hard to say. Hopefully not more than a day or two. I can take you to get a rental car later if we can find someplace open."

"That would be great. Thanks. I'll have to call for a tow too." She shifted. "I think I'll go get dressed."

❦

Sophie retreated to her room, Pippa on her heels. The woman looked adorably mussed fresh out of bed. Even in the dimness he could see the pillow crease on her cheek and the snarls in her tousled brown hair. He was glad she'd been able to sleep late.

As for himself he'd tossed and turned, thinking about last night's conversation. About her revelation, about the way she'd forgiven him. She lightened up as they played the games. He glimpsed a side of her he hadn't seen since their dating days. He'd forgotten how competitive she was. She'd never been the most gracious winner.

But he hadn't minded. He always played along, sulking, while secretly admiring his strong, sassy woman. And last night he'd been glad to see the old Sophie coming out. The one he'd fallen in love with.

Careful, Maddox. You're leaving tonight.

What was he doing? No need to go traipsing down memory lane. He'd achieved what he hoped—settled the past with Sophie. He was free and clear to go home and finally move on. This time together had been healing for him and for Sophie too. But soon they'd go their separate ways.

He'd repeated the same mantra several times during the night, but something inside him refuted the message.

Enough with the wishful thinking.

He awakened his phone. Tiffany had texted him late last night, and he hadn't responded. He replied now, letting her know about his flight. He should ask her about becoming exclusive when he got home. She'd been hinting around awhile, but he'd been hesitant. And if he didn't do something soon she was going to move on.

That notion should bother him more than it actually did. He

shook away thoughts of Tiffany. He should work on his speech for tomorrow night. He'd planned to write it on the plane, but he needed something to focus on now.

Back when he'd devised the SpringChute, he'd never dreamed his little invention would go beyond Extreme Adventures. But Ross entered him for an Extreme Sports Technology Award in the Innovations category, and Aiden was actually a finalist.

The awards ceremony was tomorrow night. He didn't expect to win the ESTA; the competition was stiff. But he was honored just to be considered. It was the most prestigious award in the industry, and a lot of influential people would be present.

Aiden had never won anything before, much less something like this. He needed to get some words down on paper or risk making a fool of himself on the off chance he did win. He wanted to do Ross proud.

Aiden looked down at his phone. How long could it take to write a one-minute speech?

Aiden had been at it for twenty minutes. He wrote three different openings and deleted them all. The first was too casual, the second too formal, and the last was a lame attempt at a joke that wasn't funny or appropriate for the audience. He needed to strike the right tone. But he'd never been a good writer.

He was so wrapped up in the speech he didn't even realize Sophie had passed by until he heard her in the kitchen.

He read his newest opening sentence. Not great. Not terrible. He had to move on. He could always tweak it later.

He made a list of people to thank—it was pretty short. Besides his dad and Ross and God in heaven, who else was he going to thank? What he'd written so far was as boring as mud and would take ten seconds to deliver. He couldn't give a ten-second speech. But how was he going to fill a full minute without a long list of names?

He googled *thank-you speeches* and spent a few minutes reading other people's work. Some were too specific, others general and boring. Maybe all thank-you speeches were dull. Maybe his expectations were too high. He reread what he'd written. The only good thing about it was it was too short to put the audience to sleep.

He jumped out of planes for a living—surely he could do better.

"That was a pretty heavy sigh." Sophie sank onto the sofa and pulled a wad of yarn from a bag.

Glad for the diversion, Aiden set down his phone. "You still crochet."

She arched a brow. "You still don't know the difference between crocheting and knitting."

"Guilty. What are you working on?"

"A winter hat for Granny. What are you working on?"

He scowled at his phone. "A speech."

"I hate to tell you this, but you already delivered your best-man toast. The good news is, you nailed it."

"That was easy. All I had to do was dredge up a few funny memories—Grant and I have plenty of those—then wish the couple well."

"As opposed to this speech . . . ?"

He read the lines to himself and winced. "It's for an award. I probably won't win, but I need something in my back pocket just in case. It'll be in front of industry professionals—people who wear suits and have a lot of money. I wouldn't care so much for me, but I don't want to embarrass Ross."

Her needles clacked together. "What kind of award?"

"It's nothing, just a project I worked on, on the side. Little doodad to make jumping safer."

"You invented something?"

He shifted. "I guess. Ross entered it for an ESTA—Extreme Sports Technology Award—and here I am."

"Aiden . . ." Sophie's mouth widened in a smile. "That's wonderful. You invented something! You always were an out-of-the-box thinker."

Pleasure bloomed inside at her words. "It's really not a big deal."

"Sounds like a big deal to me. You're up for an industry award! Read me what you've got so far."

He made a face but did as she said. It sounded just as boring out loud as it had in his head. When he was finished he made himself meet her gaze. "See? Lame."

She laughed. "You have the bones down."

"It'll take me longer to walk to the podium than it'll take me to deliver this thing. If I win—and I won't. I'm sweating this for nothing."

"Why do you do that? A panel of professionals decided you deserve this honor. Tell me about your invention."

He shrugged. "I call it SpringChute. It's just a little gizmo that makes opening the chute safer. Reduces the risk of failure."

"So basically your invention could save lives."

He opened his mouth and shut it again. When she put it like that . . . "I guess so. That's the hope anyway."

"In that case the award would just be a bonus."

That had been his motive for inventing it. But if he won, someone might want to buy his patent. It wasn't uncommon for a winner to be approached after the ceremony itself. Plus there was the ten-thousand-dollar prize, meant to help the winner take the product to market if he or she wanted.

Sophie smiled down at her needlework. "And why do you want to thank your dad?"

He did a double take. "Because he taught me everything I know. Because he showed me what hard work and discipline can accomplish. Because he sacrificed everything to give me a good life."

She held his gaze, her smile widening. "And Ross?"

"I see what you're doing here. All right, Ross. He gave me the opportunity of a lifetime. Ross believed in me."

She nodded. "Good stuff, Aiden."

"And God," he added, having the hang of it now. "Well, I wouldn't even be breathing without Him, now would I?"

"There you go then. Sounds as if you've got this."

"I need to get all that down." He opened his notes and started writing, his fingers clumsy on the tiny keypad. When he finished the acknowledgments he silently read through the speech from the beginning, correcting a thing or two as he went.

"The opening is still boring." He looked up at Sophie. "Any suggestions? And don't say 'open with a joke.' I tried that already."

"Sounds as if this whole award thing is a little scary for you."

"You know, writing's not my thing."

She gave him a pointed look. "And yet, you jump out of planes for a living . . ."

"I see the irony." As he frowned down at his phone the perfect opening line came to him. He glanced back at Sophie, a smile spreading across his face.

chapter

fifteen

From beneath her lashes Sophie watched Aiden's brows draw together as he tapped away on his phone. Helping him like this took her back to when she'd tutored him. He never needed much help with writing, really—just someone to jump-start his creativity. She completed the knit stitch and began another.

Her phone buzzed at an incoming call, and she recognized the number from the previous voice mail. Joshua had promised to call back later. She appreciated that he hadn't put the burden to call back on her like a lot of people did. And she *had* looked him up on Facebook. Not only was he a handsome doctor, but he regularly posted pictures of his family, and he had an adorable black Labrador named Bear, to boot.

She set down her knitting and answered the call. "Hello?"

"Hi, is this Sophie?"

"Speaking."

"Hi, Sophie. It's Joshua Stevens—my grandmother is a friend of your grandmother." He said the last a little sheepishly.

"I hope she didn't have to twist your arm too hard."

His laugh was a pleasant one. "Not once I found you on social media. I confess to stalking you a little."

"In the vein of honesty, I'll fess up to a little stalking myself."

"And you still answered my call?"

"It was Bear that sealed the deal."

He laughed. "Your grandmother didn't lie. You really are delightful."

"You know, she never says nice things to my face."

"I have a sister like that. Other people tell me things she's said, and when I bring it up to her—okay, hold it over her head—she denies she ever said such a thing."

Sophie laughed. She caught Aiden's eye, and her stomach gave a little wobble. She looked away. "Sounds about right. I have two siblings myself."

"Full confession, I saw them on your Facebook page. You were recently in your sister's wedding—this is weird, isn't it? I should at least pretend I don't know your life history."

"Would it make you feel better if I ask how your nephews are doing on their mission trip?"

He laughed. "It would, actually. Dating in the modern day sure is a wild adventure. I took somewhat of a break during the rigors of med school, and when I jumped back on the merry-go-round, everyone was meeting on apps and cyberstalking."

"It's a brave new world. I admit I've been on a bit of a break too."

"Your grandmother said you were opening a bookshop in Piper's Cove."

"Guilty as charged. It's been a long time in the works."

"I gathered . . ." He paused for so long Sophie nearly checked her connection. "Listen, it sounds as if you're wanting to grow roots there on the coast—and I'm stuck here in Raleigh, at least through my residency."

Sensing a dismissal, Sophie shifted in her seat. "Ah. I see what you're getting at."

"No, no. I'm just saying . . . distance is an obstacle, at least a short-term one. But I really like you, Sophie, and I'd like to get to know you better."

"I'd like that too."

☙

Aiden scrolled through his newsfeed, not seeing a thing. He'd finished his speech a long time ago. Sophie had been on the phone for a good twenty minutes. They were talking about the hurricane now, but she neglected to mention she had company. He was so glad he'd charged up her phone for this.

Aiden scowled at Sophie, but she was focused on Pippa, now curled up on her lap.

He'd heard enough of the conversation to know a man was on the other end, and her slightly flirtatious tone told him it wasn't a mere friend. She might not have a boyfriend, but she was clearly working on it.

He should give her some privacy. But hey, why not sit here and listen to her seal the deal?

His chest tightened at the thought. He had no right to feel this way. Tonight he'd go home to Tiffany and a potential long-term relationship. Sophie deserved to have someone, too, didn't she? She of all people deserved a fulfilling life after putting her family first for so long.

"I don't mind meeting you halfway," Sophie said. "All right, if you insist. Looking forward to it. I'll see you then. You too."

Aiden continued scrolling, making a conscious effort to unclench his jaw and reminding himself his jealousy was unwarranted. She was free to set up a date if she chose. Heck, she was free to run off and elope, though he couldn't imagine her ever doing something so impulsive.

The silence had grown prolonged. He glanced up and found her watching him.

"That was the grandson of one of Granny's friends."

"Matchmaking, is she?"

"You know Granny—always butting in where she's not wanted."

That he did. He also remembered the way Granny May had rebuffed him at the rehearsal and wedding. Not that he blamed her.

"She's no fan of mine anymore. Must think I'm a real dog to have left on your dad's heels."

"I'll tell her you didn't know Dad had just left. I should've already told her. Don't know why I didn't."

"Doesn't matter now. I'll probably never even see her again."

His eyes locked on Sophie's across the room as realization sank in. In a matter of hours he'd leave for the airport. For home and work and Tiffany. Sophie would stay here and start her business, find some nice man—possibly the guy she'd just been chatting with—to settle down with.

The moment drew out, his stomach growing heavier until Aiden could hardly draw breath. The love they'd shared seven years ago was still present, he realized suddenly. Maybe it was just a seedling now, but it was there. With a little nurturing it could grow once again into something sturdy and thriving.

Sophie looked toward the kitchen, her gaze sharpening. "Listen . . . Do you hear that?"

Aiden's ears perked up, noting the absence of sound. "The rain stopped."

She straightened in her seat, eyes gleaming. "The storm's over."

chapter

sixteen

The storm left as suddenly as it arrived. From the deck Sophie anchored the window shutter in place, then wiped her hands on the dishrag.

A gray abyss yawned overhead, stretching toward the horizon where it met the blue of the sea. Waves undulated on its expansive surface, rolling ashore with loud crashes. The beach itself was littered with flotsam. Small branches and twigs cluttered the backyard, but thankfully there'd been no damage to the house.

She looked to the top of the ladder where Aiden secured the bedroom shutter. He leaned in as he worked, long legs pressed against the aluminum rungs. His biceps bulged beneath his short sleeves as he struggled to secure the shutter.

They were almost done. He'd confirmed that the airport had opened, and she'd reserved a rental car and left a message at a towing facility. He'd be leaving in a couple hours.

She shook away the gloom. Alanda had texted to let her

know the boardwalk shops had also lost electricity. Sophie would have to make do with natural light as she painted and use flashlights once the sun had set. She wouldn't let that sour her mood, though. Today was the start of her bright new beginning.

She shielded her eyes against the bright sky as she peered up at Aiden. "Well, I've finished my windows; what's taking *you* so long?"

He smiled down at her, that charming half smile that was so dangerous to her well-being. "Why's everything a competition with you, Lawson?"

"That's why I win, Maddox."

"You seem to have forgotten our Yahtzee game."

"Maybe I let you win because you're such a sore loser."

He laughed as he latched the shutter in place, then started down the ladder. "Since you're so good at this, I think I'll let you do the last window."

She steadied the ladder as he descended. "I'll probably get it done more quickly anyway."

"Be my guest. I'll pick up the sticks in the yard after I return a call."

"You don't have to do that. I can clean up tomorrow. But if you can take me to Budget, I'd appreciate it."

He checked his watch. "We should have time for both."

She stepped aside as he reached the ground. Then he picked up the ladder and moved it to the last window. "It's all yours."

He secured the ladder and held it in place as she ascended. It barely shook under Aiden's firm grip. Once she reached the third rung from the top, she braced herself.

"Thanks," she called down. "I got it from here."

She went to work on the left shutter. Was that call Aiden had to make to Tiffany? He'd gone inside the house—seeking privacy?

None of her business.

She made herself think instead of Joshua Stevens with a *v* and their upcoming date. He seemed nice enough, and even though she'd initially planned to go through with the date simply to appease her grandma, she decided she'd give the guy a real chance. It would take her mind off Aiden's departure, and she was coming to realize that was going to hit her hard.

Sophie secured one shutter quickly, but the other side was trickier. Aiden had managed both sides without moving the ladder, but her reach wasn't as broad as his.

Still, she could manage. She swung the shutter outward, pushing it back against the house. This last part would take a bit of balance. She put her weight on her right leg and reached. Yes, she could do this.

As she grabbed the bracket, the ladder shifted suddenly to the right. Her weight went with it. She grabbed the frame, but it was moving. Falling.

Gravity pulled. Helplessness engulfed her. A scream pierced the air just before she hit the ground with a thud.

❧

Aiden had just tapped the number into his phone when a shriek sliced the air. *Sophie.*

He tore out of the kitchen, ripped open the sliding door, and dashed outside. His muscles froze at the sight. The ladder lay on the ground, Sophie a motionless heap in the landscaping.

"Sophie!" He was at her side in two seconds flat. "Are you okay?"

She groaned. "My ankle."

"Let's lie you flat. Careful. Let me do it." He lifted her off a bush that had likely broken her fall and laid her in the mulch.

She winced with the movement. "It hurts."

He carefully tugged up her pants leg. Her ankle was starting to swell, but there was no noticeable deformity that would indicate an obvious break.

"Don't touch it!" she said when he reached out to do just that.

"It's okay. I'm certified as an EMT now. We should see what the damage is before we move you inside."

When she gave a nod he palpitated the area gently, checking for points of tenderness and watching her face for reaction.

He thought of the ladder lying on its side and glanced at the ground where he'd set it. It was the lowest part of the property and spongy from all the rain. He should've been more careful. He should've stayed and held the ladder. He should've climbed it himself instead of passing the task on to her so he could return a stupid call to the ESTA ceremony coordinator.

He finished checking her range of motion. "I don't think it's broken."

"I heard something snap."

"Probably a ligament. You might just have a nasty sprain, but you should get an X-ray to be sure."

"I'll be fine. Take me inside so I can ice it."

"Sophie, you need to get it checked out. You could have a small fracture. Injuries like this can have long-term consequences if they don't heal properly."

"I've already got car trouble, Aiden. I don't need hospital bills on top of it."

"Insurance will pay for it."

"I have a thousand-dollar deductible."

"I'll cover it then. I shouldn't have left you on that ladder."

"Don't be ridiculous. Just get me inside."

He pinned her with a look as he reached for her. "I'm taking you to the hospital."

She leaned away. "No, you're not."

He leaned back on his haunches, glaring at her. She was too stubborn for her own good. She'd nurse the whole world within an inch of their lives, but heaven help her if she needed a hand.

"Fine. A compromise then. We'll find an Urgent Care. They'll be able to x-ray it, and it won't cost as much." He'd put it on his credit card, and hopefully she'd be none the wiser until he was miles away.

A frown creased her brow. "You have a plane to catch, Aiden."

"I still have a couple hours. It won't take that long. Come on, let's go." He picked her up before she could protest.

They drove twenty-five miles inland to find an open Urgent Care. It appeared everyone else had found it too. Sophie was one of about thirty patients waiting for help. Aiden convinced her to prop up her foot while he facilitated check-in and slipped the receptionist his Visa.

An hour and a half later they were still waiting, her cold pack having long since grown warm. The ankle was puffy and bruised red. She'd tried to put weight on it as they entered the building, but the pain was too much.

Aiden flipped sightlessly through a copy of *Southern Boating*, his mind running at warp speed. He was pretty sure Sophie didn't have a break, but at the very least she was sporting a nasty sprain.

He didn't know if she'd yet grasped what this would mean. Sprains took a while to heal. She couldn't even put weight on it and probably wouldn't be able to for a few days as yet. She was in no condition to get her bookshop ready to open. The injury being in her right foot, she wouldn't even be able to drive.

It was obvious how much this shop, this new beginning, meant to her. She'd been worried over a one-day delay. When she realized what this injury meant to her plans, it would send her reeling.

But sometime in the past twenty minutes he'd arrived at a decision—he was going to stay in Piper's Cove.

It was his fault the ladder had fallen. He'd stay and help get her shop ready to open. He'd paint or clean or whatever she needed him to do.

Of course, staying would mean missing the ESTA ceremony. He wasn't going to lie, that was a bummer. But with Sophie's sister on her honeymoon, and her brother in a new job, she didn't have anyone else. She needed him, and he wasn't going to leave her to fend for herself.

Sophie checked her watch. "You should go. You'll miss your flight. I can take an Uber home."

"I want to make sure you're okay. You're due up any time now."

"This could take all—"

"Sophie Lawson," the nurse called from the door that led to the examination rooms.

"What'd I tell you?" he asked.

chapter

seventeen

The young female doctor swept into the room and pushed a slide onto the glowing screen. "So, here it is."

The paper crackled beneath Sophie as she leaned in for a closer look, but she had no idea what she was looking at.

Aiden took two steps closer, studying the film. He'd insisted on keeping her company even though the ticking clock was making her nervous he'd miss his flight.

"Good news." The doctor pushed her glasses up on her nose and began writing a prescription. "It's not broken—just a sprain. You'll want to keep it elevated as much as possible over the next two to three days. Ice it for twenty to thirty minutes up to four times a day. Since you can't put weight on it, you'll want crutches for the next few days."

"*Crutches?* But I can't."

The doctor's gaze toggled to Aiden, then back to Sophie. "It's imperative your ankle heal correctly, Mrs. . . ." She glanced down at the chart. "Lawson."

Sophie didn't bother correcting her. "Can't you just put me in a cast or boot or something?"

"A boot's a good idea. If it's not too painful to walk on, you can go that route."

But Sophie remembered the pain that had shot up her leg when she'd tried to stand on it. Crutches or boot, she was effectively laid up for the time being.

"You can pick up either of those at the pharmacy when you fill this." She ripped the prescription off the pad and handed it to Sophie along with an instruction sheet. "Take one of these every four to six hours as needed. Ibuprofen after that. Any questions?"

"No." She couldn't keep the dejection from her tone. "Thank you."

"You're all done here then. Good luck with your ankle." The doctor swept out of the room, leaving the door open.

The full weight of the diagnosis sank in. How was she going to paint her shop? How was she going to get all the books on the shelves? How was she going to get her store open in just eight days?

Her eyes burned, and her breathing became labored.

Aiden was suddenly beside her, taking the papers from her hand. "Okay, now, don't panic. Let's get out of here. We'll talk in the car."

Aiden helped her off the table. She held on to him as she

limped through the lobby, barely registering the pain in her ankle. Once outside he assisted her into the passenger side of his car, and as he rounded the vehicle she realized he needed to get to the airport. They hadn't even picked up the rental car.

She looked down at her swollen ankle. Rental car? Who was she kidding? She couldn't drive like this. She couldn't even move her foot without exquisite pain. Now that it wasn't elevated it was throbbing again. How would she manage everything she had to do? On one foot, that was how. What other choice did she have?

She dabbed at the corners of her eyes while Aiden got in on the driver's side and started the car. "I can worry about the pharmacy later. You'd better take me home and get going. Are you packed up?"

Aiden still hadn't buckled up or put the car in motion. He regarded her with a strange expression.

"What? Why aren't you driving? You're going to miss your flight."

He buckled up, put the car in Drive, and pulled from the slot. "I'm not going home today, Sophie."

"You still have time. The airport's small—it won't take long to get through security."

"I'm not leaving you like this."

She blinked, her heart suddenly thumping like a bass drum. "I'll be fine. You can't miss your flight. Surely you have to get back to work."

"You can't even walk or drive."

"I can take an Uber."

"You're so stubborn. And once you get to the shop? How are you going to manage then?"

"I don't know. I'll figure something out."

He shot her a look as he pulled from the parking lot. "You mean you'll carry on with your plans—on your bad ankle, pain or no pain—and likely make your injury worse."

It irked her that he knew what she'd been thinking. And she couldn't believe he was willing to cancel his flight. "I can handle it. This is not your problem."

"It is now. I'm staying until you're on your feet, Sophie."

"I'm not the only one who's stubborn."

Her mouth had gone dry. Now that she saw he was serious, she went through a short list of people in her life. Anyone who could step in for a few days and help. But there was no one. How pathetic was that? She was twenty-five years old and had no one she could call in an emergency.

Aiden must've already reached the same conclusion, otherwise why would he put his life on hold for her?

She curled her fingers into her palms. "I don't need your pity, Aiden."

"Oh, for crying out loud. It's not pity. This is my fault. I placed the—"

"No, it's not."

"—ladder and left you there to manage alone. Do you use Walgreens or CVS?"

Sophie clamped her lips together. Her stomach was turning, and she didn't know if it was the pain or the conversation. And why did it bother her so much that Aiden was willing to stay? She should be grateful. But he was a threat to her mental well-being. Ever since their truce yesterday she'd begun softening toward him again.

He had to go.

And yet there was also some foolish part of her that wanted him to stay. Her stupid, gullible heart wanted what it couldn't have. Besides . . . it was incredibly sweet that he was willing to stay. And she had to get her shop open.

She had to face facts: Even if she muddled through on one foot, there was no way she'd be open in time for Nathaniel Quinn's release party. Bye-bye, instant revenue. Bye-bye, community support. Bye-bye, any chance of scheduling another book signing with the biggest publisher in the US.

She closed her eyes, defeated. How had she wound up in this impossible predicament? All she'd wanted was to get out of this with her heart intact. Yet, no matter what she did—

God, what is going on? Why are You leaving me stuck with the one man who has the power to break me?

"Sophie . . . ?"

She mentally rewound the conversation to his last question and sighed. "Walgreens."

Even she could hear the flat, hopeless tone of her voice. She couldn't stop him from staying. In fact, she needed him to do just that. And needing Aiden was never a good idea.

Moments later he pulled into the pharmacy parking lot and shut off the engine. He turned in his seat, then went still.

What was he thinking? His decision to stay stood in stark contrast to the way he'd left before. She had to admit, it showed a lot of growth. Once again she had a dream to achieve, and this time he was staying to help her achieve it.

The gesture warmed her through—and scared her silly. "Thank you for staying. I appreciate your willingness to help."

At his prolonged perusal her pulse notched up, and her cheeks went hot. Of course he didn't see the problem with his staying—it wasn't his well-being on the line.

"Hey . . ." he said softly. "It's going to be okay. I promise."

But he couldn't really promise that, could he? And she couldn't seem to control the part of her that still loved him.

chapter

eighteen

Aiden called Ross and told him the bad news. Fortunately, his boss seemed to understand and even offered to accept Aiden's ESTA on his behalf if he won. After he got off the phone, Aiden sent him the acceptance speech. The last of his regret whooshed away with the email. He was right where he needed to be. Right where he was supposed to be.

Aiden cleaned up the yard, pitching sticks into a pile he'd worry about later. He worked for almost an hour until the backyard was restored to its prehurricane condition.

He still had to do one thing and he wasn't looking forward to it. He threw the last of the sticks into the pile, pulled out his phone, and placed the call. Might as well get it over with.

Tiffany picked up on the second ring, and after they exchanged greetings she asked, "Hey, shouldn't you be in the air right now?"

"That's why I'm calling. I'm afraid there's been another delay."

"Oh no. Bless your heart. Was your flight canceled again?"

"No . . . No, that's not it." He sank onto the deck step and stared off toward the burgeoning sea. "I think I mentioned an old friend of mine is here at the beach cottage. Her name's Sophie, and she was the bride's sister. She took a fall and got hurt this afternoon. I need to stick around for a few days and help her get things sorted out."

"Her?"

"I should've mentioned that. She's someone I knew back in high school."

"Someone you dated?" He couldn't miss the thread of tension in her voice.

"Yes. The fall was my fault, and I feel I have to stay. I hope you understand."

"Wait, did you say a few days? What about the award ceremony? That's tomorrow night, Aiden. You can't miss that."

He'd asked Tiffany to be his date. "Believe me, I don't want to. But Ross is going to fill in for me. I know you bought a new dress—I'm sorry about that. I'll take you someplace nice soon so you can wear it."

"I don't care about the dress." Her voice was tight, and a long moment of silence followed—not the comfortable kind.

He'd mishandled this whole thing. He should've been more forthcoming from the beginning. Now it seemed like he'd been trying to hide something. Maybe he had been. Maybe his feelings for Sophie were returning. But the same obstacle still blocked their path. Her life was here and his was not. Besides, forgiveness was one thing, trust another. And he wasn't sure if she'd ever trust him again—or even if she should.

Tiffany released a hard sigh. "I know we're not exclusive or anything but—"

"No, you have every right—I should've been up-front with you from the beginning. It's my fault." He owed her some kind of explanation. "Truth of the matter is, I did Sophie wrong when we were together, and I need to do the right thing by her this time around. I hope you can understand that."

Waves crashed on the shore, and a seagull soared overhead, letting out a piercing cry.

"I don't have a hold on you, Aiden. You're free to date other women if you want, but if you are, I'd like to know it."

For all he knew, Tiffany was dating other men. Why did he feel okay about that? Why did he almost wish she were? He gave his head a shake.

"I'm not dating Sophie. I know this is a weird situation. I plan to stay just until she can get around on her own, then I'll catch a flight home."

A brief pause followed before she said, "All right then. Thank you for being honest with me."

He let out a slow breath at the absence of tension in her voice. They talked a few more minutes, then said good-bye.

That wasn't fun but it could've gone much worse. Aiden stood up and slipped quietly back into the house. Warmth spread through him at the sight of Sophie still passed out on the sofa, dark eyelashes feathering the pale skin of her cheeks. His fingers itched to stroke the softness of her face.

She'd taken a pain pill and had wanted to head straight to the shop once they'd changed clothes. But that foot needed rest, so he'd stalled until she drifted off.

From the coffee table her phone buzzed an incoming text, and the notification appeared on the screen. Hey, Sis! Having a great time! Hey, I hate to bother you, but could you—?

The notification ended there, and Aiden rolled his eyes. He liked Jenna. At one time he'd thought of her as his little sister. He liked Seth, too, but they'd both grown to depend on Sophie too much. Taking advantage of their sister had become a bad habit.

He toyed with the idea of letting Jenna know her sister was down for the count. But Sophie wouldn't thank him for interfering.

Her eyelids fluttered open and she stirred, wincing at the movement. She looked down at her foot, still propped on a pillow.

"I fell asleep?" She sat up carefully, tossing aside the blanket Aiden had dropped over her earlier. "What time is it?"

"Going on six. I have a sandwich for you in the kitchen. You must be hungry."

"Aiden, we have to get going. I've wasted almost an entire day."

"You have time to eat. I promise, I'll paint all night if you want me to, but you need to keep up your strength."

Her chin jutted out. "I'll eat on the way there."

He gave her a long look, imagining the way it might go—her hobbling around on one foot, roller in hand. "Promise me you'll let me do the work. You need to keep that ankle elevated."

"It hardly even hurts now."

"Because you've got prescription pain meds in your system, and you've had it elevated for an hour. I guarantee that's going to change if you start trying to walk on it. I've had a sprain or two, you know. I remember what it feels like."

The look in her eyes softened. Was she remembering the way she'd hovered over him his senior year when he'd fallen while rock climbing? She came to his house and waited on him, hand and foot. But he hadn't been hurting so bad that he resisted the chance to pull her onto the sofa and nuzzle her neck every chance he got.

She broke eye contact as she scooted to the edge of the seat. "We'll see how it goes."

✿

It was late when Aiden finally pulled up to the deserted board-walk shops. Sophie had canceled her rental car, and Aiden had been kind enough to meet the tow company when they picked up her Tahoe. He'd also gone to the store and bought some cheap tennis shoes and paint clothes to augment his meager wardrobe.

Outside the window the moon hung over the harbor, pro-viding the only light. Sophie was relieved that the dying oak tree on the street side of her shop had stayed upright through the hurricane. Even now its hulking shadow seemed threatening. She'd intended to have it taken down before now, but funds had been tight. She shouldn't take the chance, though. She had a few thousand dollars to spare; she'd get someone to take care of it this week.

Sophie surveyed the dark shops with sinking spirits. "The electricity is definitely out."

"We planned for that. It's not ideal, but I can at least get everything taped off tonight. You can hold the flashlight for me."

This was ridiculous. How many obstacles were there going to be? How would she get the shop ready in time, even with Aiden's help?

"Don't worry." He helped her from the car. "We've got this."

She settled the crutches under her arms and followed him, hobbling up the boardwalk steps. "My shop's that way."

The stores faced the seawall and went on for a block and a half. The boardwalk started at the old train depot and ended shortly past her shop with a gazebo that overlooked the busy marina. At the moment, however, all was quiet. Boat masts glowed in the moonlight, and water rippled against the seawall.

The boardwalk was a hot spot for tourists, as the price of her building had attested. Sophie and her mother had debated the location for a long time, and the boardwalk had been their preferred spot. When the old house-turned-boutique became available shortly before her mother's death, she encouraged Sophie to jump on it.

"I've never been to this part of town," Aiden said. "It's nice. Quaint."

"It's pretty busy on summer days."

"A great location for your bookshop."

Sophie observed the entrance of her store with fresh eyes.

The two-story building sported weathered, white clapboard siding. A large gray-blue canopy protruded from the building and would shade the entryway on sunny days. Empty flower boxes awaited a flat of fresh petunias, and the spacious porch cried out for Adirondack chairs. The shingled sign, bearing the name of her store, hung from the eaves, unreadable in the dark.

Sophie slipped the key from her purse and unlocked the door. Despite the painkiller in her system, her ankle throbbed from the short walk. Aiden had been right about keeping it elevated.

She opened the door and pushed inside, a musty smell assaulting her nose. The place needed airing out. The beam of Aiden's flashlight cut across the front two rooms, previously the house's living room and dining room. Worn beige carpet covered the floors, and walls the color of Pepto Bismol surrounded them.

"Yikes," Aiden said. "I see why you're so adamant about painting."

"It used to be a boutique. The carpet needs to go too. The original wood floor is under it, and from what I've seen it looks pretty good. I'll have to give it a couple coats of polyurethane, but I need to get the walls painted first." Or rather, *he* did.

"It's a nice space, though. Perfect for a bookshop." He shone the beam at the hallway, which led to two additional rooms on opposite sides. Farther down the hall were a half bath, an office, and the stairwell leading to her living quarters.

"The supplies are over here." She hobbled to the corner where she'd dropped a heap of hardware store bags and the five-gallon buckets of primer and paint.

"All right." Aiden opened the deck chair he'd carried in and set it in the middle of the room, then dragged over a five-gallon bucket of paint. "Take a seat and prop up your foot. You can hold the flashlight for me. I'll have this taped off in no time."

Pain caused Sophie to stir. She opened her eyes to the sucking sound of a roller laying on paint. The smell of paint fumes hung heavily in the air. The flashlight she'd been holding had been turned off and now lay on her lap. Blue tape outlined all the woodwork in the room. Aiden had propped three flashlights, aimed at the wall he was currently rolling with primer.

She'd fallen asleep again. She checked her phone for the time, ignoring the notifications. It was after midnight.

She must've made a sound because Aiden turned around. "Did I wake you?"

She shifted in her chair, finding her muscles stiff. The movement made her ankle throb. "I'm not taking any more of those meds. They knock me out."

"It's probably time for more."

"I'll take ibuprofen. I can't afford to sleep my life away." Her gaze skittered around the room, buoyed by his progress. "You got a lot done. It's late, though. You must be getting tired."

"Let me finish rolling the primer. Shouldn't take but a half hour or so. The hallway and other two rooms are done. Are you good till then?"

"Sure." Sophie dug in her purse for ibuprofen and popped three of them. Then she got up and hobbled around on her crutches, needing to move her stiff limbs. She noted the gap of paint between the primer and baseboards, an idea forming. Spirits lifting a little, she limped to the bags in the corner, finding a narrow paintbrush.

"What do you think you're doing?"

"I'll cut in around the baseboard while you finish rolling."

She could feel his look of disapproval. "Sophie . . ."

"I'll scoot along the floor. I'll be fine."

"I can see there's no reasoning with you."

She lifted her chin. "Nope."

She set herself up with a flashlight and a pan of primer, then went to work. Her ankle did hurt, but she didn't have her weight on it, and the pills would kick in soon.

The sound of her brushstrokes joined the slurping of paint being rolled onto the walls, making a satisfying symphony. It felt good to be making progress on her dream. To get on with the work and know they stood a chance against the ticking clock.

Aiden had opened the windows at some point, airing out the odors of must and primer. The briny scent of the sea now mingled with the other smells. She was happy to have him here. Maybe too happy.

"Was Tiffany upset you didn't come home tonight?"

"Not really." He loaded his roller. "More surprised than anything, I guess. Did you tell Jenna and Seth what happened?"

"Not yet. I didn't want Jenna to worry on her honeymoon, and there's nothing Seth can do."

"Did you get her message? A notification came in earlier while you were sleeping."

Sophie set down her brush and checked her phone. She had

a text from Granny May also. And one from Joshua, confirming a location for their date next Friday. She sent a quick response to both of them before she opened and read Jenna's text.

Her sister had remembered a juror notification she'd received, and with all the wedding stuff, she'd forgotten to respond. Could Sophie handle it, pretty please?

That niggle of reservation rolled over her again—the one that said her sister was now a married woman and should be fending for herself. But Jenna had been consumed by wedding preparations, and she was away on her honeymoon.

Pushing the reservations aside, Sophie told Jenna not to worry about a thing. She'd find the number and call in on her behalf.

"Everything okay?" Aiden asked.

After the way he'd responded earlier to Seth's request for help, she was reluctant to go into detail. "Everything's just fine."

chapter

nineteen

The last person Sophie wanted to chat with was her grandmother, but here she was doing just that. She moved the phone to her other ear, Granny's voice a constant drone through the line, and shifted on the flower box perch to elevate her foot.

It had been a busy day so far. She and Aiden had finished priming last night and worked all morning to coat the walls in Coastal Blue. It looked as wonderful as she'd hoped. Good thing, because there was no time to do it over.

Aiden came outside, passing her on his way to get a fresh pail of water from the sea. They still had no electricity in the shop—or at the house.

Her grandmother yammered on. During their lunch break Sophie had made the mistake of texting her grandma about her injury. She should've expected the phone call.

"I promise I'm fine, Granny," Sophie said when her grandmother paused for breath. "I'm taking it easy."

Aiden turned around, his pointed look accusing her of stretching the truth.

"My foot is propped even as we speak." She matched his expression with the jut of her chin.

"And yet, you're somehow on schedule to open in time? Did you decide to hire out the work then?"

"Not exactly."

"Then you are overexerting yourself. You need to rest that ankle, stubborn girl, or you'll have a mess on your hands."

"I am resting my ankle." Sophie let out a hard sigh. Might as well get this over with. "Aiden's still here, Granny. He's pretty much doing the work for me."

"Don't you say that boy's name. He was dead to me the moment he up and left you, and how you can stand to associate with him now is beyond me. What do you mean he's still there? What does he want from you, your soul?"

Sophie rolled her eyes as Aiden walked past with the full bucket. He avoided her gaze, as if he might've guessed what Granny was saying. The door opened and closed behind him. Still the windows were open, and she didn't want him overhearing this conversation.

"Hang on a minute," Sophie said, but the woman continued her rant. Regardless, Sophie pocketed her phone, hobbled over to the seawall, then lifted the phone to her ear.

"Do you hear me, young lady? Oh, I'm just wasting my breath!"

"Calm down, Granny. There's something I need to tell you, and you need to hear me." She took a deep breath, making sure she had her grandmother's attention. "When Aiden took the job in Charleston, he didn't know Daddy had just left. I didn't tell him that night. In fact, he didn't know Daddy left at all until two nights ago."

There was a beat of silence.

"He thought Mama and Daddy were together until she passed."

"Well, he still up and left you when you were madly in love with him and expecting to marry him. I haven't forgotten the mess he left in his wake even if you have."

"Yes, I was hurt. But it wasn't like he'd proposed or something. Our plans to marry someday were vague at best and probably more built up in my mind than his. And in all fairness, he did ask me to follow him there. I should've told you that at the time, but I was too busy playing the victim."

"You couldn't leave with your mama ill! Did he expect you to give up all your dreams too? For heaven's sake, what kind of boy—"

"That's right, Granny. He was just a boy, and he's apologized for being selfish. But he's a grown man now. When I fell off the ladder I didn't ask him to stay and help, but he's been kind enough to do so anyway. He's the only reason this shop will get finished in time."

"You're falling for him all over again! I hear it in your voice. He's slithered right back into your heart!"

Sophie sighed. "I've forgiven him—and now you need to do the same. And that's all I'm saying on the matter right now. I have to get back to the shop. There's still a lot of work to be done."

"Sophie, be careful. I don't want to see you hurt again."

Sophie was beginning to wonder if that was her fate, regardless of how she tried to guard herself. The universe seemed to be conspiring against her.

"I'll call you soon, Granny."

A few minutes later Sophie limped back into the store. The smell of fresh paint mingled with the sea air. The room was warm and empty, but she heard Aiden's voice drifting down the hall from her office.

"Thanks for filling in, Ross." The floor creaked beneath his feet. "This means a lot to me. I don't expect to win, but it's good to know you'll be there just in case."

Frowning, Sophie stared out the window. Filling in? He'll be there just in case?

A moment later Aiden emerged from the hall, pocketing his phone. He stopped when he saw Sophie. "I didn't hear you come in."

Her eyes sharpened on his, dread roiling in her gut. "What was that about? Ross filling in for you?"

Aiden headed to the wall where he'd left off and picked up the roller. "We were talking about the award ceremony. Going over a few details."

She shuffled over to him. He was avoiding eye contact and seemed laser-focused on the task at hand. He'd already applied paint to the roller and was now laying it on in long, careful strokes. And he'd evaded her question.

Sophie stopped a few feet away, making herself ask the question. "Aiden . . . When is that awards ceremony?"

He darted a glance her way, not long enough to meet her eyes. Not pausing in his work. "It's tonight. Ross is taking my place."

Sophie's stomach bottomed out. Aiden was trying for casual, but there was nothing casual about his sacrifice.

He'd gone through high school without a single award. She'd had her own moments: National Honor Society, salutatorian, class secretary. But Aiden had been a no-show in the academic department, and while he'd started on the football team, his efforts hadn't been spectacular enough to merit awards.

But now he'd found his niche in a field he was passionate about. He'd done something amazing on a national level and was about to be publicly recognized. Only he wouldn't be there for it.

Because he was here. Helping her paint.

No, this wasn't right. He needed to be there. "What time is the ceremony?"

"Six o'clock."

She checked the time on her phone. A mere two hours from now. There wasn't time to catch a flight or make the drive. Oh, this was all wrong.

"Aiden, why did you do this? I didn't want you to miss the ceremony! What if you win? And even if you don't, you should be there to celebrate."

"It's no big deal, Sophie." He kept rolling, the sucking sound now an irritation.

She grabbed his arm, stopping his work. Her crutch hit the floor with a dull thud, leaving her to balance on one foot.

He looked over his shoulder at her.

"It *is* a big deal, Aiden. If I'd known you'd be missing your big moment, I never would've agreed to let you stay."

"I know. It's okay." He lowered the roller to his side, the muscles contracting under her hand. His eyes pierced hers, as fathomless as the deep blue sea. "That's why I didn't tell you, Jelly Bean."

The old nickname made her heart roll over in her chest. His sacrifice brought mixed emotions, and they battled inside her. As did the realization that he was no longer that selfish boy. He was a man who'd put someone else's needs ahead of his own.

Her needs.

"I can't believe you did this," she said finally. "What if you win?"

"Then Ross will deliver the nice acceptance speech you helped me write, no doubt doing a better job than I would've. Win or lose, I don't have to be there for it, Sophie. But you needed me here—and here is where I wanted to be."

Her breath caught at the sincerity in his eyes, in his voice. But what did it mean? Was he simply making up for a past mistake? Or was it something more? She was afraid to follow that thought.

His gaze swept over her face, seemingly taking in every inch, every plane, every slope.

Her cheeks heated under his inspection, her body prickling with awareness. Tension crackled between them, making the temperature rise by ten degrees. It was familiar, this feeling. Took her right back to when she'd last been his.

He cradled her face. His thumb brushed her cheek,

awakening every cell. She was spellbound. Hopeless. At his mercy. Her grandmother had been right, and Sophie couldn't even bring herself to care.

"I want to be here for you this time." His voice was like molten honey. "It's more important to me than any award I might win."

She swayed toward him, precarious balance or magnetism, she wasn't sure. He dropped the roller, catching her at the waist. So close she could feel his warmth through her T-shirt. Smell his piney scent.

His hands twitched at her waist. Her fingers clamped onto his biceps. Her gaze followed the column of his neck to his bristly jaw, to that sensual mouth, those smoldering eyes.

When his gaze fell to her mouth, she knew a moment of longing like she'd never experienced before. She wanted to feel his lips on hers again. Wanted to feel the delicious desire he alone had summoned. Wanted to feel cherished and adored. It had been so long.

His hands tightened on her waist a moment before he blinked and released her. He cleared his throat, the sound loud in the silence. He seemed unable to make eye contact now. "We should, ah, get you off your feet."

She swallowed against the tightness in her throat. "Right."

He led her to the chair and pulled the bucket close, then went to fetch her crutches. She propped her foot and willed her heart to resume its normal pace.

❦

The back of Aiden's neck prickled, and his hand was unsteady as he worked the roller. The last few minutes played back in a surreal blend of torture and pleasure.

Sophie's expression when he'd told her he wanted to be here, when he touched her cheek. The want in her eyes—and he was certain he hadn't mistaken the look. He'd seen it enough in the months they'd dated. In the golden porch light while they glided on the swing, in the darkness of his car after a date, in the lamplight of his living room after his dad retired early.

One more second of insanity, and he would've taken those lips and reminded her of what they'd shared. But in an instant he remembered how he hurt her before. How their lives were in two different places now. How there was a woman at home expecting to become his girlfriend soon.

He shouldn't start something he couldn't finish. That wouldn't be fair to Sophie. It wouldn't be fair to him, and it wouldn't be fair to Tiffany either.

But, heaven's mercy, how he'd wanted that kiss.

There was a shuffling sound behind him. Movement from the corner of his eyes told him Sophie had sat still long enough. She lowered herself to the floor near the adjacent wall and began cutting in paint. Suggesting she rest would be a waste of breath.

"What time do you think the awards will be given out?" she asked.

He released a heavy breath at the mundane topic. "After the dinner, I guess. Probably around seven. Ross will text me when they announce the winner."

"Why don't you have him FaceTime so you can hear it live?"

He gave a wry laugh. "I'm not sure I want to hear it live. Besides, we've got a lot of work ahead of us."

"It'll take all of three minutes." The brushing stopped. "Come on, let's do it. Please? It's the next best thing to being there."

If he won the award she'd hear his acceptance speech, and he hadn't really planned for that. But he wouldn't win—and he didn't exactly relish the thought of Sophie witnessing his failure. It sounded like a lose/lose proposition to him.

But how could he deny her anything when she looked at him, eyes sparkling with hope and excitement?

"All right, fine. Let's do it."

chapter

twenty

"I'm not going to win." Aiden helped Sophie sink down to the carpeted floor. Ross had just FaceTimed him, and his nerves gnawed at his gut.

"Stop saying that. You have as good a chance as anyone." Sophie settled back against the checkout counter, setting aside her crutches.

"You don't know who I'm up against. Anyway, it doesn't matter. It's just a stupid award."

Sophie grabbed his phone as he settled beside her and turned it up all the way to check the progress. The screenshot showed a podium, center stage. The speaker's acceptance speech was winding down.

"Ross said my category's next."

"How do you feel?"

"I kind of wish it were over."

Aiden ran sweaty palms down the legs of his jeans. Man, he

was glad he wasn't there right now. The thought of losing was every bit as heinous as the idea of delivering an acceptance speech in front of all those people. He wasn't sure which he'd be hoping for if he were there. But now, with Ross as his proxy, he definitely wanted to win. He tried to tamp down his hope.

Sophie turned down the volume and set her hand on his arm. "No matter what happens, Aiden . . . I'm really proud of you. You created a device no one else has ever thought of. That's amazing."

Pleasure swelled inside at her words, heating his face. He'd forgotten how easily words of affirmation rolled off her tongue. She'd always made him feel like he could do anything. Be anything. He let the admiration in her eyes wash over him like a cool wave on a hot summer day. And just like that, all the stress of this ceremony and award was worth it, win or lose.

He smiled at her. "That means a lot to me, Soph."

She jerked her attention back to the phone, jacking up the volume. "Your category's up."

He homed in on the screen where the MC was waiting for the applause to die down. Aiden was glad Sophie was holding the phone because his hands were shaking. He crossed his arms over his chest.

"And now, for the category of Innovations in Extreme Sports . . . Lonnie Griffin for the Grappler." An image showed on the screen, but it was washed with white. "Kendra Francis for the Sure Climb Shoe. And Aiden Maddox for the SpringChute. And the winner is . . ."

Aiden swallowed, his eyes trained on the phone. His heart skipped a beat.

"Aiden Maddox, for the SpringChute."

He blinked. His breath tumbled out. A chill ran through him.

"You won!" Sophie grabbed his arm. "Aiden, you won!"

Music was playing as Ross presumably made his way to the stage. "I can't believe it. I never dreamed. The other innovations were so good, and Lonnie Griffin has been up for this award three times and won twice before. I can't believe this is—"

"Shhh! I want to hear your speech."

Ross appeared at the podium and adjusted the microphone. "Thank you. I'm Ross Givens, Aiden's partner at Extreme Adventures. Aiden couldn't be with us this evening, but he asked me to deliver his speech if he should win."

Ross looked down at his phone. "If anyone wants to know how to make a daredevil nervous, try telling him he has to deliver a speech in front of a live audience."

The audience chuckled as Aiden wiped his hands down his legs again. He was suddenly second-guessing the rest of his speech.

Ross continued. "I'm grateful to the board members of ESTA for this honor. I also owe a debt of gratitude to my father, Dan Maddox, for teaching me everything I know about life. He showed me what hard work and discipline can accomplish, and he sacrificed everything to give me a good life. Ross Givens, my partner, for giving me the opportunity of a lifetime and letting me handle the fun end of the business."

Ross smiled briefly toward the camera.

Aiden tensed at the part that was coming.

"A special thank-you to Sophie Lawson for always believing

in me. For making me feel like I could do and be anything I set my mind to."

Sophie sucked in her breath. Her fingers tightened on his arm. Aiden didn't hear another word Ross said. His mind swarmed with thoughts and emotions.

The audience applauded and Ross exited the stage, disappearing from their line of vision.

Sophie lowered the phone, visibly touched. "You acknowledged me in your acceptance speech."

He gave a wry grin. "You were never supposed to hear that."

"Well, why ever not? It was a very nice thing to say."

She was right. It was something she—not three hundred strangers—deserved to hear. But where she'd always been free with compliments, he'd been reluctant. Afraid. Of what, he wasn't sure.

He gazed at her, grateful to the depths of his soul and determined to let her know it. "It's all true. I'm sorry I never thanked you for it."

"It's all right."

The connection between them crackled like a live wire. There was so much more he wanted to say to her, but he didn't even know where to begin.

"Aiden? You there?" A voice came from his phone. The screen showed the blur of movement. "Aiden?"

Giving Sophie a grin, he took the phone off Speaker and held it to his ear.

⁊〇

Sophie listened as Aiden accepted his partner's congratulations while pacing the room. His cheeks were flushed, and he cupped the back of his neck.

She'd never seen him with so much nervous energy. He'd acted as if the award wasn't important to him, but clearly it was. And she was so thankful to see him winning at life. Even though he'd left her and broken her heart, she was glad he'd found his way. That others were seeing him for the unique and special individual he was.

Her thoughts went back to his acceptance speech and his kind words about her. She'd had no idea she'd done that for him. She never said anything to him but the truth. He always had so much potential—he just hadn't been able to see it.

He laughed at something Ross said. "I know. I know, it's crazy. All right. Sounds like a plan. Thank for doing that, man. All right. See you."

Aiden pocketed the phone, looking at her. He seemed to have grown a full three inches in stature in the past five minutes.

He chuckled. "I still can't believe it. I know it's just a silly award, but—"

"It's not a silly award. It's a huge accomplishment." She started to pull herself up, and he rushed over to help.

"Let's go celebrate," she said once she was on her feet. "Where would you like to go?"

"Aw, we don't have to do that." Aiden surveyed the room. "We've still got a lot of work ahead of us. We should get back to it."

"Absolutely not. We're making good time. We can afford

an hour to celebrate your accomplishment, and that's what we're going to do."

A smile slowly curled his lips. "I guess I could call my dad on the way. He'll be chomping at the bit to hear."

Sophie returned his smile. "Let's do it."

chapter

twenty-one

The Fish House squatted on a wharf that catered mostly to lobstermen and commercial fishermen. Sophie liked its casual, seaside setting. Inside the rustic restaurant country music poured from speakers, mingling with the chatter of patrons and the scrape of utensils. A busy bar took up the far side of the room, and booths lined the rough-hewn walls on the other side.

She and Aiden settled into a corner booth, the savory scent of crab cakes tantalizing her nose. "I'm not a huge seafood fan, but the aroma in here is heavenly."

"This place is one of my favorite things about coming to Piper's Cove. You can't go wrong with the seafood platter, and if you like hush puppies, you're in for a treat."

"I could make a meal of them."

"A woman after my own heart. I have to admit, though, I come here for the real seafood."

"You're not alone in that, I think. Your dad must've been so happy for you." They'd talked on the phone most of the drive here.

"He was thrilled in his understated way. Of course, he'd like to see me settle down to a less dangerous job." He gave Sophie a knowing grin. "Like roofing."

"He's still after you to take up his business?"

"Oh, yeah. I always tell him more people die falling off roofs than jumping from planes."

"That might be because fewer people are jumping from planes."

His eyes sparkled. "Spoilsport."

The server came a moment later. Once they placed their orders she waltzed away.

"So, tell me." Sophie eyed Aiden, pride for him welling up inside. "How does it feel to be an award-winning inventor?"

His lips pulled into a sheepish smile. "To be honest, I don't think it's even sunk in yet."

"What do you think you'll do with the cash prize? Do you have intentions of manufacturing the SpringChute yourself and selling it—to a parachute manufacturer? Sorry, I really have no idea how this kind of thing works."

"Honestly, I have no idea what I'm going to do because I hadn't let myself think that far ahead. Dad thinks I should sell the rights, but we'll see. I had a few of the devices made up for our own use at Extreme Adventures. I never expected it to go any further than that. Ross didn't even tell me he'd entered it in the contest until after I'd finaled."

Sophie smiled. "He seems like a good friend."

"The best. He's great at running the business too. We turned a profit our first year, which I'm sure you know is pretty hard to do."

"Wow. You'll have to give me some tips."

"It took a lot of work and advertising, I can tell you that. Ross is really regimented about the financial side of things. We have a dozen well-trained guides—they don't take clients out until I'm satisfied they can handle themselves, and Ross lets me have free rein over all that. I don't think I could stand working with someone who was always watching over my shoulder."

"You still enjoy what you do?"

He quirked a brow. "Jumping from planes? What's not to love?"

Sophie laughed. "Oh, I don't know . . . concussions, broken bones, death . . ."

He chuckled. "None of those have ever happened to me—or my clients—while jumping. Mountain climbing seems to be my nemesis. Still, worth it every time."

"You're a crazy man. I can't even seem to manage a ladder."

His smile dimmed. "Aw, that was my fault, not yours."

"Not true. Besides, you're not allowed to feel guilty tonight. We're here to celebrate."

As if on cue the server brought their drinks. When she left Sophie raised her glass. "To hard work and gratifying payoffs."

"Hear, hear." He clinked his glass with hers.

"Sounds like you'll have some decisions to make when you get home."

"A lot will depend on how much attention the award garners. I'll have to wait and see what kind of offers I get, if any."

"Is it possible one of those offers could pull you away from your business?"

"I doubt it. Like I said, I still love what I do. It's the thrill I love, of course, but it's more than that. The people I take up inspire me. Make it really worthwhile."

"Tell me."

Aiden studied Sophie's face as if determining if she really wanted to hear. He must've been satisfied with what he saw.

"There's this one guy who jumps regularly. Not tandem jumping, he's a proficient skydiver. So, his dad calls me one day and tells me he wants to jump with his son, for no other reason than to share the experience with him. So I set it up. The father tandem jumped with me while his son skydived on his own."

He laughed heartily. "Guy screamed all the way down. But you know what? He did it again the next month. He's been up four times, and I think it scares the bejeebers out of him every time. I don't think he really likes it, but his son does, and he wants to share it with him."

"What a great story. I guess I always thought skydiving was something people did just for the thrill of it."

"Mostly it's that. But there are other reasons. A lot of people have it on their bucket list, and I'm happy to help them cross it off. I took up a paraplegic once. Man, that was amazing. He'd always dreamed of skydiving and decided not to let his disability hold him back.

"He was beaming when we landed. I'm told by a lot of

customers that the sense of accomplishment they got from their skydiving experience gave them the courage to try other things they were afraid to do."

"I hadn't thought of that. But I know what you mean. Going through everything with my mom—it was something I feared I'd be unable to handle. Despite the terrible sense of loss when she was gone, there was also a sense that God had gotten me through it, and He'd get me through the next thing too."

"That's it exactly. And the next thing for you . . . your bookshop."

"Despite all the obstacles this week, it's working out. Thanks to you and your willingness to stay."

He ducked his head.

"It means a lot to me that you were willing to miss your big moment for me. Now that you won the award, I wouldn't blame you if you regretted it."

Their eyes locked as he set his hand over hers. His long, tapered fingers curled around hers, rough and warm. "I don't regret it, Sophie. Not for a minute."

Her breath slowly leaked out. Ever since they'd announced his name, she'd been plagued by guilt. "I feel as if you should be sharing this moment with Ross. He's your partner, the one who entered you in the contest."

"I'll celebrate with Ross when I get home. For now . . . I feel like the moment happened exactly as it was supposed to. And I can't think of anyone I would've rather shared it with."

Her stomach tightened at the sincerity in his eyes. In his voice. Sometimes the things he said brought her to her knees.

And the way he looked at her now . . . Was there more than affection flickering in those deep blue eyes? More than warmth in the gentle caress of his fingers?

"Here we are." The server lowered a tray, making Sophie and Aiden withdraw from the table, from each other.

Sophie avoided his eyes as the server set down another tray in front of him. They kept having these moments. What did it mean?

What could it mean when she was putting down roots here, and he was leaving in a few days? Best keep a rein on these runaway feelings before she lost her heart all over again.

chapter

twenty-two

The next day Sophie and Aiden were finishing up the last coat of paint in her shop when the lights flickered on.

Sophie stopped painting. Her eyes connected with Aiden's. "Electricity!"

He grinned. "Now we're talking."

Catching the mood, Pippa jumped up on the barricade, yapping.

"It's so exciting, isn't it, sweetheart? Yes, it is." Sophie pulled to her feet and grabbed her crutches. "Hopefully it's back on at the house too."

"I'll bet it is. Won't it be nice to have coffee in the morning?"

"Not to mention a hot shower."

"Amen."

Sophie hobbled over to the wall and flipped on a couple more lights. The Coastal Blue looked beautiful in the artificial lighting. She couldn't wait to see it set off by the bookshelves' honey pecan stain.

She gazed around the room, beginning to see what it would look like in its final form. *Can you see this, Mama? It's going to look just the way we planned. I wish you were here with me.*

Her phoned buzzed with a new text, and Sophie pulled it from her pocket.

Jenna wanted to know if she'd handled the jury duty notice. In fact, Sophie hadn't. So she headed down the hall and went to work on that, Pippa on her heels. It took some doing to locate the right phone number, then find someone who was willing to look up Jenna's juror number. Sophie had explained the circumstances to three different people before finally finding someone who would help her.

Thankfully, calling the recording and giving the appropriate responses only took a minute. She texted Jenna and let her know it had been handled.

As she headed back down the hallway, Sophie heard Aiden talking to someone. When she reached the main room, Alanda came into view. The woman looked every inch the mayor in her charcoal suit and fashionable glasses. Her black hair sprung from her head in tight corkscrew curls, framing her perfectly oval face.

"Alanda. How nice of you to stop in."

The woman's face fell at the sight of Sophie's crutches. "Oh no. Honey, what happened to you?"

"Just a little mishap with a ladder when we were taking off the storm shutters. It's only a sprain." Her gaze toggled to Aiden. "Have you met my friend Aiden?"

"We were just introducing ourselves. Looks like you've got some much-needed help."

Pippa gave a yap, and Alanda wandered over to the barricade. "What have we here? Who's this little darling?"

"That's Pippa," Sophie said. "She's a little put out at being kept in the hallway."

"She's adorable." Alanda squatted down and held out her hand. Pippa sniffed the woman's fingers, not giving in too easily to the attention. "Well, we can't have you in the paint, now, can we? I always wanted a Yorkie; they're so cute. But I'm not home enough to have a dog."

A moment later Pippa wandered off and curled up in the corner.

"She's a little skittish," Sophie said.

"She's precious." Alanda came to her feet, taking in the room with a long, sweeping glance. "I'd expected the shelves to be up by now at least."

Alanda had arranged the book-release party with Rosewood Press and was no doubt feeling the same pressure as Sophie. The event would provide a nice influx of visitors, who'd be spending money everyplace from hotels to restaurants.

"I admit I'm running a little behind schedule, but we're making good progress. We'll be up and running in time for the party."

"I certainly hope so. I gave the publisher my word."

"A lot is riding on this party for all of us, and I'll make sure it happens. Have no fear." Sophie infused the sentence with more confidence than she actually felt.

"So you're having the grand opening and release party all at the same time?"

Sophie smiled. "I can think of worse ways to open a store."

"True enough. I believe you mentioned Leonard Puhls is making the shelves? I heard he had a bit of hurricane damage at his house. I hope that doesn't delay things on his end."

"I hadn't heard. That's too bad. He was in weeks ago to measure, and I heard from him yesterday. The shelving's almost finished. He's staining them now. We'll do the floors tomorrow and Friday, and the bookcases will go in over the weekend. From there it's just a matter of putting out the books. It's all under control."

"I'm glad to hear that. And I'm so glad to see the last of that awful pink! I never liked it, even for a boutique. I tried to tell Millie it was gaudy, but she wouldn't listen."

"It was quite bright."

Never one to dawdle, Aiden had gone back to rolling, the slurp of paint now a constant backdrop.

"I was sorry to see her go out of business," Alanda said. "But her merchandise was overpriced. Anyway, this town has needed a bookstore for years. I'll be glad to have a brick-and-mortar store where I can smell the books before I buy them."

Sophie laughed. "Spoken like a true book lover."

"I heard you hired Ellie Peterson as part of your staff. She'll do a great job for you."

Ellie was a former librarian and a consummate reader. She currently led a popular book club and was known for her excellent taste in literature.

"She'll be holding her book club here on Thursday nights

now, and she's been very helpful in curating the books since she's familiar with the local readers. I've also hired a few college students to work part time through the summer."

"Sounds like you've got it covered. Is Schooners catering the party?"

"They cut me a great deal on hors d'oeuvres. Thanks for the recommendation. And Cheryl from Party Plus is helping with decorations."

"It'll be an exciting day for sure. Donovan Spencer from the *Gazette* wants to interview you about the party soon. I spoke with him yesterday. And of course, a reporter from the paper will be here to cover the party itself."

"I've gotten a great response from the media, including the ABC and NBC affiliates. Nathaniel Quinn will be doing a couple of call-ins to the local radio stations as well." Talking about all the promotion surrounding the party was spiking her blood pressure. There was so much riding on this party.

"It'll be a red-letter day," Alanda said. "I heard that for Nathaniel's last book release party, people lined up hours beforehand."

"I didn't know that."

"Well, I, for one, can't wait to meet him. He lives here in North Carolina, you know."

"I read that recently, but I couldn't find out where exactly."

"I'm sure he doesn't advertise it, given his popularity, but he and his wife live in Bluebell. He came to Piper's Cove a couple years ago to do some research for the novel, but he was so low-key nobody even realized he was in town."

"Can't say I blame him," Sophie said. "I wouldn't like all the attention either."

"I'm excited to read the book, though. Imagine if it becomes a film! A big movie about our little town." She gave Sophie a coy smile. "Do you suppose they might give the mayor a little cameo?"

Sophie laughed. "They definitely should."

"Boy, oh boy, can that man write a love story." Alanda fanned her face.

"He hits all the right notes. I plan to keep a whole end cap for his books. Ellie says they're popular with locals."

"And the tourists, no doubt. Everyone loves a good beach read. I'll have to introduce you to some of our local authors too."

"I plan to feature them in a special section, and I'm hoping to schedule book signings with them also."

"I'm sure they'd love that. Oh, I'm getting all excited just thinking about it."

"Me too." Excited and scared half to death. Because if she couldn't pull off this opening, she was going to be letting down a lot of people—not the least of whom was herself.

❧

Aiden peered over his shoulder at Sophie. She'd continued cutting in the paint after the mayor left, but she was unusually quiet. And he didn't think it was the focused kind of quiet. "What's wrong?"

"Nothing." The sound of the brush and roller filled the

silence for a good minute before she spoke again. "That's not entirely true. I guess I suddenly realized how much there is yet to do."

"And how many people are counting on you to do it?" He suspected the mayor had intended just that.

Sophie straightened, sporting a little smudge of blue on her cheek. "Am I that transparent?"

"You shouldn't let the mayor stress you out. You've got this. We're almost back on schedule."

"But what if something goes wrong? What if the shelves don't get finished in time, or the wood floor is in terrible shape, or—?"

"Don't borrow trouble. 'Who of you by worrying can add a single hour to your life?'"

She gave him a wry look. "Did you just quote Scripture at me?"

"Hey, there's a reason I have it memorized. If I've learned anything it's that worrying does nothing but stress you out."

Her shoulders slouched with the weight of the world. "There's so much on the line. Did I ever tell you my mom used to dream of opening a bookstore here in Piper's Cove?"

"I didn't know that, but I knew she grew up here."

Sophie went back to painting, but he watched the wistful smile curve her lips. "She worked at a bookshop in New Bern throughout high school and loved it. She was determined to save up enough money to open a store herself—she wasn't really interested in attending college. But she got pregnant with Seth and me, and then she married Daddy, and they moved to Raleigh for his job. I think she still hoped to open that shop one day. But then she got diagnosed with MS when I was in grade school, and that was that. I hate that she never got to live out her dream."

He lowered his roller. "I was around your mom enough to know her kids were her world. She wouldn't have changed a thing, Sophie."

"I know you're right." She rewetted her brush. "Still . . ."

"Like mother like daughter. The library always was your favorite place." He fondly remembered sneaking a kiss or two in the biography section. Once they'd gotten caught by a prim and proper librarian who'd promptly tossed them out.

Sophie cleared her throat. "Talking about this bookshop was one of the few things that excited her. I think it felt good for her to know what I'd be doing, and that it would be something she loved and had a part in planning."

His throat tightened and his gaze sharpened on her. "You're keeping her memory alive with this store."

She turned to him with a pained look on her face. "I guess I am. Trying to, at least. Is that foolish?"

"You shared a love of reading with her, and you want to hang on to that. I don't see a thing wrong with it. It's honorable."

She gave a wistful smile. "I have so many wonderful memories of her reading to me when I was growing up. *Charlotte's Web*, *The Secret Garden*, *Bridge to Terabithia*, all the Little House books— some of them multiple times. Seth would start out listening, too, but he'd get distracted and wander off. But those stories held me spellbound. And in her last months, when she was bedridden, I read to her for hours every day."

He felt a pinch in his chest at Sophie's loss. "She was a wonderful mother. You were blessed to have her."

Sophie's eyes widened with sudden realization. "I'm so sorry. Here I am having a pity party because I miss my mom, and you . . ."

"That's all right. You can't miss what you don't remember."

But even as he said the words, he realized they weren't true. How many times had he missed the idea of a mother? Mother's Day at church, Parents' Night at school . . . Sometimes he feared that lost little boy was still inside him. The one who'd gone without a mother's tender care when he scuffed his knees or had his heart broken by some little girl on the playground.

"I don't even remember her leaving. My dad later told me I sat outside day after day, waiting for her to come back. I just have vague memories of her, talking on the phone or baking cookies, stuff like that."

"I feel sorry for her. She's the one who missed out, Aiden."

He gave her a smile. "Thanks. Dad and I did okay. He wasn't one for sloppy affection, but I knew he loved me, and he was always there for me. He was enough."

"He didn't take off when the going got tough. That's more than I can say for my dad."

"Do you have much of a relationship with him now?"

Sophie lifted a shoulder. "We meet for coffee now and then. Things are stilted and awkward—you probably noticed at the wedding."

"I saw there was tension between Seth and him, but Jenna seems to have forgiven him."

"She was always a Daddy's girl. It's more complicated with Seth. He was disappointed and angry when Dad left. He knows a real man doesn't abandon his wife when she's down."

"For better or for worse."

"Dad was selfish, and he hasn't really changed. He still doesn't take responsibility for what he did—just offers excuses. And until that changes, I don't think Seth will let him back into his life."

"Forgiveness is one thing; trust is another."

"Yes, and his adding a new girlfriend to the mix hasn't exactly helped. I've forgiven Dad, and I'll continue the relationship, but my expectations are realistic."

"What does he think of your opening a bookshop? Surely he knows it was your mom's dream."

"I think he's happy for me, but we don't really talk about Mom or her connection to the store. I find it's best if we steer clear of touchy topics for the time being. Maybe someday we can have something more real, but for now we're just trying to find our footing again."

"Fair enough." Aiden sent up a prayer for Sophie and her family. They'd been through so much, and he wanted nothing more than a happy ending for Sophie.

chapter

twenty-three

Sophie was touching up the paint in the back room when someone entered the store. Aiden had stepped out a few minutes ago to pick up supplies from the hardware store.

"Forget something?" she called.

"Sophie?"

She frowned at the unexpected voice. "Dad?"

"It's me."

She set down her brush, gathered her crutches, and hobbled into the front room. Sure enough, there was her father, hands in his pockets, scanning the room appreciatively.

"Dad . . . Is everything okay?"

His face fell when he saw her crutches. "Honey, what happened to you?"

She gave a self-deprecating smile. "I fell off a ladder. It's just a sprain. Is everything all right back home?" Surely if something had happened to Seth or Jenna she would've been the first to hear.

"Sure, sure. I wanted to see how you were doing, so I decided to drive over and find out for myself."

"Dad, it's a three-hour drive. And aren't you supposed to be at work right now?"

"I'm on midnights this week." He paced the room, inspecting the paint job. "This place is really coming along. When's your grand opening?"

"Tuesday, Lord willing."

"*Next* Tuesday?"

"I'm afraid so."

"How are you getting anything done on those crutches?"

"Thankfully, I have help." She avoided mentioning Aiden since her dad had snubbed him at the wedding. "Let me give you the grand tour."

She showed him from room to room, explaining which genres would go where. She told him about Nathaniel Quinn's book signing, but not being a reader, he didn't recognize the author's name.

"And this will be the children's room." She pointed toward the large window seat. "I'm planning to make a cozy reading spot there, but that'll have to wait a few weeks." Or maybe longer. Sophie had gotten an estimate from the auto mechanic this morning. The repairs on her Tahoe would eat a big hole in her meager savings.

"It's coming along real nice, sweetheart," Dad said when the tour was finished. "You have an extra brush? I have a little time before I have to get back on the road."

Warmth surged through her at the offer. "That'd be great, Dad. There's an extra brush in that bag."

He retrieved it and she led him down the hall. "If you could touch up around the doorways that would be helpful. It's hard to manage on crutches."

"We can catch up while we work."

She sank onto the floor nearby and resumed painting.

They made small talk for a while, sticking to safer topics like work and Jenna's honeymoon, their brushstrokes a backdrop for their conversation. She knew she should say something about Aiden being here, but instead she hoped her dad would be gone before Aiden returned.

She was happy to have her father here, and not because of the work he was doing. It felt good to have him stepping up to the plate. Since he'd left the family, it felt as if he'd abdicated his role as parent. And even though Sophie was all grown up now, she still needed her dad.

Conversation flowed fluidly for an hour or so, and talk soon returned to her renovation.

"I was thrilled to find original wood floors under the carpet," Sophie said. "I think they'll only need a topcoat."

"Use the fast-dry stuff since you're on a deadline. I used it at my house a few years ago."

"I'd forgotten you have wood floors." She'd only been to his house twice.

"Yeah . . ." Something in his voice made Sophie look up from her work.

He spared her a glance. "Sweetheart . . . There's something I

171

wanted to ask you. I almost asked at the wedding but decided the time wasn't right. At this point things are getting pretty bad—it can't wait any longer."

She lowered her brush, frowning, her mind immediately leaping toward some kind of illness. "What is it, Daddy?"

He dipped his brush in the paint and resumed touch-ups. "This is a little embarrassing to admit, but I'm in a bit of a financial crunch. I'm afraid I'm behind on my mortgage payments."

No illness. Her breath released on a sigh. But a beat later her stomach plummeted. So this was the true reason for his visit. "What happened? I thought things were going okay with your job."

"Well, I earn a living but not enough to put much back. My furnace went out this winter, and that took my savings. Then my car's transmission went out, and I can't get to work without a car, so I had to put the repairs on my credit card. I just got a raise, and that'll help me shuffle along, but I'm in desperate straits. I'm about to lose my house, Sophie. I have till Friday to come up with the money."

"*This* Friday?"

"'Fraid so."

"Dad, I wish I could help, but I've sunk nearly everything I have into this shop."

"Sure, sure. I know you've got a lot going on here. I see that. It's just that your mom and I owned the house free and clear, and I didn't ask for my part of it in the divorce."

Sophie gritted her teeth. As well he shouldn't have! He'd left them with all the hospital bills.

"I hate to ask you for anything, but I don't have anywhere else to turn."

She forced a moderate tone to her voice. "That money's long gone, Daddy. What didn't go toward the hospital bills was divvied up between us kids. Seth's and Jenna's shares went toward college loans, and mine went toward this shop. Maybe you should get an apartment."

Her dad lowered his brush, giving her a pained look. "If they repossess the house, I'd still need money for first month's rent and deposit, which I don't have. I'd be homeless until I could save up the money. Unless Jenna and Grant would take me in for a while."

Sophie gaped at her dad. Surely he didn't expect to be on their doorstep with his luggage the moment they returned from their honeymoon. "They're newlyweds, Daddy."

"That's why I came to you first. I didn't want to put them in that position. It wouldn't take much to get me over the hump, honey. Just a few thousand dollars."

Sophie's heart twisted. She really didn't have it to give. Or did she? There was that money she'd set back to take down the troublesome tree out front. But it had been there a hundred years. What were a few more months?

The sound of the door opening stole her thoughts.

"I'm back," Aiden called from the front. "Sorry it took me so long. They were out of the—" He appeared in the doorway, going still at the sight of Dad.

Her dad's back went stiff. "What are you doing here?"

"Helping Sophie." Aiden looked at her, then back to Dad.

Her dad raked his gaze up and down Aiden. "Is that so?"

"Daddy. He's been helping me all week. And he's the only reason my dreams aren't swirling down the drain right now."

Dad fixed Aiden with a long glare before he checked his watch and smiled at Sophie. "It's time for me to get back on the road, honey. Sorry I can't stay and help out more."

"I'll walk you out." Eager to separate the men, she grabbed her purse and slung it over her shoulder. She could use a coffee.

They'd barely cleared the front door before her dad said, "You were always too good for that boy."

"Said every father on the planet. He's only a friend, and it was kind of him to stay once I sprained my ankle."

He harrumphed.

They walked side by side until he reached his blue Ford truck.

She faced him. "I can write you a check, Daddy. I can divert three thousand from my store for now, but that's all I have to give."

"That's all I need." He embraced her, holding her tight. "Honey, you don't know what this means to me."

She softened at his gratitude. "Of course."

"I'll pay you back. It shouldn't take too long now that I got a raise."

When he let go of her she reached into her purse and pulled out her checkbook. After she wrote the check she handed it over, swallowing back a surge of apprehension. With no money to fall back on, she'd better hope and pray nothing else went wrong.

chapter

twenty-four

While Aiden ripped the carpet from the tack strips, Sophie held her breath. On hands and knees she rolled the carpet and padding away from the walls, slowly revealing the wood floor beneath it.

Please let it be in good condition.

She'd pulled up a few corners weeks ago, delighted to find the original planking under the carpet. The caramel-colored wood had seemed like it only needed a little TLC, the minor scuffs and scrapes simply adding character. She hoped there were no ghastly water stains that would require sanding and restaining. She didn't have time for that.

Sophie surveyed the exposed flooring. "So far so good."

"It looks great. Nothing a coat of polyurethane won't cure, I think."

They'd finished painting yesterday. They had only to remove the painter's tape but decided to pull the carpet first thing this morning and see what they had to work with.

Aiden moved to another wall, ripping the carpet free from the strips. When it proved stubborn, Sophie joined his efforts. Finally the old carpet came loose. Some minor discolorations marred the wood near the door.

"Looks like a good place for a rug," Aiden said.

"Doesn't it?"

"How long will the shelving take to install?"

"Leonard said two days. He called last night to tell me they were ready. We just need to take care of this floor first."

"You'll have to give the polyurethane some time to cure before installing the shelves."

"I have the fast-drying type, but it needs two coats, and you can't walk on it for twelve hours. You're supposed to wait three days to put furniture on it, but we don't have that kind of time. We'll clean the floor and hopefully get both coats done today. Tomorrow, while it cures, I can price books—I should have no trouble doing that on my own."

Aiden sat back on his haunches, bringing him close enough for her to see the silver flecks in his blue eyes and the stubble on his jaw. Smell the lingering scent of his soap.

He regarded her with an enigmatic expression. "Are you saying you'll be finished with me after today?"

She shrugged, her stomach wobbling at his nearness—and at the thought of his departure. "I know you have a life to get back to. Once the shelves are in, it'll just be a matter of setting up my shop. My ankle is already a lot better. I'll be off the crutches by tomorrow, I think."

The look in his eyes might've passed for regret. Or maybe that was just wishful thinking.

"You'll still be hobbling around."

"I can work around that. There's nothing too arduous ahead of me."

"What about the heavy boxes of books? You shouldn't be carrying that kind of weight."

She hadn't really considered that. "I'll see if I can get some help. Seth might be able to come after work tomorrow, and maybe Jenna and Grant wouldn't mind pitching in once they return from their honeymoon." Though she hated to ask them.

His eyes searched hers. "Sounds like you've thought it through. I guess I should book a flight for tomorrow then."

"Sounds reasonable." The thought of him leaving made her gut twist. She'd gotten used to having him around again.

That live wire stretched between them, zinging pulses back and forth. Drawing her in. Making her wish things were different.

She broke eye contact, giving a quiet laugh. "You'll probably be glad to get away from these mundane chores and get back to your adrenaline rushes."

His gaze traveled over her face, his eyes turning thoughtful. "I'm glad I stayed."

Sophie basked in his affectionate look. Tried to memorize the straight slope of his nose, the sharp turn of his jaw, the graceful sweep of his lashes. Their time together was drawing to a close, and she wanted these details to carry her through the long, lonely nights.

As painful as the parting would be, his unexpected appearance in her life had been good for her. Had allowed them to settle the past. She was grateful for that, but that's where it ended.

She moved to stand but forgot her injury and nearly came crashing down.

Aiden was there in a blink, steadying her. "Careful."

She clutched his forearms, regaining her balance.

In an instant the mood shifted. Her focus narrowed to just the two of them. To the feel of his hands at her waist. To his piercing blue eyes, trained on her and filled with ardor.

His thumb brushed her cheek, bringing every cell to life.

Her heart threatened to escape her rib cage as her gaze fell to his mouth. To the heart-shaped curve of his Cupid's bow. Darn those lips.

He moved closer, a soft puff of breath a prelude to the kiss. Then just a brush of his lips. Unhurried. Warm and gentle. Reverent.

He paused, hovering over her for a long, desperate moment. She waited, breathless, wishing with everything in her for more.

And then, blessedly, his lips were on hers again.

Her hands glided up those solid biceps to curl around his neck and pull him closer. She still fit against him so well, the embrace as familiar as the kiss.

She yielded to his expertise. How had she forgotten how good he was at this? She marveled that the touch of his lips could send tremors through her body like an earthquake. The few other kisses she'd had were poor imitations of this. Had it been the same for Aiden?

But she was quickly distracted from her thoughts when he pulled her into the cradle of his chest. His mouth also served as a distraction, working her lips with beautiful precision. She gladly yielded to his soft exploration, lost, remembering all those other times he'd made her feel like the most desirable woman in the world.

She felt his withdrawal moments before he ended the kiss. He didn't go far, though. Their breaths mingled between them, shallow and ragged.

He cupped her face, eyes raking over her features.

She nearly melted under his smoldering gaze.

"I'm staying until your shop is open." His voice was as thick as honey.

She blinked, waiting for her brain catch up with his. "Aiden . . ."

She wasn't even sure how to complete the sentence. Were they not going to talk about the kiss? What had he meant by it? What had *she* meant by it?

"You need the help. And Ross can do without me a few more days. I want to be here for your opening."

What about Tiffany? Guilt pinched at the thought of his girlfriend, but she refused to speak the woman's name into the moment.

She backed away, letting her arms fall, needing a little space before she asked the next question. "What—what was that about, Aiden?"

His own arms fell to his sides. "I don't know. It was—me, wanting you, like I always have."

She didn't want to say it, but it needed to be said. "To what end? It can't go anywhere. I live here, and you live in Charleston."

A dozen thoughts seemed to flicker in his eyes before he responded. "You're right. I guess we should just . . . forget it ever happened."

Fat chance of that. But for now she put aside thoughts of the kiss. "Are you sure you want to stay longer? Maybe it'd be best if—"

"I'll be more careful. Do I owe you an apology?"

She gazed into his eyes and couldn't work up an ounce of regret. "There were two people involved in that kiss."

A smile played at the corner of his lips, crooked and charming. "So there were."

A smile trembled on her lips, and her shoulders sank at the breaking of tension.

He backed away, shelving his hands on his waist. "We should get back to the carpet. Then I'll sweep up and mop the floor."

Sophie surveyed the unfinished space with the dull floors and barren blue walls. They had plenty of work to distract them. She had a feeling they were going to need all of it.

❧

Aiden slopped the mop around the floor, jamming it too hard into the woodwork. Sophie had gone outside for some fresh air, and he was glad for a moment alone. Ever since that kiss it seemed like the air in the room had thickened, making it impossible to draw a full breath.

He jabbed the mop into the corner. He was such an idiot. He'd gone and taken a taste of her, and he of all people should've known what a mistake that would be. She was downright addictive—that much hadn't changed. He already wanted to get his arms around her again—and for what? Sophie was right. What future could they have?

He only half regretted telling her he'd stay. She needed the help, and he wasn't convinced her brother and sister would drop everything and come to her rescue. Besides, Sophie would do whatever it took to get this store finished in time, up to and including reinjuring herself.

It would only be five more days, and he'd feel much better leaving with the shop finished. Anyway, after all this effort he wanted to see the finished product.

He threw down the mop, pulled his phone from his pocket, and opened it to Tiffany's last message, which he hadn't yet responded to. What was one more delay in his return home?

chapter

twenty-five

So many things were left on Sophie's to-do list. But it was official—she could walk without crutches. She hobbled through the day's work, and the sun was almost down by the time Aiden applied the last coat of polyurethane on the floor. While he completed the task, Sophie headed to Schooners to finalize the party menu.

The restaurant was at the other end of the boardwalk, within walking distance even with a gimpy ankle. She felt so free without her crutches she relished every step. The waterfront eatery was rustic and quiet, being past suppertime and not quite beach season.

She met with the chef, Ramona Jenkins, an attractive redhead Sophie figured to be somewhere in her early thirties. The care and attention the woman put into the details impressed

Sophie. They sat over drinks and samples for an hour, discussing food and eventually segueing to books and authors. By the time they wrapped up, Sophie felt as if she'd found a new customer and possibly a new friend.

"Relax." Ramona smiled as they parted. "Put your worries elsewhere. I've got the food covered."

"I have no doubt."

By the time Sophie returned to the shop, Aiden was finished. And since they were unable to step foot on the floor for twelve hours, they knocked off for the rest of the evening.

"We're almost back on schedule," Sophie said from the passenger seat as she stroked Pippa's back.

"So tomorrow we'll price books. What else?"

Sophie laughed. "Believe me, that'll take up the day and then some."

"Don't most stores just use the barcode?"

"Some do. But some like to have their store's name on the cover. It also makes the returns easier. Plus, I'm stocking a small selection of used books, which always needs pricing. But back to the schedule . . . The shelves will be going in Saturday and Sunday, even though that's a bit early according to the polyurethane instructions. It can't be helped though."

"But that only leaves Monday to stock the shelves."

"How are you at alphabetizing?" she asked wryly.

"Not as good as you, I'm sure."

"You'll be fine. Ellie's coming in to help and train the other staff on the register." She'd texted Jenna to ask if she could come but hadn't heard back yet.

Just the thought of how close they were cutting it was shredding her nerves. Why had she thought she could stock shelves on Monday and be ready to open—for a release party—the very next day?

"The party starts at four on Tuesday?"

"Yes, but the grand opening will be all day, of course. I'm hoping for a good crowd but at the same time, I'm also afraid we won't be able to handle that many people. Somewhere between book pricing and shelving, I'll have to fit in a final meeting with my staff. We have to make a good first impression."

When they arrived home Sophie noticed a car in the darkened drive.

"Who's that?" Aiden asked.

"I don't know. I'm not expecting anyone."

"Maybe the Fosters decided to come for the weekend."

Surely they would've notified her. But she didn't know them well, and it was their home after all.

Once Aiden parked, she opened the door and let Pippa down, then climbed from the car. She struggled to retrieve her purse, which was tangled with the seat belt. She spun, hopping to keep her balance until she finally freed it.

Aiden closed his door, chuckling.

She must've looked like a giraffe on roller skates. Her own lips twitched.

"Are you laughing at me?"

"Wish I'd gotten that on video. It was almost as good as when you tripped over the paint pan a few days ago."

"That was not funny. I made a huge mess."

He chuckled again. "And then when Pippa ran through it . . ."

Having joined his side, Sophie nudged him with her shoulder, favoring her good foot and almost losing her balance again.

"Those little blue paw prints . . . I kind of hated to get rid of the carpet after that."

"She made a mess! And it took thirty minutes to get the paint off her paws."

"Aiden?"

Sophie jumped at the voice coming from the darkened entryway.

A woman descended the porch steps. Even though it was too dark to make out her features or expression, Sophie knew instantly who she was.

❧

"Tiffany." Aiden finally found his tongue. His humor scattered in the wind. "What are you doing here?"

Pippa yapped at Tiffany as her gaze darted between Sophie and Aiden.

"Tiffany, this is Sophie Lawson. Sophie . . . Tiffany."

They exchanged unenthusiastic pleasantries, then Tiffany addressed him. "Since you'd been delayed again, I thought I might surprise you."

Well, she'd certainly managed to do that.

"And I brought your award." She extended it to him. "In case you wanted to see it in person."

"That was thoughtful." As he received it he dimly noted the

trophy's substantial weight, but it was too dark to appreciate its aesthetics.

Sophie stooped down, gathering the yipping dog. "I think I'll head inside and get Pippa some water."

He held out the trophy. "Would you take this inside, please?"

"Sure."

Aiden watched her walk between the house's pilings and inside through the lower door, wanting with everything in him to follow her inside.

But Tiffany had driven a long way to see him. He should be glad to see the woman, but her appearance only felt like an intrusion.

And that's how he knew what he had to do. His chest weighted with the realization. "It's a nice night. Why don't we take a walk on the beach?"

"Sure."

Tiffany fell into step beside him as he walked around the corner of the house and down the flagstone path to the beach. She was unusually quiet tonight. Normally when they spent a few hours together, her chattering got on his nerves. It didn't escape him that he'd spent five solid days with Sophie and hadn't tired of her once.

When they reached the beach they shucked their shoes and continued toward the shoreline. The moon hung low, glowing in the sky, its reflection a shimmering cone on the water's surface. Aiden drew in a lungful of briny sea air as he reached the hard-packed sand and turned north, the cool water lapping at his feet. Tiffany came alongside him.

"How'd you get here so fast?" Charleston was a five-hour drive. "It had to be past noon when I told you I'd been delayed."

"I guess that says it all." Tiffany gave a wry laugh. "It was just a whim. It was a slow workday, and I thought you might be glad to see me. Guess I was wrong."

Aiden scratched the back of his neck. "I'm sorry. You surprised me is all. It's been a long day."

"Yes, it sounded like you were exhausted when you got here."

He opened his mouth to speak, but she beat him to the punch.

"Look, Aiden. I didn't mean to . . . overstep our relationship. I know we're not an item or anything—but I thought we were headed that direction. And ever since you left for the wedding, you've seemed a little distant."

"I'm sorry . . ."

"I don't want an apology. I came because I'd hoped I'd misinterpreted things. That maybe it was just the long-distance communication. That you were distracted with this project you're helping your friend with. But I see now that's not it at all."

He'd thought he'd done a better job of hiding his feelings. But he shouldn't have been hiding them at all. He should've been seeing them for the signs they were. He wasn't interested in a long-term relationship with Tiffany.

"And it doesn't take a genius to see there's still something between you and your old girlfriend."

Aiden shook his head even though the memory of their kiss still warmed him. "That's not going to happen."

Tiffany stopped in her tracks, facing him.

The moonlight touched her pretty features. She'd never looked more beautiful, but he couldn't conjure up any real feelings for her. Nothing beyond friendship at least.

"But neither is this—is it?"

"It's not you, Tiffany. I like you a lot. You're fun to be with, and I've enjoyed the time we've spent together."

Her laugh held no humor. "It feels like you should've known that weeks ago."

He'd been hoping something would kick in. Something to make him feel the way he used to with Sophie. He saw now that he'd hung on too long and had led Tiffany on in the process.

"I probably should've. I'm sorry for that. And I'm sorry you drove all this way only to—"

"Get dumped?"

He took her hand. "I'd still like to be your friend. We have a lot in common. We have fun together."

She withdrew her hand and turned back toward the house. "I don't think of you as a friend, Aiden," she said without malice.

He followed, wincing. A girl had never broken up with him, so he couldn't know how that kind of rejection felt. But he'd always hated breaking someone else's heart. Experience had taught him there was nothing he could say or do to make Tiffany feel better right now.

"It's too late to drive back tonight. You're welcome to stay at the house."

"No offense, Aiden, but this is the last place I want to be right now."

The rest of the walk was quiet. When they reached the

property, they picked up their shoes and carried them through the yard and around to the front.

When they reached her car he opened the door for her.

She lifted her chin. "We still have to work together."

"I hope it won't be too . . ." He struggled to find the right word.

"Right. Me too." She gave him a tight smile and got into the car without another word.

chapter

twenty-six

Shortly after Sophie entered the house her phone rang.
Joshua's name appeared on the screen. With her growing feelings
for Aiden, she'd been avoiding the man. She'd let yesterday's call
go unanswered and responded only briefly to his text today. He
knew she was busy with the store, after all.

But on the third buzz she looked through the sliding glass
door toward the beach. Somewhere in the darkness, Aiden
walked with his girlfriend.

She accepted the call before it went to voice mail. "Hi,
Joshua."

"Sophie. I hope I'm not calling too late."

"Not at all. I just got home, actually. How are you?"

"Fine. Busy with the residency. How goes the shop? Are you
back on schedule yet?"

"Almost. We're really cutting it close, but I think we're going to make it." She'd informed him a friend from high school was helping.

"And how's your ankle? Still hobbling around on crutches?"

"The swelling's gone down and it's not as painful, so I only use them to walk long distances—though I'm definitely favoring my good foot."

"As you probably should. In fact, an ankle brace would be a good idea, especially since you're quite active right now. You don't want to reinjure it. How's the pain—are you still on prescription meds?"

Sophie smiled. He was in full doctor mode now. "It's much better. I'm taking ibuprofen as needed."

He made a few other suggestions about caring for her ankle over the next few weeks. But when he began detailing specific exercises, her mind wandered. She looked out the window and caught sight of Aiden and his girlfriend down the beach, standing close. The moonlight glimmered on the woman's white shirt, and the wind whipped her long hair.

Sophie's heart wrenched. Even in the dim light she'd noticed the woman's beauty and lithe figure. What a nice-looking couple they made. Being a pilot, Tiffany no doubt had an adventurous spirit like Aiden too. They had so much in common. And soon he'd be going home to her.

"Sophie?" Joshua said.

She turned from the window. What was she doing, longing for someone she couldn't have while she ignored a perfectly nice—and interested—man?

"I'm sorry. I missed that last thing you said."

"I was asking if you needed help setting up your shop. I know we don't know each other very well yet, but I'm off on Sunday, and I have a strong back if you could use an extra set of hands."

She warmed at his offer. "That's so nice of you. But my carpenter will be installing the bookcases all weekend. There'll be so many people in the shop, we'll be tripping over each other."

And she couldn't imagine Aiden, Joshua, and her tucked into her small office, working together amid stacks of boxes and books.

"Well, if things change, just let me know."

"I will. We got the floor finished today, and we'll be pricing books tomorrow."

"That sounds like a good plan for your ankle. Maybe you can elevate it while you work."

"You're a regular mother hen."

He groaned. "Not what I was going for at all."

"No? Then maybe you should stop being so helpful."

"That settles it. I'm taking off my doctor's hat—metaphorically speaking. Tell me how your grandma's doing. Have you heard from her this week?"

"Oh, for certain. Barely a day goes by that I don't hear from her."

"Now, why does that sound so ominous?"

"Possibly because the woman is an opinionated nag."

He chuckled. "Since her opinion of me is favorable, I don't mind at all."

"She's called me every single day since my injury to hound me about staying off it."

"Sounds quite reasonable to me."

Sophie's lips stretched into a smile. "You're taking her side! And after I agreed to go out with you and everything."

"The woman set me up with you—how can I find fault with her?"

Sophie laughed. "Touché. How can I argue with that? Now tell me how Bear's doing. Any more squirrel adventures to report?"

"Oh, every day is a squirrel adventure for Bear. I think he's only toying with them, though. He never catches them but seems immeasurably proud just to chase them away for me."

"Pippa runs away at the sight of blowing sea oats, but she yips at strangers as if they're the devil. She's very slow to warm up to people." She instantly thought of the dog's warm reception to Aiden, then shook the thought from her head.

"So I shouldn't be offended if she hates me on sight?"

"If she does, I'm sure she'll come around soon enough."

"We should get our canine companions together. I wonder how they'd like each other."

The front door opened and Aiden entered. His dark curls were windswept, his expression unreadable. She was surprised when his girlfriend didn't appear behind him. She'd assumed the woman would end up staying the night—and Sophie hadn't been anticipating awkward small talk.

Aiden gave Sophie a little wave and headed upstairs. What had happened on the beach? Maybe the woman felt more comfortable staying at a hotel.

She realized Joshua had just spoken. "I'm sorry, what did you say?"

"I was saying Bear would probably slobber all over Pippa and possibly trample her. He tends to forget how big he's grown. He still jumps into my lap when I'm in the recliner."

"Oh my." Sophie tried to smother her yawn. "I'm sorry. I'm not bored, I promise."

"But you are tired, no doubt. I should let you get to bed. I just wanted to check in and see how your shop's progressing."

"That's very kind of you. But, yes, it has been a long day."

"I'll call you soon, if that's all right."

"I'd like that. Good night."

"Good night, Sophie."

chapter

twenty-seven

Aiden's face fell as his gaze drifted around Sophie's of-
fice. "I've never seen so many books in one room."

"You say that as if it's a problem."

"Only if you have to price them all."

The windows were open, the temperatures mild, and a refreshing breeze ruffled the gauzy curtain. Sophie sat across from
Aiden, her foot propped on a bucket. First thing this morning
they'd stopped at the pharmacy for a brace, which helped stabi-
lize her ankle. She'd sent Joshua a text thanking him for the idea.

She'd thought Aiden might spend time with his girlfriend
this morning, but he said nothing of Tiffany. Surely the woman
hadn't returned to Charleston so soon after that long drive. They
hadn't spent more than fifteen minutes together on the beach.
As curious as Sophie was, she wouldn't ask. It was none of her
business.

Aiden moved boxes around, looking for the memoirs. This sorting project was going to take a while, but it would allow them to shelve the books quickly once the bookcases were in place.

A knock came on the back door and Pippa yipped ferociously.

"Wonder who that is," Sophie said.

Aiden navigated the maze of boxes, picking up Pippa on his way to the door.

When he opened it, an unfamiliar man smiled in greeting. He looked to be in his late twenties, wore a ball cap, and sported a neat goatee. He was built like a workingman, and his rugged clothing bore out the notion.

"Brandon." Aiden shook the man's hand. "What are you doing here?"

"Just stopped by to see how the topcoat turned out for you. I saw the sign on the front door, so I'm guessing you got it down already. Who's this little critter?"

"Pippa. She's a little gun-shy. Come on in." Aiden closed the door behind the man. "Sophie, this is Brandon. I ran into him yesterday in the stain aisle at the hardware store. Brandon, this is the owner of the new bookstore."

"Pleasure, ma'am," Brandon said as they shook hands. "Can't tell you how happy I am to be getting a local bookstore."

"Nice to meet you. What's your reading pleasure?"

"Mainly biographies. Though I read up on history sometimes—the World Wars, mostly."

"We'll have an excellent selection of both. And if there are particular books you're interested in, don't hesitate to ask. We can always special order."

He took in the office. "Looks like you've got enough books to keep me busy until the end of time."

She laughed. "That's my intention."

Aiden shoved a box aside with his foot. "Brandon here saved me from buying the wrong topcoat."

"Well, not so much wrong as inferior."

"Are floors your business?" Sophie asked Brandon.

"Aw, no, I'm really just a handyman. I know a little bit about a lot of things."

"I neglected to mention his last name's Hooper," Aiden said. "His dad owns the hardware store, and Brandon launched his own business."

"I do odds and ends for people."

Aiden gave the man a tolerant look. "He's a contractor, a framer, and a licensed electrician besides. And apparently knows a good deal about refinishing floors too."

"A handyman you are then," Sophie said.

"The floor's still curing, of course." Aiden motioned for Brandon to follow as he wove through the maze of boxes. "But come take a peek. If I did it wrong, I trust you'll pretend otherwise."

Brandon surveyed the hall and the room opposite the office. "Seems like I won't have to strain my acting abilities. You did a good job."

The men chatted a bit, Brandon giving advice about the floor's upkeep, which Sophie tucked away for later.

A while later Brandon said, "I should let you two get back to your books."

When he passed Sophie he handed her a business card. "If you have any questions or need an extra hand, give me a call. And welcome to Piper's Cove."

"Thanks so much. I hope you can come to the grand opening."

"Wouldn't miss it. And my mom's excited about that author who's coming."

"Tell her to bring all her friends."

He chuckled. "Oh, she will."

"Nice guy," Sophie said once the door closed behind him.

"I seem to meet someone helpful every time I go to the hardware store."

"It's a friendly town. I hope they all like to read."

"I'll bet they do—and tourists are always after beach reads, right? You know what they say about setting up a business—location, location, location. I think you nailed it."

"Hope you're right."

Aiden lowered a box at Sophie's feet. "Here are the last memoirs I could find. What next?"

"Let's do the biographies. I think most of those are over there." She gestured to the corner, her eyes taking in all the boxes. It was a little overwhelming. "I hope I didn't underestimate how much time this would take."

"Any chance of calling in reinforcements this weekend?"

"Seth is working—wants to impress his new boss, I guess. And Jenna and Grant don't return until tomorrow night. I hate to bother them the moment they step off the plane."

Aiden said nothing, but a muscle flickered in his jaw. He

settled across from her and helped her with the books. "What about Joshua?"

She glanced at him, but he was already busy with the price gun.

"That's his name, isn't it—the guy you've been talking to?"

"Well, yes, but . . ." She didn't realize he'd noticed. "He did offer to help, but I can't accept—we haven't even met in person."

That muscle flexed in his jaw again. "Well, maybe you shouldn't turn down free help."

She had no doubt Joshua's offer had been sincere. But the thought of bringing the two men together gave new meaning to the word *awkward*. Kind of like when Tiffany had shown up on their doorstep last night.

"Maybe I shouldn't." She shot him a defiant look, which he missed entirely. "Too bad Tiffany couldn't come and help today. Did she have to go back so soon?"

Sophie applied a sticker to a Fred Rogers biography and set it aside. She felt Aiden's gaze but pretended not to as she reached for another book.

"Yeah, she's . . . headed back home."

"I thought she might stick around awhile."

There was a long pause, the *ch-chck* of the price guns punctuating the silence. Of course he didn't want to talk about Tiffany with Sophie. Truth be told, she didn't want to hear it. Even now she envisioned the romantic scene from last night: the woman's slender frame close to his, her long hair whipping in the wind.

Sophie's chest squeezed tight. She had no reason to feel jealous over someone she couldn't have. But there it was.

"It's over between Tiffany and me."

Sophie looked up but he continued working.

"It hardly even started, really. She was fun to hang around, but we're not right for each other."

"Oh." Sophie blinked. "After she drove all the way here . . . I just thought—"

"We were never exclusive. If we were, I never would've—" He sighed heavily, looking at her, his blue eyes piercing hers. "I never would've kissed you."

Her breath quickened at the yearning look in his eyes, at his words. The mere mention of his kiss made her legs feel like gelatin. "I—I thought we weren't going to talk about that anymore."

A spark of amusement lit his eyes. "If I could only stop thinking about it."

Warmth flushed through her even as warning sirens wailed inside. "Aiden . . . We live in entirely different states."

"I know, I know. There's nothing you can say I haven't already told myself." He gave his head a shake, picked up the pricing gun, and applied another sticker. "You're right. I shouldn't have said anything."

But he had—and now Sophie couldn't seem to stop thinking about it either.

❧

Aiden frowned at the price tag. Why had he said that? They'd put the kiss behind them. Or, rather, she had. He couldn't seem to shake the feel of her lips on his. The feel of her hands in his hair. The feel of her heart pressed against his.

He had to stop this. He was sending mixed signals. First he kissed her and suggested they forget it. Then he broke up with Tiffany and brought up the kiss again.

For the last time, idiot, your lives are headed in different directions.

He was giving himself whiplash. He didn't need to do the same to her. It wasn't fair. She needed to focus on opening her business. It was the only reason he was here.

Wasn't it?

But it was always possible that winning the ESTA could change his situation. It would likely open up new avenues for him. Open doors he'd never had a chance to walk through. Would he be willing to leave Extreme Adventures and his partnership with Ross for one of those opportunities?

It was the first time he'd allowed the thought to form. The notion sent a burst of adrenaline through his system. It felt good, the thought of change, of something new and exciting. An adventure of some kind, minus the business partner.

But what would he do if he left the business? And would that change allow the possibility of . . .

Sophie was pricing books like a woman with a carafe of coffee in her system. He didn't know what his future held, but he knew what Sophie's held—and they both needed to focus on that for the next few days.

chapter

twenty-eight

What a day. The fierce wind tugged at Sophie's hair and clothing as she limped toward the Boardwalk Beanery. Aiden was grabbing lunch from the deli, and Sophie had promised to bring back some much-needed caffeine.

When she opened the coffee shop's door, she held tight to the handle, then dragged it shut behind her. She drew in the pleasant aroma of brewed coffee and sighed at the promised shot of energy.

"Sure is breezing up out there, isn't it?" Haley said as she came out of the kitchen. The brunette barista was about Sophie's age and had become her favorite. Haley was a free spirit with an impish smile. Her bohemian style of dress suggested she marched to the beat of her own drummer.

"Where's my girl?" Haley asked.

"I was afraid to bring her out." Even as Sophie said it, the windows rattled in their panes. "Goodness."

"One of our table umbrellas blew away this morning. Jim went out to hunt it down."

Sophie laughed, picturing the straitlaced manager chasing the thing down the boardwalk. "Oh no. I'll keep an eye out for it."

She placed her order along with Aiden's, then paid for both and made small talk as Haley whipped up their drinks.

"How's the shop coming along? I started to peek in when I passed by yesterday, but there was a sign on the door."

"The floor's still drying. Well, technically it's dry but we can't walk on it yet. The bookcases go in tomorrow."

"How exciting! If you need help shelving books, let me know. I'm off Monday, and I'm a whiz at alphabetizing. Plus I want a preview of all your fiction so I can figure out how much of my paycheck to set back."

"I might take you up on your offer. We're running pretty tight on that deadline."

"I'd shelve every book in the store for a chance to meet Nathaniel Quinn." Haley winked.

"Have no fear. Everyone who comes Tuesday will have the privilege."

"I'm going to have to buy two books, because I'm putting the one he signs behind glass."

"I hope everyone else feels the same way. I just finished pricing his new releases. I hope I didn't over order."

Haley waved her fears away. "It'll be a huge event. All my friends are going. It'll be a regular race to see which of us finishes the book first." She gave Sophie a coy look. "I don't suppose you might let me . . ."

Sophie laughed. "Sorry. I'm not allowed to give out the copies early."

"Well, it was worth a shot." She handed Sophie the drinks. "Here you go."

"Thanks. Come down and see the shop when you get a chance."

"I'll bring you a sample of my new apple tart when it's done. I'm still tweaking the recipe, and I need feedback."

"Yum, I'll be happy to provide it."

"Don't blow away out there," Haley called as she made her way back to the kitchen.

"See you later." As Sophie neared the door her phone buzzed with an incoming call. She set down the drinks at a table and checked the screen in case it was Aiden, wanting to add dessert to his order. But it was Jenna calling.

Sophie answered. "Hey, Sis. Everything all right?"

"*Aiden* is still there?" she said by way of greeting.

"Hello to you too. I see word has gotten around." Sophie was actually surprised it had taken this long.

"This is kind of big, Soph. He's been there a week, and I'm just now finding out? I thought you hated him."

Sophie rolled her eyes, sinking into a chair by the window facing the boardwalk. "I don't hate him. And why would I bother you with the minutia of my life while you're on your honeymoon?"

"Minutia?" Jenna chuckled. "If there's one thing Aiden Maddox is not, it's minutia. You were heartbroken when he left, and we weren't allowed to even mention his name."

Sophie gaped. "I never said that."

"Granny warned us not to. She said as far as she was concerned his name was a curse word, and we'd get our mouths washed out with soap if she found out we'd uttered it."

"Oh brother."

"And now he's staying at the beach house with you, helping you fix up your store, and you didn't even bother telling me?"

"Nothing's going on, Jenna. There's no mystery here. Go back to your umbrella drinks and suntan lotion."

"Oh, come on. He's missing work to help you? That doesn't add up."

"He got stuck here because of the hurricane. His flight was canceled. Then I sprained my ankle, and he felt bad so he stayed to help. That's all there is to it."

Jenna humphed. "I remember when the two of you were dating—I wasn't that young. It was like an explosion in the chemistry lab every time you two were together."

"That was a long time ago."

"I saw you together at the wedding, Sophie. Sparks galore. Grant agrees, don't you, Grant? He's nodding his head."

"You both have very active imaginations." So did Sophie, apparently, because the steamy kiss they'd shared yesterday played back in vivid HD. Again.

Jenna laughed. "You are so in denial. You were good together once. Maybe you can be good together again. Maybe there's more to him hanging around than a little paint and varnish."

"I'm trying to open a business here, Sis. Not rekindle an old relationship."

"You can do both at once, you know."

"I realize you're on a tropical honeymoon, but real life is not a fairy tale. Aiden and I didn't work out for a reason."

"Situations change and obstacles can be surmounted."

"Spoken like a happily married newlywed. How's it going in the Bahamas, anyway? Soaking up some sun on your last day in paradise?"

"Nice change of subject. And, no, I got a little sunburned yesterday so we're going to hang out in town today. I haven't bought any souvenirs yet. How's Seth's new job going?"

"Pretty good from what he says. He's diving in headfirst."

"Sounds like Seth. Have you heard from Dad at all? He was great at the wedding, wasn't he? He seems happy."

She was glad Jenna hadn't noticed his quarrel with Seth at the reception. "He actually came to see me this week—to check out the shop and everything." No need to mention the loan.

"Aw, that was nice of him to make that drive. See, he's trying. I wish Seth would give him some credit."

"Give him time." Lots and lots of time.

"So you're still opening on Tuesday?"

"I have no choice in the matter. A bestselling author and all his fans will be at my doorstep. Speaking of which, I'd better get back to the shop and finish pricing books."

"All right. Granny, Seth, and I will be there for your opening. Can't wait to see your store."

"Looking forward to catching up. Safe travels tomorrow."

"Love you, Sis!"

"Love you too," Sophie said but Jenna had already disconnected, no doubt eager to return to her new husband.

Just as well. Their coffee was getting cold. It was nice that Jenna had taken the time to call. Even if it had only been to harass her about Aiden. Jenna obviously cared and that meant a lot to Sophie.

She fought the wind as she navigated the boardwalk, passing a few brave souls as she went. Not a single boat was on the harbor today. The waves kicked up, splashing into the seawall, shooting spray into the air.

When she reached the shop she ducked into the building, then closed the door before sand and leaves could make their way in. Pippa danced under her feet, welcoming her as if she'd been gone days.

"Who's a good girl? Mommy's so glad to see you too. Yes, she is."

"I was afraid you'd blown away." Aiden was seated on a tarp, the deli food spread before him. His hair was windblown, somehow making him look both boyish and irresistible.

She dragged her fingers through her own hair. "It's like a hurricane out there."

"Without the rain, thankfully."

He took the coffees from her while she carefully lowered herself to the floor, then they dug in. This week they'd made a habit of eating lunch at the gazebo overlooking the harbor. Sometimes their conversations outlasted the food, and they had to drag themselves back to work. Today's accommodations were far less scenic, but it was too windy to eat outside.

After a while Pippa gave up hope of getting scraps and hopped up in the box window where she watched passersby and kept an eye out for squirrels.

"We're making good headway on the books, don't you think?" Aiden took a bite of his sandwich.

They'd worked until after midnight last night and returned at dawn this morning. "I think we'll finish today. If you don't mind working on that, I think I'll clean the windows and set up my window display."

"Sounds good."

She sipped her coffee, watching him from beneath her lashes. The things Jenna said were rolling around in her brain like marbles. It wasn't as if she needed reminding about their chemistry. It was still there in spades. Working together gave her many opportunities to appreciate his broad shoulders and sculpted biceps.

But it also gave her opportunities to notice other, newer qualities. Aiden was meticulous about his work, not settling for anything but excellence even though it wasn't his store. If he didn't know how to do something, he was quick to figure it out and plunged in headfirst, fearless. He also seemed to make friends everywhere he went. He was now on a first-name basis with everyone at the deli, the hardware store, and several neighbors he'd met while walking Pippa.

All of that, in addition to the fact that he'd made a substantial sacrifice to stay and help her.

He lowered his sandwich, his gaze sharpening on her. "What?"

She'd been staring. Heat bloomed in her cheeks. "What?"

"You're looking at me funny. What are you thinking?"

Even though they were in the largest room of her shop, the setting suddenly felt close and intimate. A little impromptu picnic, just the two of them, the wind whistling in the eaves.

He was leaving in a few days, and they wouldn't see each other again. Aiden hadn't necessarily had people in his life who'd encouraged him. His mom abandoned him and his dad, though he loved Aiden, had never been quick with validation or praise.

"I was thinking . . ." Sophie bolstered herself with a sip of coffee. "That you've turned out to be a pretty great guy."

His eyebrows jumped, but she saw the real effect of her words in his eyes. Felt it in the pause, when he seemed to struggle to find words. "That's—that's really nice of you to say, Soph."

Those soulful eyes of his drew her in and wouldn't let her go. They were still hungry for approval, perhaps because he'd lost his mom so young.

"I mean it." She suddenly wanted more than anything to fill that deep, empty well inside him. "Not only have you stayed to help me at considerable personal cost, but you've poured yourself into this place as if it's your own. No paint drips on your watch. And when you weren't sure how to apply a topcoat, you researched it and went after it like a pro. You've worked long hours without complaint and won't even let me pay for your meals."

There was so much more she could say. But she couldn't get too personal. There was a line she couldn't cross—for both their sakes.

chapter

twenty-nine

Aiden couldn't look away from Sophie if he tried. He soaked in her words like a dry sponge soaked up water. He didn't know why she was suddenly so keen on saying all these nice things, but she had his attention.

She'd always had his attention. With her long, glossy brown hair, expressive brown eyes, and warm, caring spirit. She was like balm on a wound, soothing and refreshing. She always had been. Had he ever told her that?

A crack sounded somewhere outside, barely registering. He was too busy trying to formulate the words he wanted to say. Who could think when she was looking at him like that?

Something crashed overhead, loud and close. He looked up. The ceiling was caving in! He dove for Sophie, laying her flat. A cascade of debris rained around them.

The crash reverberated through the room. Rubble clattered and thumped to the floor around them. Something hit the back of his head. He tucked Sophie's head beneath his own, vaguely aware of her shrieking.

Time slowed, turning seconds into minutes. When the noise finally stopped, Aiden cautiously lifted his head. He frowned at the branches and chunks of bark nearby. He ducked as a piece of drywall thudded belatedly to the floor a few feet away.

"What's happening?" Sophie's voice trembled. "What's going on?"

He scanned the room, taking in the tree. A tree whose branches almost reached them where they lay. It sprawled across most of the room and had dragged the ceiling down with it. Pieces of drywall and insulation littered the floor. Drywall dust floated in the air like smoke. Above them, a light fixture dangled by a wire, the bulb still lit somehow. He looked beyond it, up into a clear blue sky.

He eased off Sophie, who stared stricken at the same sight.

"Are you all right?" he asked.

"Pippa!"

He was suddenly aware of the dog, barking from her window perch.

"She's fine."

He needed to get Sophie out of harm's way before the rest of the ceiling came down. The tree had only missed them by a few feet.

"Sophie . . . Come over here, honey." He helped her up and tugged her to the far corner of the room.

She couldn't seem to take her eyes from the grotesque sight of the ceiling.

"Are you okay?" he asked. "Is anything hurt? Your ankle?"

"I'm all right," she said on a breath. "You?"

"I'm fine." He rubbed the back of his head, surveying the disaster that was her shop. It seemed surreal—a tree lying in the room they'd been working so hard to perfect. The sky visible through the gaping hole in the eaves. The wind rushing through what was supposed to be an enclosed space.

"It's over," Sophie said, her tone flat. "We'll never make it now."

He touched her arm, hating the sound of defeat in her voice, the look of hopelessness in her eyes. "Maybe we can get it cleaned up. Patch up the ceiling. We'll work all night."

But even as he said the words, he realized the roof framing had caved in with the ceiling. This was no patch job. It would require more than tutorial videos and elbow grease. It would require a carpenter, a drywall crew, and a lot of money. "You have insurance, right?"

"That'll take days if not weeks to process. And I sure don't have the money to fix"—she gestured to the disaster—"*this*. That stupid tree. I knew it was trouble."

Her words jogged his memory. "Wait a minute. You said you had a few thousand dollars set back for that tree. You were going to have it taken down. You can use that. It might not be enough, but it's a start."

"I don't have that money anymore. I—" She gave a humorless laugh. "I loaned it out."

Loaned it out? She'd mentioned having the money only several days ago. "Loaned it to who?"

Her eyes slid silently to his. "My dad."

He recalled Craig's recent visit to the store. Aiden had thought the man was taking an interest in Sophie's new business. But that hadn't been the case at all. Aiden's blood pressure shot up, his chest going tight.

It took great effort to speak in a measured tone. "That's why he came here? To borrow money from you?"

She lifted a shoulder. "He was going to lose his house."

"You're going to lose your store." His voice was too loud in the quiet.

Her face took on a stricken look that made him wish he'd kept his big mouth shut.

"No, no," he said quickly. "You're not going to lose your place. We're going to take care of this."

She lifted her gaze to the ceiling, a shadow shifting in the brown depths before a strange expression came over her face. Her shoulders started shaking a moment before laughter escaped, erupting like it was busting loose from prison. It was too high-pitched for humor, nothing like the usual melodic sound of her laughter.

Aiden blinked, wordless, at a loss for how to respond. He rubbed his forehead. He'd never seen this side of her. "Sophie."

"A tree!" she squeezed out between guffaws, staring at the monstrosity in the room. "I have . . . a *tree* . . . in my shop."

His chest ached at the anguish hiding behind her laughter. "Sophie. Come on."

Her eyes swung to him, lit maniacally as she pointed at him. "Look at you! You think . . . You think I've gone stark raving mad."

"Settle down now. It's going to be all right."

Something shifted in her eyes as she took in the mess again. Her laughter petered out, dying one chortle at a time. Her breaths came hard. Her smile gradually fell away, and her eyes took on a distant look as tears filled them.

✸

Even as the disaster in front of her blurred, Sophie couldn't take her eyes off the tree. Its sprawling branches reached the farthest corners of the room. Rafters and sheeting and drywall littered the floor. It didn't seem real.

The ceiling was on the floor. The thought brought another bubble of laughter, but it escaped as a choking sound. She was officially losing it.

Aiden stroked her arm, and the touch grounded her somehow.

"It's going to be okay, Sophie. We're going to get through this. You'll see."

She swallowed audibly. "I have a tree in my shop, Aiden. A tree. In my shop."

He wrapped his arms around her, gathering her close.

She sank into his chest, trying to slow the thoughts spinning through her head. But no matter how fast they spun she couldn't see a way to fix this. Not with her deadline.

She'd have to call Alanda and cancel the release party. Cancel her opening. She'd need to post the changes on her website and social media sites. There would be no way to reach everyone, not with all the fliers and all the people who'd seen the newspaper article. The author would be upset—not to mention Rosewood Press. They'd never trust her with another book signing.

She had so much to do. She pushed back from Aiden. "I need to call Alanda."

"Hold up, not so fast. Don't give up just yet. Let's see if we can figure this out."

"There's nothing to figure out, Aiden. I have a—" She looked over his shoulder and back at him. "Situation. A very expensive situation, and I have no money to fix it. And even if I put it on a credit card or something . . . I'm out of time. We can't get all this done by Tuesday." The very idea was absurd. "We were cutting it tight as it was."

He squeezed her arms. "I have money, Sophie. We can hire people to do the work. Brandon, from the hardware store, remember? He'll know what to do, and he'll know the people who can get it done. I'll call him, and we'll get the ball rolling, okay?"

"I can't take your money, Aiden."

He framed her face and brushed a tear away with his thumb. "Yes, you can. I have that prize money, remember? And I have a little set back besides. That should be enough to—"

"That award money is for *you* to use on your invention. I'm not taking that away from you."

"You can pay me back when you get your insurance check."

The door to the shop opened, sending Pippa on a rampage. Sophie grabbed the dog and soothed her as Haley appeared.

The young woman gaped at the sight of the tree. "Holy mackerel. Sophie, are you all right?"

Sophie wiped her face. "I'm fine. We both are. But my roof . . ."

"I heard the noise all the way from the coffee shop, but I couldn't figure out what it was or where it came from. Holy mackerel." Her gaze shot to Sophie. "Your grand opening!"

"I was telling Sophie we could get a crew in here and get this cleaned up."

Sophie shook her head. "Give it up, Aiden. I appreciate it, I really do, but I'm not taking your money, and there's no way we can fix this in time."

"My dad has a chainsaw," Haley said. "I'll call him and ask him to come down and help. And I just got off work. We'll have this mess hauled out of here before you know it."

The door opened again, and the owners of the deli stepped inside. "Are you guys all right?" Anna asked.

"We saw the tree go down," her husband, Dave, said.

"We're fine," Sophie said.

Haley had stepped away and was already on the phone.

"But as you can see we have a real mess on our hands." Aiden looked at Sophie, his eyes piercing hers. "I'd like to call Brandon and see if he can come down. Is that all right with you?"

She started to remind him of her financial situation, but he spoke before she could verbalize it. "Let's see if he'll work with us. It can't hurt to have him take a look, can it?"

"Brandon Hooper?" Dave said. "He'll get that roof fixed right up. He's well connected too. He and his dad know every tradesman in town."

"He built the extension on our deli," Anna added. "And he came in on time and under budget."

Sophie gave a hopeless smile. The Morrisons had no idea her budget was nonexistent.

"Sophie?" Aiden said.

She honestly didn't know how anyone would be able to fix this mess in time. The bookcases had to go in tomorrow if they were going to open on time, and the main room of her shop had no ceiling.

But the hope in Aiden's eyes was her undoing. She sighed. "All right. I'll give him a call and see what he says."

Haley joined them in the corner. "My dad and brother are coming down with a chainsaw."

"We can help too," Dave said. "And you can use our Dumpster for the debris."

"Thanks, guys." Sophie looked at him and Anna, tears welling in her eyes again. She didn't know if Brandon would come through, but just knowing she was part of a caring community made her want to hug every neck in the room.

chapter

thirty

The next nine hours passed in a whirl of activity and noise. Sophie called her insurance company while they waited for Brandon to arrive. Since she was on a deadline and her agent was out of town, his assistant advised her to take plenty of pictures before they began cleanup.

Haley's dad and brother arrived after Sophie finished snapping photos. They went to work with the chainsaw, and by the time they started hauling out branches, others had shown up to help. People she hadn't even met.

When Brandon arrived with his two-man crew, they were well on their way to having the tree cleaned up. Sophie gestured to Brandon to follow her out front where they could talk.

He already knew about her deadline, so when he said they could have the roof reframed and sheeted by nightfall and the shingles replaced tomorrow, Sophie stopped him.

"Brandon, I appreciate your willingness to dive right in, but

I don't have the money for this right now. And to be honest, I don't know when I'll get the insurance check or how much it'll even cover." She knew what she had to do. Her stomach sank. "I'm going to have to postpone the opening."

Brandon tugged down his ball cap, peering at her with earnest eyes. "Sophie, this is an emergency, and you're a neighbor. I'm volunteering my time, and so are Steve and Derrick. Now there's still the matter of materials, but I think my dad would be willing to start a tab for you."

"Brandon . . . I can't let you do that."

"Sure you can. There'll come a time when someone else around here has a need—maybe me—and you'll pitch right in. That's the way we roll around here."

Tears stung the back of her eyes. Just then a man she didn't even know exited her store with an armful of branches, heading toward the Dumpster. She didn't know half the people working in her shop right now, but they'd seen a need and lent a hand. Brandon was right about this town. What a generous and caring community.

Was it possible they could get this shop done on time yet? Maybe with all this help it was possible. She had to try, didn't she?

She couldn't stop the smile of gratitude from tilting her lips. "I'll pay you back when I get the insurance money."

Ever since Sophie's chat with Brandon, the progress had stepped up another notch. By the time the handyman and his crew returned with materials, the tree had been cleared from her shop.

The wood floor had some new scratches, but she chalked them up to character and called it a day.

Once the tree was gone, Haley's dad and brother moved outside with the chainsaw and took down the rest of the tree so it wouldn't pose further problems.

Ramona from Schooners brought pizza and water for the volunteers. After supper, it was just Sophie, Aiden, and the roofing crew. While they finished up outside, Aiden and Sophie cut and placed drywall for the ceiling.

Brandon, true to his word, had the roof reframed and sheeted by nightfall. It was after ten by the time they left, promising to finish early the next morning. They'd tarped the roof in case of rain.

When the door closed behind them, Sophie let Pippa out of the office and took a few minutes to comfort her. "My poor sweetheart. All those mean old saws and unfamiliar people. It's okay now. It's quiet and it's just us three."

She let Pippa down, and the dog went about sniffing every inch of the place. Sophie surveyed the space with renewed wonder. She could hardly believe what had been done in one day. Not only had her neighbors helped with this disaster, but she'd gotten numerous offers for further help once the bookcases were installed. She was overwhelmed by the generosity of this town.

Aiden drove a nail into the last piece of drywall, then descended the ladder, surveying his work. "That does it for the drywall. Now I just need to do the mudding. It can dry overnight, and I'll finish in the morning. Dave and Jim are coming to help paint midmorning. Leonard and his crew can install the shelving in the other rooms and finish this room last. What do you think?"

"I didn't think it was possible but . . . I think we're going to make it." Sophie took in the room that had, only hours ago, housed a tree. Someone had even swept the floor and put a tarp down to protect it.

Aiden gave her a hopeful smile. "I think maybe we are."

"I can't believe everything that's happened today." As if suddenly realizing how many hours she'd been on her feet, gravity pulled at her shoulders, and her ankle began throbbing. She felt every hour of hard labor she'd put in.

When she swayed Aiden's gaze sharpened on her. "Sit." He grabbed the chair they'd pushed into the corner and placed it behind her. "You've been on your feet for hours. Your ankle's probably swollen up like a watermelon."

"You might be right." She did as he said, and when he dragged over an empty five-gallon bucket, she gladly propped her foot on it.

He pulled over another bucket and took a load off. "I should take you home and come back to finish. You can't be up on the ladder anyway."

She scowled. "I'm not going home while you work on *my* shop. I can at least fetch you tools so you don't have to come down off the ladder."

"I admit it would be nice to have the company. Can you believe we've been at it for . . . fifteen hours? And we had at least that many people here today." He propped his elbows on his knees. "As my dad always said, 'many hands make light work.'"

"He wasn't kidding. A few of the women are even coming on Monday to help me shelve books. Isn't that nice of them?"

He gazed at her thoughtfully. "I think you've found yourself a really nice community."

Sophie let her gaze drift around the room, now quiet and still after the hubbub of bustling people and buzzing saws. "I'm starting to see why my mom loved it here. Seeing the way everyone pulled together today was . . . inspiring. Humbling."

"You need people like that in your life, Sophie. I've been a little worried about you, uprooting yourself, living away from your family and all."

Sophie eyed him with a raised eyebrow. "You did the same thing when you moved to Charleston."

"And it wasn't easy, starting over like that. But I had Ross at least. You're all alone here. But I'm not worried anymore." His face softened. "The town's already in your corner, and the more they get to know you, the more they'll see how special you are."

Sophie warmed at his words, falling headlong into his soulful gaze. She wanted to thank him for his kindness, but the words caught in her throat.

"You've always been such an encouragement to me, Soph. Always saw the best in me. It's time someone did the same for you."

He touched her jaw as if he were handling fragile porcelain. "I'm amazed by you. I always have been. You're surprised at how your neighbors came through for you today, but that's exactly what you do for everyone else. You dropped your entire life to take care of your mom and siblings. You gave up a scholarship to a prestigious university—" When she started to speak, he placed his finger over her lips. "I know you were happy to do it, but that doesn't negate the sacrifice.

"You're selfless and caring, and you inspire me to be a better person. Consider how you're going after your dream with everything you've got. Literally, every penny you've got." He pinned her with an unswerving look. "Your mom would be so proud of you, Soph. I know I am."

No one other than her mom had ever said such things to her. She wasn't even sure how to respond.

His finger slid slowly from her lips, making them tingle with want. His eyes pierced hers. That familiar tension crackled between them. And then he was leaning forward.

He kissed her tenderly, his lips brushing hers with a softness and reverence that melted her heart. He pulled away, his eyes searching hers. He must've found what he was looking for because he drew her closer and kissed her again. This time his lips began a soft exploration that narrowed the world, once again, to just the two of them. There was no store, no deadline, just Aiden and his wonderful kisses.

She touched his jaw, the bristles a pleasant scrape against the palm of her hand. She never wanted it to end. Wanted to stay in his arms forever because his embrace felt like home.

Home.

Home for him was in Charleston. He'd be leaving on Wednesday, and she'd be staying here, starting her new life. They'd once again lead separate lives. She didn't want it to be so, but there it was. When he left last time he'd asked her to drop her plans and follow. Would he ask the same of her this time? And was she just as bad, hoping he'd leave the business he'd worked so hard to build and move to Piper's Cove for her?

He must've felt the tension coursing through her because he pulled away again, searching her face.

⁂

Aiden's pulse was still pounding out a wild tattoo as his breath mingled with Sophie's. He hadn't wanted to stop kissing her. The taste of her was still on his lips, an addictive drug that made him desperate for more.

But he'd felt a shift in her, a withdrawal. And he understood her reservation. As much as he wanted to make out with her the rest of the night, they needed to have a conversation. One that had been a long time coming.

Sometime between yesterday and today something had shifted inside Aiden. It started last night when he passed her room and looked in at her, sleeping so peacefully. And it continued all day as he watched her organizing the crew of volunteers who'd shown up on her doorstep. All evening he could hardly take his eyes off this amazing woman.

He knew it now with every beat of his heart: He didn't want them to go their separate ways. He didn't want to give up something that, he was only beginning to understand, was a once-in-a-lifetime kind of thing.

"What are we doing, Aiden?" she asked softly, a pained look on her face.

"What we should've done days ago." He cradled her face, drew a deep breath, and dug deep for the courage to put words to his feelings. "I still care for you, Sophie. I'd like to see where this could go."

She shook her head regretfully. "This is a mistake. We live *five hours* apart."

"I know there are obstacles, and I don't know how we'll overcome them. I only know we have to try." His gut clenched at the question he had to ask. "Do you still have feelings for me, Sophie?"

"Of course I do. But my business is here and yours is in Charleston."

"Can't we try the long-distance thing?" His eyes pierced hers, needing her to see how fervently he wanted this. "What we have is . . . It's too special to give up on. Can't you see that?"

The pause that followed tightened his chest and made his throat ache. It wasn't possible the feelings were one-sided. Not after that kiss. But she still had reservations. Were they enough to make her call it quits before they'd even begun?

Her lashes swept down. "I'm afraid, Aiden."

If she only knew. He hadn't forgotten that constant low hum of fear he'd experienced when he'd been in love with her the first time. It was still there, running in the background like an obnoxious computer program.

A rueful chuckle slipped out of him. "You don't think I'm afraid too? But you know what I decided? I'm even more afraid of losing this—of losing *you*."

Slowly, the worry fled from her eyes, and her lips turned up at the corners.

He couldn't stop his own from doing the same. Couldn't stop the floating sensation as the weight lifted from his body. He settled his forehead against hers. "Does that little smile mean I can kiss you again?"

She didn't answer. Didn't wait for him. She just lifted her face and pressed her soft lips to his.

chapter

thirty-one

They didn't get home until after midnight. So many things were spinning through Sophie's head—the shop and her new relationship with Aiden—that she feared she'd lay in bed fretting half the night. But she fell asleep as soon as her head hit the pillow.

She didn't wake up until her alarm chimed at six o'clock. It was still dark outside, the sun only beginning to creep over the horizon. She thought of last night as she headed toward the shower. A smile curved her lips as she remembered the sweet way Aiden had held her hand. The tender way he looked at her. She still saw the boy he used to be in those looks, but she also saw the man he'd become. Just thinking of all he'd done for her this week made her eager to see him this morning.

As she rushed through her shower, worry bubbled up inside. Had his declaration last night just been an impulse? She hoped not. She was at peace with the decision to see where their relationship led. And after the internal fight she'd been putting up since seeing him at the Dock House, this surprised her.

The smell of brewing coffee quickened her steps. She opened the sliding door to let Pippa out. The dog was good about staying nearby, mainly because she was afraid of the sea oats that lined the yard.

"Good morning." Aiden was seated at the kitchen bar, reading the newspaper and sipping from what had become his favorite mug.

"Morning."

By the time Sophie slid the screen door closed, Aiden was there, hands on her waist, drawing her close. He set a soft kiss on her lips, and all Sophie's anxiety drained away. The passion in his eyes made her pulse flutter.

"Sleep well?" he asked.

She slid her hands up his arms, enjoying the solid feel of his muscles. "Like a baby. I didn't wake up until my alarm went off."

"Coffee's ready. Want some toast?"

"Sure. Thank you." Pippa was back at the door, never one to linger when breakfast waited.

While she fetched Pippa's food and a bowl of fresh water, Aiden made her toast and poured her a mug of coffee, fixing it the way she liked it. They settled at the kitchen island, as had become their habit.

"Brandon's crew will be there at seven," she said after she'd taken her first delicious sip of java. "And Leonard will arrive with the bookcases at eight. Get ready for a crazy day."

While she ate her toast Aiden went over his plans to finish the drywall and painting. It was much the same as it had been every morning this week, except Aiden's hand had settled on Sophie's leg, and he kept casting delicious little glances her way.

As she finished breakfast a text came in. Seth wanted to know if she was awake yet. Seconds after she replied her phone buzzed with an incoming call.

"It's Seth." She rose to take her plate to the sink as she answered the phone.

"Hey, Sis. You're up and at 'em early."

"It'll be a long day. The bookcases are going in. You won't believe the day I had yesterday." She filled him in on the tree crashing through the roof and all the efforts to restore order.

"Wow, good thing you had all that help."

"You're not kidding. I couldn't have done it otherwise. How's your job going?"

"So far so good. They actually want me to fly to Chicago for some training. It's kind of last minute—this Tuesday through Thursday."

Sophie's heart sank. "My grand opening is Tuesday."

"Oh, shoot. Is that this week? I'm sorry, Soph, but they asked me last minute, and I didn't feel I could turn them down, new job and all. I want to prove I'm a team player, and this training only comes around once a year."

Sophie beat back the disappointment as she leaned against the sink. "Sure, I understand."

"Well, would you mind booking the flights for me? You always find the best deals."

"Isn't the company paying for it?"

"Well, yeah, but I want to show them I'm frugal with their money. And I wouldn't have the first idea how to book a flight online."

She rolled her eyes. Only because he'd never had to. She glanced at the kitchen clock. It wouldn't take her long. "Sure, I can do it."

She took down the dates and times and his credit card information, then told him she'd forward the itinerary to him when she was finished.

"What was that all about?" Aiden asked after she'd pocketed her phone.

"Seth's company is sending him to Chicago for training next week."

"He's going to miss your grand opening?"

"Unfortunately, yes. The trip came up last minute, and his boss expects him to go."

Aiden took a sip of coffee, his silence speaking louder than words.

Sophie turned to rinse off her plate.

"Why was he giving you his credit card information?"

"I told him I'd book his flight for him—I'm kind of the family travel agent." She meant it as a joke, but it fell flat. "The company he works for is a new start-up. They don't have someone on staff to handle that kind of thing."

"And when are you going to find time to do that? You have a busy day ahead."

Sophie stuck her plate in the dishwasher and glanced at the

clock again. "I can do it right now if you don't mind waiting a bit."

He opened his mouth to say something, then seemed to change his mind. "I'll take Pippa for a walk. She's been cooped up a lot lately, and I need to call Ross about some work-related stuff."

After Aiden slipped out the back door with Pippa, Sophie went to work on her laptop. It didn't take her long to find the best deal, and within twenty minutes she had Seth's flights booked.

She'd just forwarded the itinerary to her brother when Aiden returned. They loaded Pippa in the car and headed to the shop. She'd forgotten to charge her phone last night so she plugged it in.

Aiden was quiet. He'd wanted to have the sanding finished before Leonard arrived with the bookcases, but that wasn't going to happen now. They'd have to hang plastic sheeting to keep the dust off the new shelves. Leonard's crew probably wouldn't be happy about having to work around them, but it couldn't be helped.

Tension hovered between them in the car, and it stemmed from Seth's phone call. Sure, she babied her siblings sometimes. But growing up with an emotionally absent father and chronically ill mother, they'd had to count on her. Aiden couldn't understand that when he'd had a present father and no siblings.

"Is everything okay back home, with the business?" she asked.

"Yeah, Ross just had a couple questions about the schedule. I usually handle that kind of thing."

"Has he been overwhelmed with you gone all week?"

"A little, I think, though he'd never admit it. I'll definitely have to leave Wednesday morning. Our other skydiver's on vacation next week, and we have a jump scheduled that afternoon."

Her phone buzzed, and she glanced down to the console where it was charging. A notification on the screen showed a text from Joshua.

Good morning. Praying all goes well today with the bookcases.
Have a great day!

She glanced at Aiden, who was looking at her phone. His gaze swung back to the road, face unreadable.

She hadn't given Joshua a single thought since she and Aiden had had their heart-to-heart last night. As far as the other man knew, they still had a date Friday.

"I haven't had a chance to talk to him yet," Sophie said into the silence. "I'll call him today."

Aiden shot her a thin smile as he put on his blinker but didn't say anything. The level of tension had gone up another notch. This morning was not going the way she had hoped. First Seth and now Joshua.

Of course, Aiden could hardly blame her for not contacting the other man yet. It had only been a matter of hours since they'd decided to give their relationship a try—and she'd spent almost all of them sleeping. But at the same time, it couldn't feel good to see a friendly text from another man on her phone. A man who was supposed to take her out soon.

She reached for Aiden's hand and offered him a tentative smile. His big hand engulfed hers, giving a reassuring squeeze, and his own smile warmed a few degrees.

Relax. She was worrying for nothing. They were both on edge because of everything they had on their plates at the moment. He was here helping her through a crisis and probably stressed about his business back home.

Once they arrived at the shop Aiden went to work on the drywall while Sophie hung plastic to keep the dust down. She'd already let Leonard know what they'd be working around today. Aiden hoped to have the ceiling painted by midafternoon, which would allow the bookcases to be installed in the main room.

Once the shelving crew arrived, chaos broke loose. The high-pitched whine of cordless screwdrivers joined the scratching sound of Aiden's sanding and the chatter of the crew.

In between answering questions Sophie worked in the office, pricing nonbook merchandise: necklaces and earrings made by area artisans, locally made candles, magnets, bookmarks, and pens. She stocked a wooden rack, to be placed near the register, with luxury stationery, journals, and planners. She'd put a lot of thought into her selections, and she was proud of the unique appeal and diversity of her merchandise.

Dave and Anna were kind enough to deliver lunch from the deli, which kept the crew going. Aiden worked right through the meal. Having finished with the sanding, he was already applying a coat of primer.

While the crew ate, Sophie slipped outside to call Joshua. She got to the point pretty quickly, admitting that her relationship with her old friend had recently flared up. Joshua was obviously disappointed, but he handled the news gracefully. He even told her he'd welcome a call from her if things didn't work with Aiden. Sophie hoped that wouldn't happen.

She went back inside, relieved to have the call over with, and wolfed down a sandwich. While she ate she replied to Jenna's text—the newlyweds were about to board their last flight home. Next Sophie went to work on the window display, which showed off Nathaniel Quinn's new release and advertised the party.

She hadn't gotten far when Haley stopped by, offering her help. Sophie was happy to have a second opinion from someone with artistic flair. The other woman had good ideas for the seaside display, which Sophie incorporated.

"When things settle a little for you," Haley said as they put the finishing touches on the display, "we should grab a bite to eat or something."

Sophie smiled, feeling as though she'd found a new friend. "I'd like that. I've been dying to try out some of the restaurants around here. You know, someplace I can actually go to, sit down at, and be waited on."

"You've had a crazy week. But things will slow down a bit once you're past the opening."

"I hope they won't slow down too much." But Sophie had to admit regular hours and real meals—not to mention time to read—would be a welcome change.

"So . . ." Haley nodded toward Aiden, who was up on a ladder rolling on paint. "You and your handsome friend . . . Am I imagining things, or has something changed between the two of you?"

Sophie couldn't help the private little smile that curved her lips. "Your spidey senses are spot-on. As of last night we're officially dating. Which might be a little tricky, being as how we live five hours apart and he's going home Wednesday morning."

"Well, you never know. Maybe he'll move here eventually."

Sophie didn't see him leaving the business he and Ross had worked so hard to establish. But maybe his recent award would open another door—one that would bring him closer to Piper's Cove.

"I guess we'll have to wait and see," Sophie said.

chapter

thirty-two

It was after eight o'clock when the last of Leonard's crew left. Aiden put down the dust rag and went to find Sophie. She was carrying a box of books into the nonfiction room.

"Whoa, whoa, whoa." He took the box from her and set it down. "You don't need to be putting that weight on your ankle. I'll get the boxes. Anyway, I thought we were doing this tomorrow."

She ran her hand along one of the shelves lining the wall. "It's only eight. I thought we could at least get the books to the right rooms. It's finally starting to resemble a bookshop, isn't it?"

He came up behind her, putting his arms around her and pulling her close. "It looks great. Let's go out to eat and celebrate. You need to prop that ankle, and I'd like to spend some quality time with you."

The hours were ticking away quickly. Before he knew it, he'd be boarding a plane for home.

She leaned back against his chest, tilting her head to the side. "But we still have a lot to do."

"We'll have plenty of help tomorrow." The angle of her head gave him the perfect opportunity to kiss her long, graceful neck. He inhaled her familiar scent as he ran his nose up to her jaw where he pressed another kiss.

"You're making some excellent points." She sounded a little breathless as she turned in his arms.

"I can be very persuasive." He gave her a soft, lingering kiss. He'd been wanting to get his arms around her all day, and he'd been very patient. But it was time for a little gratification.

She didn't seem to mind. Her arms roped around his neck as she let loose a little mewling sound that urged him to take the kiss a little deeper. He could hardly believe she was his again. In some ways it seemed like nothing had changed since seven years ago. In other ways . . . both of them had changed so much.

Back in the day he'd rushed things physically between them. And as tempted as he was to do so now, he cared too much about their future. With that in mind he slowed things down, giving her a series of soft kisses, ending with one on the tip of her nose.

Even though the exchange hadn't lasted more than half a minute, his heart thudded and his breaths were ragged. What she did to him. And not just physically either. She had a way of soothing him. She was a nurturer, and she filled something inside him, reached a place that no other woman had.

I love her. His pulse sped at the realization. It was true. He didn't need more quality time to figure that out.

But instead of reveling at the insight, fear seeped into his bloodstream. What if it didn't work out? What if she didn't feel the same way? Sophie had always been too good for him; he knew that. What if she figured that out? What if she broke things off? His palms grew sweaty like they did when he leaped from the door of an aircraft.

He set his forehead against hers and forced himself to move on from the disturbing thoughts. "Hungry?"

"Starving."

"Let's try that seafood restaurant down on the wharf that you mentioned. I could go for some crab cakes."

He was just tired, he thought as they locked up the building. Sophie had loved him once before. Surely she could love him again.

※

The Captain's Hook was every bit as wonderful as Sophie had heard. She splurged on the seafood platter since they were celebrating the near completion of her store.

She and Aiden talked about everything that had happened today, some of it frustrating, some of it humorous. He complimented her on the window display, and she told him about Haley's offer to hang out sometime.

When she asked about Extreme Adventures she could tell he was worried about how Ross was faring alone. She felt bad that she'd kept him so long. But when he gave her that warm, inviting look, she couldn't seem to regret it. This extended stay had given them a second chance.

"Were you able to call Joshua today?" he asked during a lull in the conversation.

"I did, and he took it well." She didn't mention that he'd given her an open invitation. "He was kind and gracious."

Aiden wore an enigmatic expression. "That's good."

"What about Tiffany? Have you heard from her since she left?"

"Not a word. But I didn't expect to with the way we left things."

"You still have to work together . . ."

"I'm sure we'll fall back into a professional relationship soon enough."

There was no point in worrying about Tiffany. Sophie had better get used to trusting Aiden if they were going to make a long-distance relationship work.

Her phone buzzed with an incoming call—her grandmother. "I missed Granny's call earlier."

"Go ahead and take it."

"Hi, Granny. What are you up to?"

"The question is, what are you up to? You canceled your date with that nice Joshua Stevens?"

"Now, Granny, I'm a grown-up. You'll have to let me make these decisions for myself."

"I know what you're up to—that boy got his hooks into you again, just like I told you he would. He's going to drop you like a hot brick, and who's going to be there to pick up the pieces this time?"

She rolled her eyes at Aiden while her grandmother lectured

her on what a great catch she was letting off the hook. Sophie bore with her for what seemed like a long time but was probably only a few minutes.

"Listen, Granny," she said when the woman paused to take a breath. "I'm kind of in the middle of something, so I'm going to let you go. I'll call you tomorrow."

"He's there right now, isn't he? Put him on the phone."

"What? No, I'm not going to—"

"Put him on the phone!"

Apparently she'd said this loudly enough for Aiden to hear. He reached for the phone.

Sophie gave him an apologetic look as she handed it over.

"Hi, Granny May. How are you?"

Sophie wished she could hear what her grandmother was saying. All she knew what that the woman wasn't giving Aiden a chance to say much.

He gave Sophie a reassuring smile. "Yes, ma'am."

Her grandmother must've launched into another lecture because he was quiet for a while. Sophie hoped the woman wasn't being mean. She could be blunt to the point of rudeness. But once her grandma got to know Aiden again, she'd forgive him. She'd already softened a little after finding out Aiden hadn't known about her father leaving her. At least Sophie thought she had. The way she was responding now made her wonder.

"Yes, ma'am," Aiden said again.

The server came and refilled their water, then gathered their empty plates. "I'll be right back with the bill."

Sophie watched Aiden's face for some sign of what her

grandmother was saying, but his face was a blank slate. He wasn't smiling anymore, however. Or making eye contact. She didn't feel good about this and wished she hadn't handed him the phone at all.

"I will," he finally said into the phone. "All right. Here she is."

Sophie took the phone. "I hope you were nice to him."

"I was truthful."

Sophie winced, knowing well what that could mean. She watched Aiden, but the server had brought the bill, and he was reaching for his wallet.

"I'll let you get on with your evening," Granny said. "Jenna's driving me over for your grand opening, so I'll see you Tuesday."

Sophie was eager to talk to Aiden so she wrapped up the conversation and disconnected the call. "What did she say to you? Was she mean?"

He gave Sophie a mirthless smile. "She was fine. Just needed to have her say."

Sophie wished he'd be a little more forthcoming. "I'm sorry if she was rude. You know Granny May. She's never been one to hold back. But she'll get past it eventually."

He squeezed her hand, his smile warming. "It's fine. She loves you and wants the best for you. I can't fault her for that."

Maybe so, but she was also a busybody and lacked boundaries, and Sophie could tell from the look in Aiden's eyes that she'd said hurtful things. And sometimes those things had a way of sticking with you.

chapter

thirty-three

Monday didn't start the way Sophie would've liked.
Pippa had had an accident during the night, and the spot didn't
come up with carpet cleaner. She'd have to buy a different product later. She couldn't leave a stain behind after the Fosters had
been kind enough to let her stay.

The problems didn't go away once they reached the shop.
The ceiling clearly needed another coat. They'd have to work
around the bookshelves and move tables. Somehow the dust had
settled overnight, leaving a fine grit on the shelves they'd just
cleaned the night before.

Sophie groaned. Her help would be here in ten minutes, and
she wanted to make good use of the extra hands.

"Where did all this come from?" she mused.

Aiden grabbed a dust rag and threw her the other. "We'll
take care of it."

They went to work, but there were so many shelves they were still wiping them down when Haley arrived. Sophie helped her get settled in the religious section, instructing her on which books got the end caps. She'd returned to the main room when Anna entered, bearing a box of doughnuts.

"Bless you." Sophie grabbed one even though she didn't have time to eat. It would be a nice treat for the volunteers.

Some of her staff joined them a little later and got to work in the nonfiction room. Aiden was still perched on a ladder over the tarp-covered bookcases in the main room. Brandon's crew showed up and began working on the roof. They tromped overhead as they laid new shingles.

After lunch the mayor stopped in to check their progress. Her face looked stricken as she surveyed the sight. The shelves in the main room were still bare, and Aiden was painting.

"It'll be fine," Sophie said. "We're right on schedule. Books are going onto shelves as we speak."

"My goodness, girl, you're cutting it close."

"No worries. We'll have it all in place by the end of the day."

Alanda's gaze swept over the construction zone. "If you say so."

"I promise. And everything's set for the party. The decorations will go up tonight, and tomorrow Ramona will have the hors d'oeuvres set up thirty minutes before the signing begins. Everything's taken care of."

"Where will Nathaniel do his signing?"

"Right here." Sophie gestured around the room. "I just need to set up the podium, book table, and chairs."

"The window display looks nice. And I like your grand-opening sign out front. Really draws attention."

"That's the hope."

"I have to hand it to you, Sophie. When I heard about that tree crashing through your roof on Friday, I thought we were sunk." Alanda had stopped in that day in time to see all the people who'd shown up to lend a hand.

"I would've been in trouble if it hadn't been for so many helpful people."

The mayor gave a satisfied smile. "I told you you'd love living in Piper's Cove. When there's a need, people 'round here step up to the plate. Makes my job a little easier."

"You should be very proud of your town."

The woman gave her a pointed look. "*Our* town."

Alanda had half an hour to spare so she carried boxes of books to the correct rooms, then helped Sophie move the podium and large wooden table into the main room. When the mayor left, Sophie set up chairs, then unboxed Nathaniel's new release, arranging the books just so on the book-signing table.

At that point Haley had to go to work, and shortly after that Anna had to pick up her granddaughter. The woman returned half an hour later with the baby carrier in tow. But little Lilly was fussy, hardly allowing Anna to work. The crying put everyone on edge, and after an hour Sophie wished Anna would just take the baby and go.

It was about that time that Aiden dropped his phone from atop the ladder. It hit the edge of a shelf and clattered to the floor.

With nerves already strung out from the baby's screaming, she was surprised when he only pressed his lips together.

Sophie picked up the phone, wincing at the cracked black screen. "Oh no."

"Great." Aiden took it and pressed the power button. "It's not coming on."

"Why don't you take it down to the phone store?"

"Later." He pocketed the phone. "I'm almost finished here." The baby wailed on.

He gave Sophie a pained look, and she could hardly blame him. The noise was on her last nerve too.

She went into the back room where Anna was bouncing the unhappy baby. "Can I take her outside for some fresh air?"

"Sure, honey. She's cutting a tooth. But she loves the ducks. Don't you, sweet thing? Go see the duckies with Sophie now. Grammy'll be right here."

But Lilly didn't seem to care about the duckies today. When that failed to distract her, Sophie walked her up and down the boardwalk, trying to interest her in everything from airplanes to waving flags to a caterpillar crawling on one of the pilings. While the baby wailed pitifully Sophie fretted about everything she should be doing back at the shop.

They were down to just Anna, two of her staff, plus Aiden, and Sophie still had so many books to shelve. At least Aiden was almost finished with the ceiling.

Giving up, Sophie sat on a bench and checked her phone, letting the baby cry. It seemed as if everyone Sophie knew had tried to reach her today. The insurance adjuster needed pictures of the damage. Ramona had questions about the hors d'oeuvres. The publicist from Rosewood Press touched base with last-minute details. Jenna inquired about the jury duty notice she'd received in the mail, and for some reason Seth needed her to resend his flight itinerary. Granny texted her—something about Joshua. But the woman had apparently used voice-to-text, and it was impossible to make sense of her garbled message.

With one hand Sophie responded to everyone, then walked Lilly back to the store. When Anna finally decided to take the baby home, they all breathed a sigh of relief. Sophie joined her staff, shelving books and answering questions as they arose.

Ellie, her librarian-turned-bookstore-helper, was a little bossy with Amber, the well-read college student Sophie had hired. The younger woman was patient with Ellie, but Sophie could tell it was wearing on her nerves.

To separate them, Sophie asked Amber to help her with the fiction section. But she would have to talk to Ellie soon. The woman seemed to regard Amber as one of her former high school students instead of as a fellow employee. Sophie would hate to lose Ellie, as the woman was a big help in curating the books, but Sophie couldn't let her chase away other employees either.

The afternoon flew by, and soon the roofers finished. She thanked the men and gave Brandon a big hug. "Thank you so much for your help. I'll let you know when the insurance check arrives."

"Sounds good. I'll see you tomorrow for the grand opening."

It was amazing how quickly the shelving went once the four

of them were focused on the task. They were making such great progress, they worked straight through supper. They did the local shelves last, a section Sophie was particularly proud of. She and Ellie had put a lot of thought into books that might appeal to tourists and locals.

Sophie took the empty boxes to the Dumpster and returned. As she passed the different rooms, she surveyed the shop as though for the first time. The wood bookcases gleamed under the lights, burgeoning with beautiful books. The blue walls were a soothing backdrop, and the wooden floors, creaking here and there, gave the place a homey feel.

She placed her palm over her thumping heart, a feeling of contentment overwhelming her. *What do you think, Mama? Is this what you had in mind?*

She didn't need an audible answer. Her mother would've loved the spacious children's area, the huge selection of classic literature, and the comfy chairs where readers could curl up and sample a book. It was just the way they'd planned.

Tears stung her eyes as it sank in: Despite the obstacles, and thanks to Aiden and all her neighbors, her bookshop—her new home—finally had become a reality. She entered the main room where the others were making quick work of the local section and drew in a lungful of her favorite smell—new books.

Aiden rose with another empty box, his eyes locking on hers, giving her a look that aligned with her thoughts. "What do you think?"

"I can't believe we're almost finished. We made it."

"Here you go, Sophie." Ellie handed her a book on the

history of Fort Macon. "This is the last one—you should do the honors."

Sophie took the book and placed it in the correct spot on the local history shelf. The others applauded, almost as thrilled as Sophie to have all the books shelved at last.

"That was a lot of books!" Amber said. "But I'm well trained in our inventory now."

"The store looks amazing." Ellie's gaze flittered around the space, her eyes filled with the kind of wonder only a book lover could appreciate. "I'm so thrilled we finally have a bookstore in Piper's Cove. I've wanted this a long time."

"I can't thank you enough for your help." Sophie checked her watch. "And we actually got done early. I thought I'd be here until midnight!"

Aiden chuckled. "Me too."

"I have a few things to finish up." Sophie addressed the women. "But after that, why don't you let me take you to supper? It's the least I can do after all your help."

"That's so sweet," Ellie said, "but I should get home to my husband. Once the store's open, I'll be working a lot of hours, and he's used to me being around all the time. Heaven forbid he should have to cook his own supper!"

"I told a friend I'd come over after I was done," Amber said. "But thanks for the offer."

The women cleared out pretty quickly after confirming they'd be here by nine the next morning to go over last-minute details.

And then it was just Sophie and Aiden.

She touched up a few things in the window display and set up the cardboard cutout the publisher had sent. She arranged the end caps closest to the signing area with a selection of Nathaniel's backlist.

When she stepped away to survey her work, Aiden came up behind her and pulled her close. "Is everything the way you want it? Anything else you need done?"

She leaned back against him, her gaze sweeping the space. "I can't believe I'm saying this at seven o'clock on the eve of the opening, but . . . everything's perfect."

He chuckled when her stomach gave a loud growl. "Not quite everything."

"I'll admit I'm starving. All I had today was that sandwich."

He pressed a kiss to that spot on her neck that always made her shiver. "Know what I'd like to do?"

Another shiver ran through her at the question. "Hmmm?"

"I'd like to grab a couple steaks from the store and grill out for you."

She laughed. "That wasn't quite what I was expecting you to say."

"That's high on my list too," he whispered into her ear as he nuzzled it. "But my girl's hungry, and I can't believe I've been here for over a week and haven't yet made her my famous filet mignon dinner."

"Famous, huh?" She smiled as he kissed the ticklish spot near her ear and tried not to think about all his satisfied customers.

"Fresh asparagus, grilled with my own special blend of seasonings, and steaks brushed with a butter and garlic sauce.

There's one other ingredient . . ." He lowered his voice. "But it's a secret."

"You can tell me. I won't tell anyone."

"I'll think about it." He turned her in his arms and gave her a lingering kiss.

By the time he let her go, her knees had gone weak.

"I'm so proud of you, Jelly Bean. You've worked really hard to make this store happen."

The beaming gleam in his eyes warmed her through. "I couldn't have done it without you, Aiden."

He gave her one more kiss. "I was kind of glad when Ellie and Amber bailed on supper. I wanted to have a nice evening together, just the two of us."

Tomorrow would be madness, and the party didn't end until nine o'clock, after which there'd still be cleanup. This would be their chance to spend time together.

"That's the best idea I've heard all day," she said.

chapter

thirty-four

Sophie stepped onto the cottage deck, inhaling the delicious aroma of grilled steaks. "Yum, those smell good."

"Shouldn't be much longer. This grill is top-of-the-line. Makes me want an upgrade."

"I wish we'd been able to put it to better use. Are you sure there's nothing I can do?"

He gave her that charming half smile. "You can sit down and prop up your foot. You've been on your feet way too much this week."

She'd definitely felt it. Even now it was aching. "Aye, aye, Cap'n."

She sank onto the Adirondack chair, propping her foot on the stool, and leaned back. A heavy bank of clouds hung low on the horizon, and even though the sun hadn't quite set, it was as dark as twilight.

The repetitious sound of the surf was soothing, but her mind whirled. She was excited about tomorrow. But the opening also signaled Aiden's last day in Piper's Cove. It was hard to prevent that thought from crowding out the optimism surrounding her opening. What would a long-distance relationship with him look like?

Aiden searched the darkening sky. "It's looking like rain."

"Smelling like it too."

Her phone buzzed with an incoming call, and Sophie checked the screen. "I hope Jenna isn't calling to say she can't come tomorrow."

"She knows what this means to you." But the tone of his voice conveyed his concern.

"Hi, Jenna, what's up?"

"Hey, Sis. Still at the shop?"

"We actually finished a few hours early if you can believe it."

"Oh, good. I was hoping you'd say that. I have a favor to ask you."

Sophie pushed back the feeling of disappointment sweeping through her. "What's up?"

"Well, you know Grant's twenty-fifth birthday is in two weeks. I've been looking for a Jet Ski for him, and I wasn't having any luck finding one in my price range. But the exact model he admired on our honeymoon popped up on Craigslist today, and it's in my budget."

"That's great. So what's the problem?"

"The seller's in New Bern, and I thought that would be

ideal, right? Since it's only forty-five minutes from Piper's Cove, and I'm coming there tomorrow anyway. I can borrow Dad's truck and tow it back—the Jet Ski comes with the trailer and everything."

"Okay . . ."

"But I've been talking to the seller today, and he has a serious buyer coming in the morning. I could PayPal him the money now, but I'm afraid to pay him without making sure it's legitimate. Could you go check it out? If everything goes well, you could tow it back to the beach house."

Sophie's stomach shrank. She could do it; she'd gotten her Tahoe back from the shop yesterday.

"I know it's a lot to ask when your grand opening is tomorrow, but you said the shop was all ready . . ."

"Right."

Aiden gave her a searching look as he closed the grill lid.

"I'm afraid if I wait," Jenna continued, "it'll sell in the morning, and this is the perfect gift for Grant. He gave me the ideal honeymoon, and I want to give him something special for his birthday."

Aiden was still studying Sophie, but she turned her gaze to the undulating ocean. The first drop of rain hit her cheek.

"Sophie? Can you do it? Please, I wouldn't ask if it wasn't important."

Sophie sighed. It wasn't as if Jenna was being selfish. It was a gift for her new husband, after all.

Hopefully Aiden wouldn't mind the change in plans. They could enjoy his steak dinner first. And they could still spend time

253

together if he rode to New Bern with her. In fact, he knew a lot more about Jet Skis than she did.

"Um, sure," Sophie said finally. "I guess I can do that."

"Oh, thank you, thank you, thank you! You're the best sister ever. Grant's going to love it so much."

"I'll head up there after supper. I'll call you once I've checked it out."

"Oh . . ." There was a wince in Jenna's tone. "I forgot to mention, the seller said you'd need to be there by nine o'clock."

"*Nine?*" Sophie glanced at her watch. She'd have to leave in the next few minutes.

"I'm sorry, I know it's really last minute, but he has to leave for work."

Judging by Aiden's irritated expression he'd figured out enough of what was going on.

Guilt pinched hard as the savory smell of his steaks rose to her nose. And yet, she'd already told Jenna she'd do it. She gave Aiden an apologetic look as she spoke to Jenna again. "All right, fine, I'll do it. I'll call you later."

"Thank you, Sophie! You're a lifesaver."

But as she hung up the phone she couldn't help feeling she was saving her sister at Aiden's expense.

⁂

It didn't take a genius to figure out what was going on: Jenna had asked another favor, and Sophie was rushing to her rescue.

A drop of rain hit Aiden's forearm as Sophie disconnected the call. Aiden set down the tongs.

She gave him a chagrined look, and he forced himself to wait for her explanation.

"I'm afraid I need to run over to New Bern tonight." She went on to explain that Jenna wanted to buy Grant a Jet Ski but was afraid to send money, sight unseen.

He could understand that, really he could. If it wasn't for the fact that Jenna—and Seth—always seemed to need something from Sophie. They took advantage of her. Couldn't she see that?

So much for their evening together. He bit his tongue, just barely. He didn't want their last evening ruined, and he didn't want to upset her the day before her grand opening.

"The steaks are almost ready," Aiden said. "I guess we can eat supper, then head over that way."

Sophie grimaced. "Um, I hate to say this, but . . . I have to be there by nine. This guy has to leave for work, and another buyer's coming in the morning."

Aiden checked his watch, his body tensing. "We'd be cutting it close even if we left right now."

"I know and I feel really bad about your meal. Could we refrigerate it and eat it when we get back?"

Sure they could. And by the time they reheated the steaks they'd be overdone and dried out. Not to mention the mood of the evening had definitely gone to pot. He wasn't feeling so amorous anymore. Instead he was remembering all the dates she'd canceled years ago because of her family obligations. And now it was happening again. It didn't feel very good taking second place all the time.

He opened the grill's lid and plated the steaks. "Fine."

"You don't have to go. You can stay here and relax, eat your steak. You've worked hard this week."

"You haven't even driven since your sprain."

"Only because I haven't had to. It'll be fine."

His eyes blazed with disbelief. "I'm not letting you go off alone to meet some stranger from Craigslist, Sophie."

She rose, a sheepish look on her face as she checked her watch.

He plated the food, took it inside, and placed it in the refrigerator, trying to quell the sense of injustice. "Jenna has the money for a Jet Ski but not the money to loan your dad?"

"I had no idea she had that kind of cash, and I'm sure Dad didn't either. He didn't even ask her for a loan."

"Because he knew he could count on you to say yes—they all know that."

She bristled. "So I'm a giving person—is that such a bad thing?"

"And I'm selfish for wanting one quiet evening with you, is that it?"

They made their way silently to Sophie's vehicle. Aiden beat her to the driver's side and she didn't argue. As he started the car she programmed the address into her phone.

Aiden flipped on the windshield wipers as he pulled from the drive. Tension had climbed into the car with them and seemed to multiply by the minute. This issue would be a problem going forward if they didn't address it.

He turned onto the main road. "Sometimes when it comes to your family, you can be a little unreasonable, Sophie."

"You haven't even been around the last seven years."

"In the past eight days you've risked life and limb in a hurricane for Seth, loaned your dad your very last dollar, played travel agent for Seth when you had a full plate of your own, and now this. And that's just the stuff I know about. Where are their boundaries? Don't they know how busy you've been this week? How important this store is to you? Or do they just not care? Maybe it's been seven years since I've been around, but it's clear you're still coddling them—and they're still taking advantage of you."

"You don't understand because you don't have siblings. We're family. We help each other out."

"It looks to me like all the help is going one direction."

"Maybe I do baby them a little, but they've been through a lot."

"So have you, and you're the same age as Seth. Besides, what's your dad's excuse?"

A long pause ensued. "He never got any money for the house in the divorce."

He narrowed his eyes. "He guilted you into that loan? He didn't deserve that money, Sophie. He deserted you guys."

"Well, the house belonged to him and Mom, nonetheless."

"Parents aren't supposed to borrow money from their children, for crying out loud. I can't even imagine my dad asking me for a loan."

"Your dad's in a different financial situation than mine is."

Aiden bit his tongue. Craig had always been a poor excuse for a father. Sophie had been taking care of her siblings, doing the laundry, and grocery shopping long before her mom became bedridden. Their dad was always working or out with his friends. But her siblings were adults now. There was no excuse for the way they imposed on Sophie.

"I already said I was sorry for ruining our evening," she said. "I don't know what else to say."

Maybe she could promise to stop indulging her family.

Aiden turned the windshield wipers up a speed. Tonight's favor might've appeased Jenna—for now—but the good deed had come at his expense.

"Why does your dad always get a pass, Sophie?"

She looked at him. "What? He hasn't gotten a pass."

"He abandoned your family. He's the reason you had to give up so much, and yet you forgave him. You let him borrow money you needed even though you're only finally able to start your life. But it took you seven years to forgive me."

A long thread of silence hung between them. The air quivered with tension.

She crossed her arms. "I don't want to talk about this right now."

Fear tightened his chest. Sophie's incessant need to please her family had triggered his own issues—that he hadn't been enough for his mom. The pain still cut to the core. It was probably making him overreact. But he couldn't seem to push back the sense of doom.

And he couldn't seem to stop the familiar feelings of

unworthiness rising like a tidal wave. He didn't want to be disregarded again and again. Would he ever be enough for Sophie? Once the doubts started creeping in, he couldn't seem to stop them.

He drove in silence a long time, reservations eating away at him with each mile. Sophie hadn't changed in the past seven years, and the issue wasn't likely to go away anytime soon. Especially when she didn't even recognize it was a problem. In the long run, could he continue to play second fiddle to her family when it dredged up so much insecurity in him?

His stomach clenched at the thought of giving up what he'd only just reclaimed. He wasn't sure. This upcoming break might be a blessing in disguise. Give them both time to think about things. Maybe it would be even better if he left earlier than planned. This tension between them wouldn't serve her well on her big day. And as much as he wanted to be here for the grand opening, maybe it would be best to clear out.

～

Sophie swallowed against the lump in her throat. Those words about her dad had hit a soft target. It was true, she'd forgiven her father more easily than Aiden. She didn't know why. But she didn't want to think about that right now.

Aiden was so quiet, and she didn't know how to fix things between them. She was sorry their evening had been interrupted, but couldn't he see Jenna's side? Her sister couldn't pay for a Jet Ski sight unseen. It was just one of those situations that couldn't be helped. Sophie hated that it had ruined their last evening together. Maybe there would be time tomorrow night after she closed to grab a meal together. She didn't want to part like this.

They entered New Bern, and Aiden followed the GPS instructions, turning onto a road that ran along the water.

"Maybe it would be best if I just left in the morning," Aiden said.

Sophie blinked at him, her heart plunging.

"Tomorrow's an important day. I don't want to be a distraction for you."

Oh, he was doing her a favor, was he? No, he was doing what he always did when things got too serious. "By all means, Aiden, you should definitely leave first."

He eased to a stop at a traffic light. "What's that supposed to mean?"

"Am I getting too close? Are you feeling a little too much for me again?" She huffed a laugh, turning to stare out her window into the darkened landscape. "I should've known. You haven't changed at all."

"I have no idea what you're talking about." His words were clipped.

She swung to look at him, her surface temperature shooting up ten degrees. "You leave first, Aiden. You leave before others can leave you. You did it to me seven years ago, and you've been doing it to every woman you've been with since."

He gaped at her. "That's not true."

"The light's green," she snapped.

A muscle twitched in his jaw as he put the car in motion. "I invited you to go with me last time—that's not the same as leaving you."

"Some offer—you knew I couldn't go. Even if you didn't know about my dad leaving, you knew my mom was critically ill and I'd never leave her. And you knew I dreamed of going to Duke. Was I just supposed to drop all that for you?"

"You're absolutely right. How silly to think you might put me first."

Put him first? Her family had needed her! She was supposed to desert her dying mom and siblings because he'd made an impulsive decision to move away?

Sophie bit back words she'd later regret. She faced the windshield where rivulets of water trickled down until the wipers swished them away. She only wished she could so easily sweep away the last hour of her life.

chapter

thirty-five

The house was dark and quiet when Sophie left her room the next morning. She flipped on the living room light as Pippa trotted to the patio door and stood waiting, tail wagging furiously.

"Don't let those mean ol' sea oats get you." Sophie let the dog out, then stared up the staircase.

Was Aiden awake yet? Once they'd arrived at their destination last night, they inspected the Jet Ski, which seemed to be in good shape. Aiden asked some questions, then Sophie called Jenna, who promptly sent the funds.

Despite the successful trip they drove home in silence, towing the Jet Ski along with a load of tension. Sophie had been afraid of making matters worse, and judging by Aiden's clenched jaw, she guessed he felt the same.

But now, a full night's sleep to her credit, Sophie was willing to admit he might've been right. She probably should wean her siblings from her care. Hadn't she been feeling convicted about that lately? Perhaps coddling them might be more about meeting Sophie's needs than theirs. She liked feeling helpful. Perhaps she even basked in the glow of their appreciation. Maybe she was even a little afraid of losing them.

But she had to consider Aiden's feelings too. She winced, thinking of the things she'd said last night. She hadn't meant to throw the past in his face. It had been insensitive—especially since she'd already forgiven him for the way he'd left.

But it was a fresh new day. Calmer heads would prevail this morning. They could talk this out, then get on with her grand opening. She had every reason to be optimistic.

Once she let Pippa back inside she headed to the kitchen, dished out the kibble, and went to start the coffee. She was still several feet from the machine when she spotted the note on the counter.

Her stomach sank at the sight of Aiden's familiar scrawl.

Sophie,

I'm sorry to leave without saying good-bye. There was an early flight this morning, and I didn't want to miss it. As much as I'd like to be there for your big day, I think I'd only be a distraction. You have plenty of help, and I know you'll have a terrific grand opening. Plus, I've been away from work too long. Ross has been eager for my return.

I'm sorry things got out of hand last night. We obviously

have some things to work through if we're going to be together. Maybe we should take a step back. Maybe some time apart would serve us well. I don't want to pressure you when you've got so much on your mind with your big day and your new business.

I'm praying your store is a big hit. Don't forget to enjoy the fruition of your dreams.

Love,

Aiden

Her vision was so blurry she could barely finish the letter.

If we're going to be together? Take a step back?

He'd said nothing about getting in touch soon. Mentioned no plans to return to Piper's Cove or invite her down for a visit. She'd thought their dispute could be easily resolved with a conversation and a little patience.

The paper trembled in her fingers. She recognized this letter for what it was—an ending. Aiden had left her yet again. How could this be happening?

She looked backward, searching for clues. She thought of his suitcase, sitting on his dresser all week, overflowing with clothes. He'd never unpacked. Maybe he'd had one foot out the door the whole time. As Granny liked to say, it was all over now but the crying.

The show must go on. That was Sophie's motto as the day progressed. Her staff arrived early, and the balloons were delivered on time. When they opened the store at ten o'clock, Haley, Anna, Dave, and Alana were waiting on her stoop.

"Congratulations!"

"Happy grand opening!"

Sophie greeted them with hugs. They all bought books and hung around until more customers arrived. The newspaper reporter came in just before lunch, and Sophie gave him an interview. He promised to return to take pictures at the release party. There would be a big write-up in tomorrow's paper.

Jenna arrived in the early afternoon. Granny had a migraine and had stayed behind. But her sister sported a fresh tan and a glowing smile. Sophie was glad to see that marriage seemed to agree with her so far.

She gave Jenna a hug. "I missed you. What a crazy week this has been. We need to catch up."

"I missed you too. This place is hopping!" There were ten or twelve people browsing shelves at the moment. "Just look at this place. It's beautiful, Sophie. I'm so happy for you."

"Thanks." Sophie took in the compliment for the umpteenth time today, wishing she felt as accomplished as she'd felt yesterday. She glanced toward the checkout counter where a long line snaked around the shelves. "Feel free to browse. I need to help with the registers."

The afternoon hours passed quickly. Sophie was busy every moment, hand-selling books, chatting with customers, or answering staff questions. Worry swirled around her as four o'clock passed.

Ramona from Schooner's appeared with a helper and

numerous foil catering pans. The shop filled with the delicious aromas of grilled chicken skewers, meatballs, and seafood tartlets. As they set up along the far wall, people flowed into the shop. One moment there were a few people seated in the chairs and the next it was standing room only.

And it was still thirty minutes before Nathaniel was due to speak. Sophie was glad she'd lined up extra help to welcome people since Ellie and Amber were swamped at the registers.

A text came in. Sophie pulled out her phone, once again hoping it was Aiden, but it wasn't. It was the publicist—he and Nathaniel had arrived and were waiting at the back door.

Sophie went to let them in. Everyone knew Nathaniel wrote under a pen name. Should she call him Nathaniel or Adam? Her legs wobbled at the thought of meeting the famous author.

As soon as she opened the door her eyes homed in on Nathaniel. "Welcome! Please come in. I'm so glad you could come."

With short brown hair and faded blue eyes, hiding behind a pair of smart glasses, Nathaniel Quinn looked just like his publicity photo. He extended a hand. "I'm Nathaniel. Thank you so much for having me."

"Sophie Lawson, owner of the shop. And it's my pleasure, truly. I love your books, and you've got a lot of fans coming tonight."

"Thank you." He poked his glasses into place. "This is my wife, Molly."

"Hi, Molly."

The pretty brunette's eyes sparkled with life. "Nice to meet you, Sophie. I come along to support my husband when I can." She lowered her voice to a whisper. "But it's also a terrific excuse to check out another bookshop."

Sophie laughed. "Well, feel free to browse to your heart's content, and let me know if you have any questions."

Nathaniel gestured to the shorter blond-haired man. "This is my publicist, Drew. I believe you spoke with him on the phone."

"Yes, of course." Sophie shook his hand and exchanged pleasantries.

"Today's your first official day then?" Molly asked. "I can still smell raw lumber and just the faintest hint of paint—my siblings and I renovated the inn I own, so I'm well acquainted with the smells of construction."

"How interesting. Yes, today's our grand opening. We definitely had some challenges getting the place open on time, but I had a lot of help from friends and neighbors."

Molly placed her hand on Sophie's arm. "Small towns are great that way, aren't they? I can't tell you how many times our hometown has come through for my family."

"I've never seen a community so eager for a bookstore. I think we're going to do good business here."

Molly beamed. "I'm sure you will. What a wonderful setting, and I love the name of your shop."

"Thank you." Sophie turned to Nathaniel. "Everything is all set up out front, and you already have a crowd waiting."

"Would you like me to mingle with the group or wait until it's time to speak?"

"Either way," Sophie said. "Whichever you'd prefer."

Drew checked the time. "In general we've found it works better to mingle after the speaking—you'll sell more books that way."

Sophie laughed. "I'm all about selling books. Please make yourselves comfortable in my office. I'll send Ellie back just before five, then you can come out when I introduce you."

Nathaniel smiled. "Sounds like a plan."

chapter

thirty-six

Sophie turned the Closed sign, locked the shop's door, and fell back against it. She was bone weary despite the adrenaline still coursing through her veins. It was thirty-eight minutes past closing time, but the crowd had lingered, and Nathaniel had kindly accommodated his fans by mingling long after he'd finished signing.

They'd sold every one of his new books and quite a few of his backlist. She was a little embarrassed when they were seven books short, but the publicist quickly promised they'd send signed copies for the latecomers who'd missed out.

Ellie came back into the room with an empty garbage can. "What a night. You must be ecstatic with the turnout."

"I'm thrilled. It exceeded my expectations, but it passed so quickly, I haven't had time to process it all."

"I wonder how many people came through today."

Sophie smiled. "I think we may have broken the fire code during the party."

"I won't tell if you won't." Amber began clearing out the register. "Nathaniel was really interesting. I loved hearing how he researches his settings, and I can't wait to read his new book. His wife was super nice. She bought eight books!"

"I bought Nathaniel's new release for my book club," Ellie said. "You should join us, Amber. We're meeting here on the last Thursday of the month."

Amber smiled. "I'd like that. I've never been part of a book group."

It appeared Amber had gained Ellie's respect today. She'd proven herself to be competent. Sophie had chosen well in both women.

Amber pushed the cash register drawer shut. "I don't know about y'all, but my doggies are barking."

"It's been a long, busy day," Sophie said. "Thanks for helping me get the place back in order. That'll make tomorrow morning easier."

Ellie shut off the front room light as they made their way to the back. "Where'd your sister run off to?"

"She went to my place to let Pippa out. She's spending the night and leaving in the morning."

"It'll be nice when you're living right upstairs, won't it?" Amber said. "Talk about convenient."

"I can't wait." Sophie didn't even want to think about more construction, especially given her financial situation. But she didn't have much choice.

They said good-bye and Sophie locked up. She was limping a little as she walked to her car. What a day. She pulled out her phone to check the texts that had come in during the party and knew a moment of despair when none of them had come from Aiden.

∽

Aiden weeded through the emails that had come in while he was gone. There were many congratulations from both clients and industry professionals. Ross had informed the *Post and Currier* of Aiden's award, so word had spread far and wide.

Beyond Aiden's door the office was dark, and only the quiet hum of the air conditioner broke the silence. Ross had left around six, but Aiden had a lot to catch up on and a full day scheduled tomorrow.

He glanced at the clock on his office wall for the dozenth time in the last hour. Sophie's shop was closed now. How had her grand opening gone? Did she have a good turnout for the release party? Sell a lot of books?

He looked at his phone, which he'd gotten repaired today. His fingers twitched with the need to call her. To hear her voice and revel in what he was sure had been a successful opening. He wanted to know every detail. Wanted to congratulate her and tell her how proud he was of her.

But he wasn't sure how his call would be received. How had she responded to the note he'd left? To his actual departure? He'd thought she might call. After their argument she couldn't have been surprised that he left. When he'd written the note he planned to call her at some point today. But the longer he was away from Piper's Cove, the more certain he was it would be a mistake.

"She deserves better than you, and eventually she'll figure that out."

Granny May's words on the phone played back, heaviness weighing his stomach. Granny was right. Sophie was smart and beautiful and good. Even in high school he'd known he was lucky to have her love. Of course he'd fallen for her—who wouldn't?

But in the back of his mind, he'd been waiting for the other shoe to drop. When would Sophie realize she could do better? When would she realize he couldn't measure up? And when she did, would she leave him?

He'd been a fool to pursue her again—that type of reckless hope could only have one kind of ending. Sophie had been right when she said he'd left before that could happen. He wanted to deny it even now. But he could no longer refute the statement when it pierced his heart in a direct hit.

She was better off without him. She might not see that now, but she would eventually. Maybe she'd get together with Joshua after all. Maybe the two of them would hit it off, get married, and have two-point-five children. And a dog. He couldn't forget Pippa, and even imagined the cute little mutt warming up to the other man.

Gritting his teeth, he closed his email program, pocketed his phone, and rose from behind his desk. As hard as it would be to stay away, it was best for both of them. Because nobody knew better than him—when the going got tough, people left.

chapter

thirty-seven

The next morning was a rush. Sophie threw together a quick breakfast, but by the time Jenna appeared, they only had a few minutes to eat. They still had to hitch the Jet Ski trailer to their dad's truck, and Sophie didn't want to be late to work.

Once outside Sophie directed as Jenna backed up the truck to the trailer parked at the curb. It took a few tries before they were properly aligned. Then Sophie showed Jenna how to hitch the trailer.

"Grant's going to love it," Jenna said once she was settled in the driver's seat again. "Thanks so much for picking it up for me."

Her sister had no idea what the favor had cost Sophie. "You're welcome."

"Did you see my necklace?" Jenna held the pretty silver necklace, which sported a small ruby, her birthstone. "Grant got it for me on our honeymoon."

273

"It's beautiful. Oh, that reminds me. Did you happen to bring Mom's necklace with you?"

Jenna winced. "Oh, I forgot to tell you. I kind of lost it. I wore it on the flight to Nassau, but when we arrived at the hotel that night it was gone. I guess it fell off somewhere along the way. That's why Grant bought me this necklace. I didn't have anything nice to wear when we went out to dinner."

Jenna kept talking, but Sophie didn't hear a word. The diamond necklace was her heirloom. It had been a gift to their mom from their dad on their wedding day. Sophie had allowed Jenna to wear it for her wedding, assuming she'd guard it with her life.

Heat flushed through Sophie's body, and her pulse thumped in her ears. She worked hard to level her tone. "Jenna. Did you try to locate the necklace? Did you call the airports or the airline's lost and found?"

"I haven't gotten around to it yet. Besides if someone found that necklace they wouldn't turn it in. It's worth at least a thousand dollars."

It was worth so much more than that to Sophie. "You have to at least try!"

"I'll call them tomorrow. But I'm sure it's got to be long gone by now."

Sophie's chest squeezed tight. She couldn't believe how flippant Jenna was being about the precious heirloom. "I was going to wear it for *my* wedding, Jenna. You said you'd take care of it."

"Well, I tried. I can't help if it fell off, can I?"

"You didn't even try to track it down."

"Calm down. I said I'd call the airport."

Jenna was looking at Sophie as if she'd morphed into a monster or something. She'd never flipped out like this on her sister. But enough was enough. It was bad enough that Jenna had lost the necklace, but her cavalier attitude was infuriating.

Sophie forced herself to take slow, deep breaths, but it took everything she had to calm herself and part with Jenna on good terms.

Losing herself at work was easy enough. They'd sold so many books yesterday that they needed to restock shelves. They had a steady stream of customers. The article in the *Gazette* was on the front page, above the fold. The headline read *Grand Opening for Bookshop by the Sea*. The accompanying photo had been taken outside her shop and featured Nathaniel and Sophie, the store's sign visible in the background.

There were just two on staff today, and Sophie had sent Ellie to lunch. She smiled at the twentysomething woman approaching the counter, two books in hand. She'd come in a while ago and spent her time browsing the fiction aisles.

"Did you find what you were looking for?"

"Sure did." The woman set the books on the counter, one of them a Nathaniel Quinn novel. "I guess I missed my favorite author by one day. My friends and I just got into town last night."

"Oh, I'm sorry you missed him."

"I was hoping to pick up his new release."

"I'm sorry. We sold out last night. We have more coming, but you'll probably be gone by the time they arrive."

"Yeah, I'm only here through the weekend. We come to Piper's Cove every year." The woman handed over her credit card. "I haven't read his last release, though. As you can see I'm planning to rectify that this week on the beach."

"Sounds like a good plan."

"I'm so glad there's a bookstore in town now. I'll probably be back for more before the week's over."

"Then I hope to see you soon." A moment later Sophie stashed the receipt in the bag and handed it over. "Enjoy your vacation."

"Oh, I plan on it." The chime tinkled as the woman left.

A few customers were in the store, but Sophie had already offered to help them. Her phone had vibrated when she was checking out the customer, so she pulled it from her pocket. *Stop hoping every text is from Aiden.*

It was her brother.

I just realized the return flight you booked leaves too early in the day. My conference ends at four. Can you try and reschedule it please?

Sophie felt her blood pressure rising. Her hand balled into a fist, tightening until her nails bit into her palms. Beyond a short text yesterday, wishing her a successful grand opening, she hadn't heard from her brother in days. And now he was asking another favor?

At the sound of footsteps Sophie pocketed her phone and dredged up a smile for the brunette approaching the counter with her little girl.

"I see you found some books," Sophie said to the girl.

"She just loves the Ramona books," the mother said. "And you have all the ones she's missing."

"Wonderful. I love those books too. My mom used to read them to me when I was your age."

"I can read them all by myself." The girl's smile showed a missing tooth.

"You must be a very good reader."

"She's been reading since she was five. If only I could get her older brother interested in a book—any book!"

Sophie rang up the five books and chatted with the patrons briefly. As they slipped out the door, Ellie breezed back in. "Your turn. The deli has a special on the Italian sub and it's delicious. Go easy on the banana peppers—they're very strong."

"Duly noted." Sophie tidied up the counter and headed toward the exit. "There's a customer in the biography section, but he seems content to browse."

"I'll check in on him in a bit. Have a great lunch."

The Italian sub sounded wonderful, and she wanted to support Anna and Dave. Sophie headed down the boardwalk and across the street. The sun beamed down today, heating the skin on her arms and face. A seagull cried out, soaring on the wind overhead.

At the deli she chatted with the owners as they made her sandwich, then she took a seat at a patio table. Before she unwrapped her sandwich she responded to Seth's request to rebook his flight.

Sorry, but I can't today, she typed. Her finger hovered over the Send arrow for a few seconds before she finally tapped it.

"There. I did it." See? She was capable of saying no. No matter that her heart was beating too fast, and she had a nasty case of instant regret.

But no. She was doing the right thing. This mothering of hers had gotten out of hand. It wasn't good for her, and it wasn't good for them. They were adults who needed to learn to fend for themselves.

She only had to recall when Jenna told her about the necklace to strengthen her resolve. Sophie had become more and more enslaved to the needs of her siblings. And she was as much to blame as they were—after all, she'd catered to their needs. Her growing frustration was as much her fault as theirs. She'd been reluctant to admit the problem. But you couldn't change what you didn't acknowledge.

She glanced across the street at her pretty little shop. Maybe moving away from Raleigh, building a business here, had been a subconscious effort to put some boundaries in place. But a geographical change had not been enough. She needed to step back. She needed to leave her siblings in God's capable hands.

The phone buzzed with an incoming call, and when she checked the screen, Seth's photo appeared. She steeled herself against his boyish smile. He wasn't fifteen anymore.

"What's going on?" he asked when she answered.

"What do you mean?"

A slight pause followed. "Are you upset with me? You seemed kind of short in your text. And Jenna said you went crazy over Mom's necklace this morning."

Sophie resisted the urge to defend herself. "You didn't even ask how my grand opening went yesterday."

"I didn't have to—Jenna already told me the event was a grand slam."

"You still could've asked, Seth. Or at least congratulated me instead of plunging right into the next favor."

There was a long silence, during which Sophie literally bit her tongue. She would not take it back. She had to put her foot down if she was ever going to resolve this.

"You're right," Seth said finally. "I'm sorry. I've been distracted with this conference, but that's no excuse. I know your shop is important to you, and I'm thrilled your first day was a success. Is that why you're upset with me?"

"I'm not upset with you, Seth. I've just decided to make some changes in my life."

"That sounds ominous."

"Not at all." She let out a huge breath. "Listen. Somewhere along the way I became a mother figure to you guys, and I don't regret that. It was necessary at the time. Mom was unwell and Dad wasn't around much, and then he was gone altogether. Someone had to do the laundry and make you guys do your homework. But you're adults now. You're capable of handling things on your own, and I'm stepping back. I'm doing it as much for you as for me."

"Stepping back? You already moved away from us."

"That doesn't mean I don't want to be close to both of you. I do. But I'm not your mom. And even if I were, it's time for you guys to fend for yourselves. More than anything I want to be your sister again—just your sister."

She squeezed her eyes closed, awaiting his response.

"Does this mean you won't rebook my flight?"

She frowned at her phone. Seriously?

Seth chuckled. "Kidding. I'm kidding. I'll call the airline myself. And you're right. You have made a lot of sacrifices for us, and I guess it was just easy to let you keep making them. I'm sorry I took advantage."

This was the last thing she'd expected. She huffed a laugh. "I appreciate that."

"To be honest, I feel kinda bad that I didn't step up to the plate more when we were teenagers. We're the same age; I should've helped instead of letting you do it all."

She blinked. "I honestly didn't mind too much. The role suited me—maybe too well. I'm obviously having a hard time giving it up."

"Well, consider yourself officially fired as our mom."

"I'm not sure Jenna will feel the same."

"She'll come around. Listen, I have to go. I have a workshop that's about to start."

"All right, have a good day, Seth."

"You too, *Sis*."

Sophie's smile spread as she disconnected her phone, a wave of relief breaking over her. Would it really be as simple as telling her siblings things needed to change? And, if so, why hadn't she done it a long time ago?

chapter

thirty-eight

"So, how's it going with that hunky boyfriend of yours?"
The wind ruffled Haley's dark curls, and she pushed them behind her ear. "I haven't seen him around this week."

Sophie gave a wan smile. "I'm afraid he's not really in the picture anymore."

They'd just placed their orders at the Galley. Patrons gathered around small tables on a deck strung with globe lights. The sun was just setting, and Sophie was content to be out on a Friday evening with a new friend.

Haley grimaced. "I'm sorry. You seemed so happy over the weekend. Am I allowed to ask what happened?"

That was the question of the hour. "We had words Monday night, and he left on Tuesday. He left me a note saying he thought we needed some space."

"Has he called since then?"

"Nope. Nor has he texted. I don't know what I expected. We go back a long way. We were high school sweethearts, and it ended when he left town, left me behind for a job opportunity in Charleston." Sophie sighed. "I was crazy to let myself fall for him again."

"He seemed really into you, though. The way his eyes devoured you . . . I'd give my right arm for a man who looked at me like that."

"I do think he cares. He just has some issues. What am I saying? I have plenty of issues of my own." Was it too early in their friendship to expound on that? Haley had already owned up to a rocky relationship with her dad. Might as well return the favor.

"You met Jenna on Tuesday," Sophie said. "But I also have a twin brother. I think I mentioned our mother passed away recently, but I didn't tell you she was chronically ill or that my father abandoned us when things got bad."

Haley winced. "I'm so sorry. What did you do?"

"I basically became the parent." Sophie told her about her caretaking and her difficulty shifting from the parental role as her siblings became adults. She told her about all the favors, the heirloom necklace, and how glib Jenna had been about losing it.

"It's like you're a mother at the empty-nest stage."

"Exactly. This week I broke down and told Seth things needed to change."

"Good for you. How did he handle it?"

"Surprisingly well. He texted yesterday just to see how my day was going and didn't ask for a single favor." Sophie's smile slipped at the next thought. "I think Jenna might be upset with me, though. She texted me saying she'd had no luck finding the necklace, and it was short and to the point. I need to call her."

"Sounds like you're just putting some boundaries in place. That's perfectly healthy. Trust me, I know what I'm talking about—my mother is a therapist." She gave a facetious smile. "I've been on the receiving end of much advice."

"Lucky you. People don't always respond well to boundaries, though. I've always been close to Jenna and Seth, and I don't want that to change."

"She'll come around. She knows you love her."

Sophie drew her thumb through the condensation on her water glass. "This is what Aiden and I argued about Monday night. I'd agreed to do yet another favor for Jenna and disregarded him in the process. He said some things, then I said some things . . . It got out of hand, and poof, he was gone."

"Seems a little rash. What are you going to do about it?"

"No idea. I've been so busy this week, it's been easy to put it on the back burner." Well, not as easy as she might like to believe.

"Do you love him?"

Sophie stared at her friend, unseeing. Instead she remembered how safe she felt in Aiden's arms, how loved she felt when he turned that smile on her. And how empty she'd felt since he left.

"I do love him." Sophie swallowed hard. "But loving Aiden is a big risk. He has abandonment issues. When things get difficult he runs. He did it seven years ago, and he did it again Tuesday."

"Is it possible," Haley asked softly, "that he's not the only one with abandonment issues? You said your dad also left when the going got tough."

"The fear is definitely there, especially since Aiden already left me once before." The achy feeling returned, and her eyes burned. "I don't ever want to be abandoned again. It really hurts."

Haley set her hand on Sophie's. "I don't blame you. That's got to make this even harder. For both of you."

As much as it had hurt when her dad left, it had to be all the worse for Aiden. He'd been so young when his mom deserted them. How was a five-year-old child supposed to understand such a thing?

Haley squeezed Sophie's hand. "Do you suppose your lack of boundaries with your siblings might also be connected to your fear of abandonment?"

Haley's words punched Sophie in the heart. Was she so afraid of being left that she felt she had to earn Jenna and Seth's love? She reflected on that for a beat.

Yes. Yes, she was.

"Sorry . . ." Haley winced. "Was that out of line? I kind of have a habit of doing that."

"Not at all." Sophie blinked at Haley. "You know, you're really good at this. I think you missed your calling."

Haley released a wry laugh. "I'd fall into depression if I had to sit in an office all day. But I'm glad if anything I've said is helpful."

"Oh, it is." A tear broke loose, trickling down her face. Sophie let out a self-conscious laugh as she swiped it away. "But I'm pretty sure you're not supposed to talk about deep-rooted insecurities with brand-new friends."

Haley squeezed her hand. "Next time we'll talk about favorite drinks and whether we prefer milk or dark chocolate—and by the way, dark is the only right answer."

"Hear, hear. Don't even get me started on white chocolate."

Sophie planned to call Jenna when she got back to the house, but Jenna beat her to the punch. The call came as Sophie pulled into the garage.

"Hey, it's me," Jenna said. "Are you busy?"

"No, I just got home. Everything okay?"

Jenna sighed hard. "Not really. I feel bad about the necklace and about the way I handled the whole thing. I'm sorry, Soph. I didn't know it meant so much to you—and I should have. I mean, you made me promise to take care of it, but I got so swept away with the wedding and honeymoon that I—I was selfish. I'm really sorry I lost the necklace, and I'm even sorrier I didn't take it seriously."

Sophie softened. She hadn't realized how worried she'd been about her relationship with Jenna until this moment. "Thanks, honey. That means a lot to me."

"I feel terrible. I wish I could replace it."

"I know you do. But I don't want to fight over a necklace. You mean too much to me."

"So, we're okay now? You're not mad at me?"

"I'm not mad at you." She steeled herself for the upcoming conversation. "But we do have to talk. I already spoke with Seth about this, but it's harder with you, because you're my little sister."

"What is it?" A note of uncertainty rang in her tone.

Sophie covered the same ground she'd covered with Seth, going back from the time her mom became seriously ill to when their dad left and on to present day.

"I think I see where this is going," Jenna said. "We're not kids anymore, and we've been taking advantage of you."

"I didn't mind taking care of you both. I don't want you to think I resent that. But you're adults now, and it's time for me to be your sister again. Because you're a perfectly capable young woman. And because I really miss being your sister."

"I'm sorry, Soph. I guess with Mom so ill and then when we lost her, I started seeing you as a mother figure. I keep forgetting you're only three years older than me."

"I like that we're close, and I don't want this conversation or the geographical distance to come between us."

"Me neither. Will you answer me honestly about something?"

"Of course."

"Did the favor I asked you for Monday have anything to do with Aiden leaving early?"

Sophie winced, not sure what to say. She didn't want to lie, but she didn't want to make her sister feel bad either.

"Oh, Soph, it *did*. I'm so sorry! I can call him and explain— I'll apologize. You two are so right together, and you'd finally found your way back to each other."

"No, don't do that. If we're right together, we'll work it out." And suddenly Sophie was more certain than ever that was the truth.

chapter

thirty-nine

Aiden didn't know what it would take to get his mind off Sophie. He'd had a busy day with two jumps, an interview with a potential raft guide, and loads of paperwork. And still, thoughts of Sophie lingered like the remnants of a potent fragrance.

He forced himself to return to the emails he'd been wading through. He opened one sent days ago, his foggy mind clearing as the words registered.

Dear Mr. Maddox,

I'm the CEO of Parajump Systems, Inc., and we'd like to offer congratulations on your recent ESTA honor. We commend your ingenuity and your desire to make parachuting safe for all. Our team is always on the lookout for ways in which we can improve our products and deliver the best safety measures for our customers. To that end we are very interested in talking with you about purchasing the patent for the SpringChute.

If you are interested in selling, we feel we could put your innovation to very good use. Please call me at the number below if you'd like to talk further. We hope we can work together to bring safer methods to the market.

Martin Sweeney

Aiden exhaled a breath he hadn't known he was holding. Parajump was the nation's leader in parachute manufacturing. And they wanted to buy his invention.

He'd heard of patents for inventions such as his going for seven figures. His heartbeat pounded in his temples. He'd known when he won the ESTA that this was a possibility, but it didn't feel real until now.

If he decided to sell, what would he do with the money? He was happy enough at Extreme Adventures, but that kind of windfall certainly presented new possibilities. He could open up his own business. He liked partnering with Ross, but he also wouldn't mind being the sole owner.

It was too late to call Parajump tonight, but he'd call Monday, at least hear them out. He wouldn't agree to anything, of course. He'd have to hire an attorney to represent his interests.

His mind whirled with the possibilities as he stared at the email. He wasn't getting any more work done tonight. He pushed away from his desk and left his office, heading down the hall.

Aiden stopped at Ross's office on his way out the door. His partner was bent over his keyboard, hunting and pecking with impressive speed. With his black hair and high forehead, he'd always reminded Aiden of Tom Hanks.

"Hey," Aiden said. "I'm taking off for the day."

Ross looked up, shoving his glasses into place. "All right. Good jumps today?"

"Yeah, the clients were safe and happy."

"That's all we can ask."

Aiden shifted in the doorway. "I was just going through my backlog of emails and found one from Parajump. They're interested in buying the patent to SpringChute."

Ross's smile widened. "Hey, that's great, Aiden. I wondered if you'd hear from them. They approached me after the ESTA ceremony, and I gave them your contact information."

Ross's positive reaction made Aiden sigh. He hadn't been sure how Ross would feel about Aiden having new opportunities. "Why didn't you tell me they'd spoken with you?"

"Didn't want to get your hopes up. You should definitely call them Monday. I know you weren't sure what you wanted to do with the device, but you should at least hear them out."

"I'd be foolish not to."

"Try and get some rest tomorrow. We've got a big week coming up—and don't forget we're short a raft guide."

"I hired someone to fill that spot today. He's got two summers' experience in Colorado, and he's starting Monday."

"Great. That'll make your week a little more manageable."

"Here's hoping." He gave the door frame a rap. "See you Monday."

"Aiden, wait." Ross gave him a steady look. "Just to be clear, I realize winning that award is going to open doors for you. I love being your partner here, but we're friends, first and foremost. I don't want this business or our friendship to hold you back."

A weight lifted from Aiden, making his shoulders sink. "You're a good man, Ross. And a good friend. I appreciate that."

They said good night and Aiden locked up behind him before heading to his Jeep. Darkness was falling on this Saturday night and he had nowhere to go but home. That was okay since he had plenty to think about.

It had been an interesting day. Earlier he'd seen Tiffany for the first time since their breakup. She'd been more cordial than he'd anticipated. He even got the impression she was still keeping her options open where he was concerned.

But Sophie or no, his relationship with Tiffany was officially over. In retrospect he couldn't believe he'd ever settled for the lackluster feelings she'd inspired. Nothing compared to the way he felt when Sophie was in his arms or when she gave him one of her cute smiles or pecked him on the lips. Tiffany had been the safe choice.

Aiden started his Jeep and turned toward home. What was Sophie doing tonight? Had her first week been everything she'd hoped? He'd found an article online about the grand opening. It had been a relief to hear the day had gone well. He was also glad she'd made so many friends in the community. He wouldn't like the thought of her being alone in a new town.

When he reached his apartment he parked and headed inside. The clean scent of pine greeted him, reminding him the cleaners had come today. The flip of a switch verified the thought. Although he wasn't a slob, the space had obviously been tidied up—cereal bowl in the dishwasher, throw pillows in their proper places, vacuum lines on the carpet.

He tossed his keys on the table and headed toward his bedroom, a hot shower on his mind. The helmet and jumpsuits were hot, and it had gotten up near ninety degrees today. Having someone strapped to the front of his body didn't help matters.

Before he pulled off his shirt, his phone buzzed an incoming call. He checked the screen and felt a pinch of disappointment when it wasn't Sophie's pretty face smiling back at him.

He accepted the call anyway. "Hey, Dad. How are you?"

"Not bad. Just getting ready to head to Hooley's to watch the Braves game with the guys. They're off to a great season so far."

Aiden had forgotten they played tonight. "Sounds fun. Tell the guys I said hi. And I have some exciting news for you—there's a company that wants to buy the rights to SpringChute."

"Well, how 'bout that. My son, the inventor!"

Aiden chuckled. "I'll be calling them Monday, see what they have to offer. It could be substantial." Aiden expounded on who the company was and what could happen. After his dad ran out of questions, he turned to another topic.

"So what's your girl think about all this? And how's her business going? I've been praying she'd have a good week."

Aiden had been putting off this conversation. "To be honest, I haven't talked to Sophie since Monday—I don't think it's going to work out between us."

"What? Why not? You two are meant to be."

"Come on, Dad. She's way out of my league and you know it."

"I know no such thing. That girl was head over heels for you back then and I'll bet she still is."

Aiden caught an image of the way she'd looked at him after they kissed last Saturday night, eyes hooded, full of want. His legs nearly buckled at the memory. Had it only been a week ago?

"There are issues at play here, Dad."

"Why do I get the feeling you've pushed her right out of your life again?"

"Thanks for the vote of confidence." Never mind that it might be true.

"I didn't hear a denial anywhere in there."

Aiden sighed. Was his dad going to make him spell it out? "She'll be just fine, Dad. Sophie's a strong woman, and eventually someone else will come along that's better for her."

"Better than you, is that what you're saying? Hogwash. There's not a thing wrong with you that a wallop upside the head won't fix. You're scared is all. And running away isn't going to fix anything."

"I'm not running away." Or was he? Hadn't Sophie accused him of the same thing? "You don't know what happened between us."

"You're doing just what you did last time. When we spoke on Sunday you were on cloud nine because you two had worked things out. Now you're all down in the dumps because—"

"I'm not down in the—"

"*Down in the dumps* because something scared you, and you ran home with your tail between your legs. How am I doing so far?"

Aiden locked down his jaw, not liking the picture his dad painted. Aiden told himself he'd left because of Sophie's issues with her siblings. Had that just been an excuse? He had a bad feeling his dad had nailed it. But that didn't mean Aiden was ready to accept it just yet.

"Listen, Son." His dad gave a hard sigh. "It doesn't take a genius to see that your mom leaving messed you up. Shoot, it messed me up too. Have you seen me dating seriously? Have I gotten anywhere near a marriage altar in the last twenty years? I see what your problem is because I've been just as bad as you. But you're not fifty-two. You're only twenty-five, Aiden—got your whole life ahead of you and an amazing woman who loves you for who you are. You'd better wake up quick or you're going to lose her for good."

Aiden palmed the back of his neck as anxiety wormed through his veins. Was his dad right?

"You said something a minute ago," Dad said. "That she's out of your league. And that's just not true, Son. If I've let you go off into adulthood thinking that, it's my own fault. But I get where it comes from—my wife left me, remember? You think that doesn't leave a mark on a man? But I've come to learn a thing or two over the years, so you listen up.

"Other people's mistakes—your mom's included—are no reflection on you. She didn't leave because something was wrong with us. She left because something was wrong with her."

Aiden took in his words. It wasn't really a new thought. But hearing it from someone else, from his dad, made it more believable somehow. He'd never really thought too deeply about how his mom's departure had affected his dad. But of course it would've.

"I hear what you're saying," Aiden said. "And I know you're right."

"Knowing it and believing it are two different things."

Aiden sank onto the edge of his bed, releasing a long sigh. "Well said."

"It's taken me a lot of years to believe it. I wish I'd been more proactive about helping you through it too. Maybe if I'd gotten you counseling as a kid . . ."

"Don't blame yourself, Dad. I'm an adult now—it's my responsibility. I'll give some thought to what you said, though." He paused, hoping he wasn't overstepping. "And it's not too late for you either, you know. You're not exactly over the hill. I'll bet there's a woman out there for you too. You deserve to have someone special."

"Funny you should mention that." There was a grin in his dad's voice. "You remember Gayle Winters from church?"

Aiden pictured the pretty middle-aged brunette who'd been head of the children's department for years. "Yeah . . ."

His dad gave a self-conscious chuckle. "Looks like your old dad's finally got a date."

chapter

forty

Sophie set down the cleaning supplies and surveyed the space that would soon be her apartment. After her long, crazy hours this week, she wished she could take the afternoon off. But she had to whip this place into shape quickly; she only had use of the beach house for one more week.

Once the upstairs of a home, her new apartment consisted of three bedrooms and a bath, all having the same wood floors they'd refurbished downstairs. The two largest bedrooms would become her living room and kitchen, and the smallest would be her bedroom.

The kitchen was going to take time and money. For now she'd make do with a microwave, hot plate, and coffeemaker, all of which she had in storage back home. The bathtub and commode were rust stained and disgusting; they'd have to go. The dingy white walls would have to wait.

For now the place needed a good cleaning, and with all the garbage and dust bunnies, she had her work cut out for her.

She slid on rubber gloves and got to work, starting with a good sweeping. She stifled a yawn. She hadn't slept well this week. She'd been rehashing Monday's argument with Aiden. He'd accused her of coddling her siblings—and he'd been right. She'd accused him of running at the first sign of trouble—and she'd been right.

But what good did being right do when it only drove them apart? His words had made her angry, and she responded by dredging up his past. Last week he'd opened up about his mother's abandonment, and in a moment of anger she used it against him. Shame crawled over her, flushing her face with heat.

An image formed in her mind of five-year-old Aiden sitting on his porch stoop waiting for his mother's return. Maybe he didn't remember the moment, but it still happened, still left an indelible impression.

If Sophie loved him—and she did—shouldn't she have protected that wound instead of exploiting it?

When she'd argued with her siblings as a child her mother used to lecture them on giving each other grace. *Think the best of one another,* she said.

Sophie had neglected to do this the first time he'd left, and she hadn't done it when he left last week. Furthermore, she was starting to see that she'd transferred some of her resentment from her dad to Aiden. They'd both deserted her on the same day, but it was her dad's abandonment that changed her life. He was the one who was supposed to tend to his wife and family. It was his fault she'd had to put her life on hold—not Aiden's.

Why was it so much easier for her to extend grace to her family?

The answer came as she gathered a pile of garbage and grit into a pile. Her love for Aiden went to the deepest recesses of her heart. The threat of losing it activated a depth of fear she'd never felt outside her relationship with him.

But didn't that kind of love require even *more* patience, *more* kindness, *more* grace? Didn't she owe it to Aiden—and to herself—to model what true love really was?

She dropped the broom and pulled out her phone, opening it to her texts with Aiden. Her fingers hovered over the digital keyboard as her mind whirled with what to say.

It all boiled down to one simple thing. Her fingers went into motion as she tapped out two simple words: I'm sorry.

Her finger hovered over the button for only an instant before she tapped the button, sending the message.

Aiden plugged his phone into his kitchen charger and flipped on the TV. He lounged in his shorts and T-shirt, belly full, the smell of pizza lingering in the air. The commentators droned on about the Braves' excellent season, reciting statistics that went in one ear and out the other.

He was mulling over last night's conversation with his dad. Last night he'd tossed and turned. All through church he'd been preoccupied. Now the baseball game was also failing to hold his attention.

Even though Aiden had been too young when she left to remember much about his mom, her leaving had undoubtedly left its mark. Everyone knew such events in early childhood could have a lasting impact.

There had always been a part of him that felt defective. He felt inferior in school even though his grades weren't terrible and he had his share of friends. His elementary years were filled with insecurity for no reason he could actually define.

Of course, he didn't admit his feelings of inferiority to anyone. No, he wore bravado like armor and hoped no one noticed the insecure boy beneath. He became the class daredevil, taking every dare issued and usually faring quite well. The stunts were exciting and earned him the approval of his classmates—if not his teachers. But that deep reservoir inside him seemed to empty as soon as it filled, as if it bore a gaping hole.

Then his freshman year he shot up several inches and began getting facial hair. The girls noticed him, even the pretty, popular ones, and that went a long way toward restoring his self-confidence. But it was false security based on the shallowest terms. The sudden attention had nothing to do with who he was or how much he was worth.

It wasn't until Sophie came along that he began to grow in that area. Sophie had high expectations. She was the first person who told him he was creative, that he was smart. She encouraged him. Believed in him. When he was with her he felt stronger and more capable. He felt worthy.

She established an important foundation he would later build on. His success at Extreme Adventures had furthered those feelings of value. He was blessed with a successful career that paid his bills and then some. Still those things were based on what he did—not who he was.

It wasn't until he resumed going to church and growing spiritually that he was introduced to the idea that his worth, everyone's worth, was God-given, intrinsic. There was nothing anyone—not even his mother—could do to take away his innate value.

This concept had been working beneath the surface for a few years now, but after Monday night he wasn't sure he'd fully embraced it. He'd said some regrettable things to Sophie. And when she'd lost her temper the conflict and tension had lit that spark of fear inside him. It kindled the fires of his insecurity. He'd been angry with her because she'd been right. His feet had itched to leave because he'd known, as sure as the sun rose the next morning, Sophie would leave him too.

And he couldn't bear for that to happen. So he'd left her first, just like she'd said. How could a man who jumped from the sky without reservation lack the courage to love?

The sound of cheering pulled him from his reverie. The Braves had scored another run, putting them up by three. But the ball game held little appeal in light of his sudden realization.

Leaving Sophie had been a terrible mistake. A decision based on fear instead of love. And this was the second time he'd left her. Sophie might have loved him once. She might have even loved him twice. But given the fool he'd been, why would she give him another chance?

He slumped in his seat. He'd be an even bigger fool to hope. She hadn't contacted him since he left. He had no reason to think she still wanted him. Sure, she had her own issues. But hers seemed minor compared to his own.

He flicked off the TV. What had he done? How could she ever trust him to stick around when he'd proven himself to be a flight risk?

God, what do I do?

His phone buzzed with an incoming text. Sophie. His hopes rose like an underwater buoy popping to the surface. He pressed it down, the wishful thinking. But that didn't stop him from going to the kitchen where his phone was charging.

The notification on the screen squelched the last of his hopes. The long text was from his dad. Aiden opened it and managed a small smile at his dad's request for advice on what to wear for his date. Two photos of outfits accompanied the long text. He could hardly believe this was his dad—a man who lived in blue jeans and T-shirts, on or off the job. He must be desperate if he was asking Aiden's opinion.

He suggested the first outfit—dark jeans and a black button-up. He was just about to set down his phone when he saw that another text had come in.

Sophie. He opened it.

I'm sorry.

His breath hitched, and his fingers tightened on the phone. He read the message over and over. It had come in fifteen minutes ago.

Was this a sign? Did she still want him? She wouldn't have reached out otherwise, would she? He was afraid to believe it. Hope was a dangerous thing—a riptide threatening to pull him out to sea.

And what should he do? His thumbs poised over the phone, his heart thrumming in his ears.

I'm sorry too, he typed, his hands shaking.

He reread the simple phrase. The words didn't say nearly enough.

I love you, Sophie, he added.

He frowned at the proclamation. He couldn't tell her that in a text. And even that monumental truth wasn't enough. He could fill a book with his feelings for her.

He should call. He should've called her days ago, in fact, instead of leaving the ball in her court. He was the one who'd left, after all.

But he didn't want to declare his love over the phone. What he had to say needed to be said in person. And after he had his say, he wanted to wrap his arms around his girl and kiss her senseless.

chapter

forty-one

Fifteen minutes had never passed so slowly. Sophie had finished sweeping and now pushed a string mop back and forth. Had Aiden gotten her text yet? And if he had, why hadn't he responded?

It had been too little, too late. She should've explained herself better. Maybe she should've told him she loved him. It was hard to know what she should've done. Surely he'd gotten her text by now—he always kept his phone in his pocket. But he'd broken it on his last day here. Was it possible he hadn't gotten it fixed yet?

Her phone vibrated, and her heart leapt in her chest. *Please, oh, please.* With a shaking hand she pulled it from her pocket, eyes eagerly seeking the notification.

Jenna.

Sophie's lungs deflated like a week-old party balloon.

Open the door, the text read.

Sophie frowned as she responded. I think you meant to send this to someone else.

The shot of adrenaline dissipated in her bloodstream, leaving her weak and shaky. If only Aiden would respond. If only he would say something. *Anything*. But maybe he'd had enough of her and her coddling ways. Maybe he'd decided a long-distance relationship wouldn't work after all.

She was just about to pocket her phone when another text came in from Jenna.

It was for you, goofy. Open the door.

Sophie looked up, the meaning sinking in. She dropped the mop, dashed downstairs, and rushed down the hall, navigating the bookshelves and tables on her way to the front door. Then she stopped, eyes widening at the sight on her patio.

She grabbed the handle and pulled open the door. Jenna and Grant, Seth, her dad, and Granny May stood there, bearing all manner of cleaning supplies and tools.

"What are you doing here?"

Grant smiled. "Isn't it obvious?"

Her dad held up a roller and paint pan. "We're your minions for the day, sweetheart."

"Put us to work," Jenna added.

Sophie released a breath. Her family—all of them—had shown up for *her*. Her throat tightened.

Dad gestured toward the parking lot. "We got your belongings out of storage and brought them in a trailer."

"Good thing you left me a key," Jenna said.

Sophie covered her mouth, her eyes stinging. "Oh, you guys." It felt nice to be the one taken care of for a change.

"Well, are you going to let us in or what?" Granny asked. "These old legs can only hold me up so long."

"Of course!" Sophie gave a tearful laugh as she opened the door wider and stepped aside. "Come in, come in. Thanks, you guys. This is so nice of you."

"We owe you about a thousand more days." Jenna laughed, squeezing Sophie's hand.

"We're going to whip this place into shape." Dad hugged her as the others admired the store. When they parted he slipped her an envelope. "My first installment."

Sophie smiled. "Thanks, Dad."

Seth brushed past Sophie, giving her a wry grin. "You know tears make me uncomfortable."

Sophie rolled her eyes, edging around the walker to embrace her grandmother. "Thanks so much for coming, Granny."

"I'm sorry I had to miss your grand opening, but I'm dying to have a look around. You'll have to give me the grand tour." Granny released Sophie and gave three sharp claps. "All right, soldiers, carry this stuff upstairs and get to work." She gave Sophie a wink. "I just came to supervise. It's what I do best."

Eight hours later her apartment was sparkling clean. Sophie and Jenna rolled a coat of Dove Gray onto her living room walls. The other rooms were already finished.

Seth and their dad worked together to replace the shower/tub enclosure and install a new commode. Things seemed better between the two of them. Seth had told Sophie a few days ago that Dad had apologized for leaving them, and Seth was working on forgiving him. At the very least they seemed to have reached some kind of truce.

Sophie also had a little more work to do in that department. Forgiveness was a good thing. But their dad didn't always act in healthy ways, so they would all need to keep boundaries in place with him.

For now, she was just enjoying the moment. They'd all come together to help her—that was a start. And her apartment was coming along quickly.

Earlier Jenna had located cheap, secondhand cabinets on Craigslist, and the men had gone to pick them up. Sophie would need a plumber before she could have them installed, but she was one step closer to an operable kitchen.

A few hours after they started their project, Granny took Pippa back to the beach house. The dog was no doubt happier there, and the others could work in peace without Granny May peering over their shoulders.

The smell of paint fumes mingled with the scent of pine cleaner, the open windows diffusing both. The slurping sound of their rollers accompanied the tunes coming from Jenna's iPhone.

Sophie set down her roller and pulled out her phone. She'd checked it compulsively all day long. But no matter how many times she looked, Aiden's response didn't appear.

She had to face facts. He wasn't going to answer her text. Her apology had come too late. The ache inside spread, tightening her chest. She hadn't felt heartbreak in so many years she'd forgotten how much it hurt. It was worse than last time somehow.

"What do you think?" Jenna asked. "You like the color?"

Sophie swallowed against the lump in her throat. She surveyed the space, dredging up a smile. "I love it. It's so soothing."

"I agree. We made good progress today."

Thanks to her family, her apartment had gone from bleak to beautiful over the course of one day. "I could move in tonight if I wanted."

"Might as well get your kitchen in first—and enjoy a few more days at the beach cottage—you're hardly roughing it there."

"That's true."

How much would Brandon charge to run the plumbing and install the cabinets? After receiving the insurance check Friday, she'd insisted on paying him for the roof, but she had a little left over. Hopefully enough to finish the kitchen.

"We're coming back next Sunday," Jenna said. "If you get the plumbing roughed in, we'll be ready to go."

"You guys don't have to do that."

Jenna tilted her a look. "I think I can speak for everyone when I say we want to. Let us do this for you, Soph. You've done so much for all of us."

For the second time that day, Sophie blinked away tears. "I love you guys."

"We love you too," Jenna said. "And it's about time we showed it."

chapter

forty-two

Sophie gave her family one last wave, shut the door of her shop, and turned the lock. She should get home to Pippa, but she wanted to take one last turn around her newly finished and furnished apartment.

As she ascended the steps she pulled out her ponytail holder and ruffled her hair, giving her scalp a short massage to alleviate the tightness. The scent of paint fumes lingered, reminding her to leave the windows cracked tonight.

She surveyed the warm gray walls, crisp white trim, and polished honey floor. Her bed, dresser, and nightstand were set up, though the mattress was still bare. In the living room, her sofa and armchair took up one wall, opposite the TV, and a plush area rug hugged the floor spanning the distance. In the corner her bookshelf stood proudly, burgeoning with all her favorite novels, alphabetized by the author's last name. Some of them were newer, but a lot of them dated back to childhood, as evidenced by their faded covers and loose spines.

She sank onto the sofa, propping her bad foot on the ottoman. Her familiar belongings looked strangely wonderful in her new apartment. She reached for a framed photo of her mother, taken during better days here on the beach in Piper's Cove. She lounged in a modest black one-piece, shading her eyes as she tilted a smile at the photographer.

"What do you think, Mama? Like my new apartment? I wish you could be here."

Sophie gave a wan smile. That wasn't entirely true. Her mother was at peace in heaven and not suffering as she had for so many months. Sophie was grateful for that.

While they'd planned the bookshop to the smallest detail, they hadn't talked much about Sophie's new digs. But, she realized suddenly, her mom hadn't really cared so much about the paint colors, the layout of the store, or even the children's area, complete with its story-hour nook.

She'd only wanted Sophie to be excited about her future—a future without her. Her mother had wanted Sophie to find joy despite her absence.

Her eyes stung at the revelation. The hope of owning a bookshop had carried Sophie through the dark days after her mother's death. It gave her something to look forward to. Something to live for.

"Thank you, Mom," she whispered. "Your plan worked beautifully."

But now the shop was finished, and Sophie had to find joy

in the day-to-day. She had no doubt that a life revolving around books would allow her to do just that, despite the heartache of losing Aiden.

She nearly reached for her phone but stopped herself. There was no text awaiting her—she would've felt it come in. No amount of compulsive checking would change that fact.

She looked into her mother's smiling brown eyes, her chest tightening painfully. "I've lost him again, Mama. And this time you're not here to help me through it."

Last time there'd been so many distractions: her father's desertion, her mother's illness, her siblings' care. Darkness surrounded her. Aiden's abandonment was just one more thing to deal with. She could hardly separate one loss from another.

This time she was surrounded by wonderful things: her new bookshop, her new apartment, her new friends. The only negative was Aiden's absence, and the weight of that loss was overwhelming.

God, help me. I have so much to be grateful for, but I miss him so much. I wanted to build a life with him, and now he's gone, and the hole he left seems impossible to fill.

A knock sounded on the door downstairs, breaking her train of thought. Her family must've forgotten something. She set down the photo and rose to her feet.

When she reached the main level she didn't flip on the bright lights. Her burning eyes would give her away, and she didn't want her family worrying. Anyway, the boardwalk lights filtered through the front windows, guiding her way through the maze of shelves and tables.

A tall, male figure was silhouetted on the other side of the door; Seth must've forgotten one of his tools.

She pulled open the door, and her lungs emptied at the sight.

"Aiden." Moonlight shone on his face, highlighting the features she loved so much. The deep-set eyes, the prominent cheekbones, those sensual lips curved in a hopeful arc. Was he really here, standing on her doorstep?

"What are you doing here?"

His smile slipped, uncertainty flickering across his features.

Sophie gave a hard blink, opening the door wider. "I mean, come in. I didn't—this is so unexpected."

"You're here late." His voice rumbled through the darkness. "I stopped by the house first."

She closed the door and turned to face him. "I was working on my apartment. You just missed my family."

His eyebrows rose. "What were they doing here?"

"Helping me clean and paint. It's almost finished. They brought my stuff from home and everything."

"That's great." His gaze shifted downward before he looked at her again, his eyes growing intense. Time suspended, the moment drawing out between them. "I got your text, Sophie. Thank you for that. I wanted to talk in person—obviously."

He'd come such a long way. That had to be good, right? Sophie's lungs struggled to keep pace with her heart.

"You want to go upstairs? I have furniture and everything."

He huffed a laugh. "I couldn't sit still right now if I tried. I've done a lot of thinking over the past week. I talked to my dad. I came to some realizations."

"You did?"

He pinned her with an unswerving look. "Monday night when we argued—I was pushing you away. And you don't deserve that."

Nerves jangling, she gave him an encouraging smile, hoping he'd continue.

He ran a hand over his face. "I don't know if I ever told you, I remember my parents arguing. My dad told me they'd always gotten along well until he got laid off. Then he and my mom hit a rough patch, and she up and left. So I guess somewhere along the line I started believing that when the going gets tough . . . people leave."

Sophie's heart went soft and squishy at his words, his vulnerability. At the little boy who watched his mother drive away from him and never return.

"Oh, Aiden."

"You and I had that argument seven years ago—do you remember? And right on the heels of that, Ross presented me with an opportunity. But I see now it wasn't just the business opportunity that appealed to me. It was my chance to leave you—before you left me."

"But, Aiden . . ." Sophie set a hand on her throat. "I was never going to leave you."

"I know that now. But after that argument I was having so much anxiety. I couldn't sleep, I couldn't eat. I didn't understand it at the time, but looking back, I can see what was going on. I let fear take control. I might've even sabotaged our relationship. I loved you so much, and I was afraid you'd break up with me. I kept waiting for the other shoe to drop, and when it didn't . . . I dropped it myself. I'm sorry for that."

Sophie'd had no idea how that argument had affected him. She'd had so much on her plate at the time, she hardly gave it a second thought.

"And last week," Aiden continued, "when we had words about Seth and Jenna, there was that fear again. It just crowds out everything else. So you were right, Sophie. Losing you—having you leave—is the worst thing I can imagine. I'd do anything to avoid it, up to and including leaving you myself—as crazy as that sounds."

Sophie opened her mouth to speak.

He held up a hand. "I know. You were never going to leave me. But when you give fear a voice, it's louder than logic or reality. It overshadows everything you know to be true, and all you can hear are the lies you fear most."

Because of fear, trusting Aiden the second time around had been so hard. "I understand more than you know."

He took her hands in his. "I need to learn to turn down the fear. I need to listen to God's voice instead. I'm going to work on it."

She held on to his hands, never wanting to let go of him again. But could they get beyond this? Could he work through this issue, or would she have to always worry that he'd sabotage their relationship and take off? The fear was still there—in both of them.

He stepped closer, his eyes searching hers in the dimness. "I know I don't deserve a second chance after all I've put you through. But I'm asking anyway because . . . I love you, Sophie. I never stopped, and I can't imagine a future without you."

Her breath left her body, her eyes stinging with tears. "I love you too, Aiden."

His eyes lit with a smile just before his mouth curved. He leaned forward and brushed her lips with his, the sweetest caress. His fingers feathered her cheeks, the softest touch. He felt like a dream and tasted of heaven. She would never tire of the way he kissed her.

His arms went around her, drawing her closer until his heart beat against hers. Her fingers plunged into his hair, reveling in the softness. When he deepened the kiss she lost herself in him.

She couldn't believe he loved her. The empty space inside her filled until she was ready to burst. Their road had been long and hard, but the journey had been worth it. Because it had brought him back to her.

He ended the kiss, setting his forehead against hers, his half-mast eyes fixed on hers. Their ragged breaths mingled in the space between them.

"Thank you for giving me another chance." His voice was thick as honey. "I'm sorry for hurting you. Again."

"I forgive you. And I really am sorry for the things I said. I also realized you were right about my dad. I was resentful about his leaving me to take over, and I transferred some of that to you. I think that's why I held on to it so long. But that wasn't fair to you. I'm sorry."

"I get it. You lost two people you loved on the same day, and it altered the course of your life forever."

"Thank you for understanding. But, Aiden . . ." She touched his face, pinning him with a look. "No more leaving. Talk to me instead. There's nothing we can't work out if we're open with each other."

"I promise." He dropped a lingering kiss on her lips.

When he drew away he gave her a smile she couldn't help returning. She still couldn't quite believe he was here saying all this. That they were together again. But it would be different this time because they'd both grown. They both understood the issues they faced and would work together to overcome them.

"Tell me about your family," he said. "They came over just to help you get settled?"

"We've come a long way in a week. I have so much to tell you. But the short version is, you were right about my siblings. I had a heart-to-heart with them, and we agreed I'd go back to being just their sister."

"I'm glad to hear it. That'll be better for all of you."

"I'm sure we'll have our bumps along the way, but they showed up today out of the blue to help me—even my dad and Granny May. That says something."

"It's a good start."

"It is." As thrilled as she was that Aiden was here, that he wanted to give their relationship a real chance, there was still a major obstacle.

His gaze sharpened on her. "What's wrong? I don't like those little furrows between your brows."

She put some space between them, her lips easing into a wan smile. "We haven't talked about the logistics yet. You still live five hours away, Aiden, and we both own businesses. That's a pretty big hurdle."

His eyes lit with hope. "I haven't had a chance to tell you my news. The largest manufacturer of parachutes in the US wants to buy my patent for the SpringChute."

She squeezed his hand. "Aiden! That's wonderful. Is that what you want to do? To sell the rights? You'd mentioned you might want to manufacture them yourself."

"I decided not to go that direction. I'll be calling Parajump in the morning to discuss the particulars and hiring a lawyer to handle the details. But the short of it is . . . I want to move here, Jelly Bean. I want to live in Piper's Cove with you. I want to open up my own tandem-jumping business." He tilted a smile at her. "What do you think of that?"

"Really? Are you sure? What about Ross and your business?"

"Ross will be fine. He's more or less given me his blessing to go off on my own. We'll figure out what to do with my shares later. For now, I just want to assure you that I'm coming here. I want to be with you—everything else comes second to that."

Sophie stared at him in disbelief. "Is it really going to be that easy?"

His lips quirked. "Don't worry, I'm sure there'll be plenty of challenges to keep things interesting."

"You always did like an adrenaline rush."

"You give me the best rush of all," he said just before he claimed her lips once again.

And just like that, Sophie decided that she, too, enjoyed the sensation of free falling.

Epilogue

Sophie turned the store's Open sign over, then held the door for Ellie as she slipped out.

"Busy Saturday," the woman said. "I hand-sold at least thirty books today."

Sophie flashed her a teasing grin. "Were twenty-nine of them Nathaniel Quinn's new novel?"

"Only twenty-eight. The other one was a nonfiction title. Big plans for tonight? I don't recall you wearing a dress to work before."

Sophie locked up behind them. "Just a picnic with Aiden. It's sort of a six-month anniversary."

"Sort of, meaning . . . ?"

"It's been six months since we reunited at my sister's wedding rehearsal."

"Good for you. I'm always in favor of a celebration. I'm going home to cook dinner for the hubs. You kids have fun."

"See you Monday." Sophie started down the boardwalk, heels clacking on the planks. She smiled as she recalled her so-called reunion with Aiden. It definitely hadn't been a romantic one. She'd been filled with anger and resentment. Still, if she was honest, she'd yearned for him even then.

If not for that hurricane . . .

She swept her gaze over the peaceful harbor, and she inhaled the briny scent of the ocean, a smell she never tired of. They'd had unseasonably warm temperatures the first week in November, which was good for Aiden's new business.

He'd opened a shop just down the street—not much more than a booth, really—and he'd hired George Buchanan, a crusty old sailor with a marshmallow heart, to operate it. Between the reservations from his shop and website, he stayed busy at the airfield, while Sophie tried to forget he spent half his days falling from the sky.

When he'd opened for business, Sophie was his first tandem jump. She wouldn't describe the sensation of free falling as an adrenaline rush so much as a surge of pure terror. One jump had been enough to last her a lifetime. He often teased her that his ears were still ringing.

The sale of Aiden's patent had been so lucrative he'd also managed to buy a cute little cottage within walking distance of his store and the beach. For now, he maintained his shares in Extreme Adventures. Ross had hired a fellow adrenaline junkie to take Aiden's place, and he seemed to be working out.

The bookstore was doing well, thanks to a community of avid readers and tourists seeking beach reads. Sophie turned a tidy profit most months and had been setting some back to help them through the off-season.

In the distance the sun was setting. Sophie loved the way the sky lit the harbor this hour of the day, bathing the water and sea grass in golden light.

A seagull cried out overhead, swooping down to land on the harbor. The boardwalk was all but deserted, the shops already closed, off-season hours in effect. Aiden was bringing their favorite foods from the Dock House.

She peered down the boardwalk where the gazebo overlooked the harbor and marina. Aiden was already there, setting out their food. He must've gone home for a shower because he wore a blue button-up and dark jeans. She took in his broad shoulders and slim waist, his handsome face and dark curls, now ruffling in the breeze. Her boyfriend was quite the looker.

They'd had a relatively smooth several months, though starting two businesses had contributed a bit of stress. But true to Aiden's promise, he opened up to her when things started going sideways. There'd been a few arguments followed by heartfelt apologies and forgiveness. This was the way relationships were supposed to go.

He looked up as she approached, a smile lighting his face. "Well, don't you look nice."

Targeting that sensual mouth, she leaned in for a kiss. "We're celebrating, after all. How was your day?"

"Excellent. I was in the air more than I was on the ground."

"I don't want to hear any more."

He chuckled. "Let's dig in before the food gets cold."

As they ate they talked about Sophie's efforts to set up another book-release party and the launch of two more book clubs.

She wanted her bookshop to be a place where people gathered frequently over the love of books.

"That was delicious," Sophie said when she finished her last bite of mashed potatoes. The sun had gone down, the pink glow of twilight reflecting off the water.

She set her napkin on the plate. "On the night of the rehearsal dinner I was too preoccupied to taste a single thing."

He pushed his plate back, eyeing her. "About what, exactly?"

"Oh, I don't know—trying to be a good maid of honor, attempting to be a buffer between Seth and Dad . . . And then there was you."

His eyebrows lifted. "What about me?"

"Oh, I don't know." She gave him a wry grin. "Trying to ignore the fact that after seven years apart you still gave me butterflies."

His eyes twinkled as he took her hand. "Oh, really? I couldn't tell between all the glares and snubbery."

She lifted her chin. "That's not a word. And you didn't exactly make it easy on me either."

"Because I was apologetic and contrite?"

"Because you were handsome as sin!"

He chuckled and Sophie couldn't help smiling in return as she remembered the way he'd looked in his suit that night. The way he held her in his arms as they danced. The way he gazed at her, his heart in his eyes.

She shivered.

An impish gleam lit his eyes. "Chilly?"

"Maybe." Sophie gave him a stubborn look as she stood,

gathering the trash. "I thought I was prepared to see you, but I wasn't. Not even close."

"You hardly even looked at me."

"That took supreme effort on my behalf." She grabbed the bag and carried it to the trash can. "I couldn't believe the way you filled out that suit coat."

"Well, for the record, Lawson, you took my breath away too."

Sophie dumped the bag and turned back to the gazebo with a ready smile.

Aiden was on his knees, picking up a napkin or something.

But no. She stopped in her tracks. He was on *one* knee, and the object he held was no napkin.

It was a ring box. Her gaze flew to his face.

His mouth curved in that crooked smile she loved so much. And his eyes . . . Those blue eyes gazing back were saying so many things.

"Sophie Lawson . . . Seven years ago I made the worst mistake of my life when I left you. But God saw fit to bring you back into my life, and I'm so grateful He did because I never stopped loving you. It took me a long time to realize that loving you is the best rush of all. And there's nothing that would make me happier than to spend the rest of my life loving you. Will you marry me, Sophie?"

Her eyes burned with tears. She hadn't seen this coming at all.

"Yes." The word was muffled by the hands that were cupped over her face.

"Um . . ." Aiden looked adorably unsure. "What?"

She lowered her hands. "Yes! Of course I'll marry you."

She rushed toward him, and he stood just in time to catch her. She gazed into his eyes, feet dangling above the ground.

"I love you, Sophie. I can't wait to spend the rest of my life with you."

"I love you too." She barely got the words out before he captured her lips in a kiss that warmed her through. That caused her to tremble with joy. That made her forget they were in public.

Was this really happening? They'd talked in terms of forever, but they hadn't talked rings or wedding ceremony. But ever since he'd returned, she knew he was hers forever.

A long moment later he drew away, wearing that sleepy look she loved so much. He would be hers, and she would be his—for as long as they both shall live.

"You really proposed to me," she whispered in wonder as she drank him in.

"And you really said yes."

She laughed. "I said yes!"

"Without so much as even looking at the ring."

"The ring!" She laughed. "I got a little distracted."

He set her on the ground and opened the blue velvet box.

She sucked in a breath. "Oh! It's gorgeous." The ring featured a round diamond center that twinkled in the evening light. A shimmering row of diamonds highlighted the open-twist shoulders.

"Are you sure? My feelings won't be hurt if you want to pick out your own."

"I feel like I already did." She waggled her fingers. "Put it on, put it on."

"Patience, woman." He chuckled as he pulled it from its velvet nest and set down the case. He slid the ring easily into place—a perfect fit.

"I love it." She admired the ring for several long seconds, turning it this way and that before peering up at Aiden. "I love *you*. I am so happy right now."

His smile widened. "Me too, Jelly Bean."

"When do you want to get married? And where?"

"You know, some people say their vows while they're free falling . . ."

"Aiden Maddox." She gave him a pointed look. "Don't even."

"On the other hand . . ." He pressed a kiss to her lips, making her go all soft and squishy. "A beach wedding is always nice too."

Coming October 2021!

RIVERBEND GAP

Don't miss the first book in a new romance
series from Denise Hunter, set in the fictional
town of Riverbend Gap, North Carolina.

Acknowledgments

Bringing a book to market takes a lot of effort from many different people. I'm so incredibly blessed to partner with the fabulous team at HarperCollins Christian Fiction, led by publisher Amanda Bostic: Jocelyn Bailey, Matt Bray, Kimberly Carlton, Paul Fisher, Jodi Hughes, Margaret Kercher, Becky Monds, Kerri Potts, Savannah Summers, Marcee Wardell, and Laura Wheeler.

Not to mention all the wonderful sales reps and amazing people in the rights department—special shout-out to Robert Downs!

Thanks especially to my editor, Kimberly Carlton, for her incredible insight and inspiration. You not only help me take the story deeper but you make the process enjoyable, and for that I am so grateful! Thanks also to my line editor, Julee Schwarzburg, whose attention to detail makes me look like a better writer than I really am.

Author Colleen Coble is my first reader and sister of my heart. Thank you, friend! This writing journey has been ever so much more fun because of you.

I'm grateful to my agent, Karen Solem, who's somehow able

to make sense of the legal garble of contracts and, even more amazing, help me understand it.

To my husband, Kevin, who has supported my dreams in every way possible—I'm so grateful! To all our kiddos: Chad, Trevor and Babette, and Justin and Hannah, who have favored us with two beautiful granddaughters. Every stage of parenthood has been a grand adventure, and I look forward to all the wonderful memories we have yet to make!

A hearty thank-you to all the booksellers who make room on their shelves for my books—I'm deeply indebted! And to all the book bloggers and reviewers, whose passion for fiction is contagious—thank you!

Lastly, thank you, friends, for letting me share this story with you! I wouldn't be doing this without you. Your notes, posts, and reviews keep me going on the days when writing doesn't flow so easily. I appreciate your support more than you know.

I enjoy connecting with friends on my Facebook page, @authordenisehunter. Please pop over and say hello. Visit my website DeniseHunterBooks.com or just drop me a note at deniseahunter@comcast.net. I'd love to hear from you!

Discussion Questions

1. Who is your favorite character in *Bookshop by the Sea* and why?

2. If you were going to open a bookshop, what would you name it and where would it be located?

3. Aiden's mom's abandonment left him feeling unworthy and insecure. Discuss the ways the desertion impacted him and the decisions he made. Have your insecurities ever led you astray?

4. Sophie has always been the person who encourages Aiden. Who is your biggest cheerleader? How has he or she impacted your life?

5. Sophie had trouble letting her siblings fend for themselves. Have you ever found yourself in a similar situation?

6. If Craig Lawson were your dad, would you have been able to forgive him for abandoning your family? Did he deserve a second chance with Sophie and her siblings? Why or why not?

7. Aiden is a daredevil who jumps from planes but is afraid

to risk his heart. Have you ever been afraid to love? Discuss.

8. What is the most adventurous thing you've ever done?

9. Aiden grew tired of playing second fiddle to Sophie's siblings. Was he justified in his feelings? How did his past make this a trigger for him?

10. In the same way that Sophie is refurbishing her shop, she is also renovating her life. Have you ever had a chance to start over? If you had that chance now, what changes would you make?

About the Author

Photo by Neal Bruns

Denise Hunter is the internationally published bestselling author of more than thirty books, three of which have been adapted into original Hallmark Channel movies. She has won the Holt Medallion Award, the Reader's Choice Award, the Carol Award, and the Foreword Book of the Year Award and is a RITA finalist. When Denise isn't orchestrating love lives on the written page, she enjoys traveling with her family, drinking good coffee, and playing drums. Denise makes her home in Indiana, where she and her husband are currently enjoying an empty nest.

❧

DeniseHunterBooks.com
Instagram: @deniseahunter
Facebook: @authordenisehunter
Twitter: @DeniseAHunter